# the lottery

# the lottery

## Beth Goobie

ORCA BOOK PUBLISHERS

*National Library of Canada Cataloguing in Publication Data*
Goobie, Beth, 1959 -

The lottery

ISBN 1-55143-238-2

I. Title.

PS8563.O8326L67 2002   jC813'.54   C2002-910677-X

PZ7.G613Lo 2002


First published in the United States, 2002

*Library of Congress Control Number:*   2002107487

*Summary*: When Sal Hanson "wins" the lottery run by the secret Shadow Council
at her high school, her fate seems set — she will be shunned by all. But her refusal to
be a victim might ultimately set her free.

Orca Book Publishers gratefully acknowledges the support for its publishing
programs provided by the following agencies: the Government of Canada through
the Book Publishing Industry Development Program (BPIDP), the Canada
Council for the Arts, and the British Columbia Arts Council.

Cover design by Christine Toller
Cover photo: www.eyewire.com
Printed and bound in Canada

*IN CANADA:*
*Orca Book Publishers*
PO Box 5626, Station B
Victoria, BC  Canada
V8R 6S4

*IN THE UNITED STATES:*
*Orca Book Publishers*
PO Box 468
Custer, WA   USA
98240-0468


04 03 02 • 5 4 3 2 1

*for Mike*

*with thanks to Roger Waters for* The Wall

*and Robert Cormier for* The Chocolate War
*and the possibilities he brought
to young adult literature*

The author gratefully acknowledges the Saskatchewan Arts Board grant that partially funded the writing of this book, as well as Kim Duff's invaluable and expert advice regarding autism.

# Chapter One

Every student at Saskatoon Collegiate knew about the lottery. It was always held in the second week of September, during Shadow Council's first official session. Rumor had it that a coffin containing the name of every S.C. student was placed in front of the blindfolded Shadow president. The lid was lifted, the president dipped a hand among the shifting, whispering papers, and a name was pulled. The Shadow vice president then removed the president's blindfold. Reading the name aloud, the president nodded to the Shadow secretary, who dipped a quill pen into blood-red ink and inscribed the selected name into Shadow Council's *Phonebook of the Dead*, a black leather binder with a silver skull and crossbones on the front. The secretary then picked up a scroll tied with a black ribbon and handed it to the vice president, with instructions to deliver the message to the lottery winner within twenty-four hours, and a bell was rung, finalizing the fate of the poor sucker whose name had just been drawn.

Every S.C. student imagined each step of the lottery in slow vivid detail, and every student pictured the ritual differently. Some added the human skull rumored to be present, others threw in a murdered cat, but everyone settled on a room that flickered with candlelight, or at least a lone flashlight beam. Sal Hanson usually added a stack of cheese-and-mustard sandwiches, figuring the intense drama would work up a few appetites, and mentally ducked the rest of the details. Shadow Council already had the imagination of every other student slaving away full time — they'd hardly notice the absence of a single third-clarinet player's terrified heartbeat.

Still, when she opened clarinet case #19 on the morning of September 14, her first grade ten Concert Band practice, to find a white scroll wrapped around the lower joint of her clarinet and tied with a black ribbon, she immediately understood its significance: *Lottery Winner. Shadow Council's Dud For The Year*. Her mouth swallowed itself, her heart skipped a double beat, and the lid of her clarinet case slipped against her suddenly sweaty hands as she lowered it and snapped the latches.

"Don't tell me — you've decided you'd rather play tuba!" Brydan Wallace, her music stand partner, stuck his clarinet reed into his mouth and began to masticate.

"Nah," said Sal, avoiding his gaze. "My reed split, and I forgot my new ones in my locker. Be right back."

"Make it fast," said Brydan. "I hear the first tune this year's going to be Choppin' Ettood."

Mr. Pavlicick, the Concert Band instructor, was Czechoslovakian and seemed to have great trouble pronouncing French. Every time Pavvie had announced that the band was about to play Chopin Étude last year, Sal had felt the reverberations coming all the way from Paris as Chopin rolled over in his grave. Normally, she would have shot Brydan a quick comeback, but today she grinned vaguely and hoped he didn't ask why she needed her clarinet case to fetch a pair of reeds from her locker. Maneuvering between the heavy cast-iron music stands, she slipped around the conductor's podium. The school was old, the music room cramped. The current joke was that everyone was going to have to link arms and learn to play their instruments as a human chain to conserve space. Most of the third-clarinet section sat on the first row of risers, but as Brydan was in a wheelchair, he and Sal were parked floor level in the front row between the oboe and first clarinets, which placed them directly in front of Pavvie's emphatic conductor's wand.

"Which means everyone gets to watch Pavvie's dancing butt instead of our beautiful beet-red, puffed-out faces," had been Brydan's complacent response to being assigned front-row seats.

Sal had liked him immediately — something about the grin in his eyes that refused to give up, and the large floppy ears he said came in handy as sails on windy days to give him more speed. "Okay, Bry — mission for your mind," she'd replied, testing him out. "Pavvie gets to pin a secret message to his butt and display it to the entire student body next time we perform at assembly. What does the message say?"

Pavvie was an active baton-waver who liked to conduct, knees bent, surging forward as if about to leap straight down the throats of his front-row players. This positioned his butt at a blasphemous angle, slightly closer to heaven than hell, about eye level to the watchful student body.

Sometimes Sal wasn't sure who deserved applause for the greatest entertainment value. Last year, he'd worn bright yellow pants to the Spring Concert performance. "Follow the yellow butt road" had become the catchphrase that drifted in his wake from that day forth.

"Secret message from Pavvie's butt to the universe?" Brydan had leaned back, eyes closed, as he'd blissfully contemplated the options. Then he'd deadpanned, "I am from the planet Marduk, where we have no auditory organs. This is the only reason I can stand this crazy job. You have my sympathy. Please feel free to plug your ears."

Sal hadn't practiced much over the summer and neither had Brydan. Although he was one grade ahead, he'd accepted his doom as a repeat third clarinetist with the same casual shrug she had. A scroll tied with a black ribbon showing up halfway through the second week of school, however, fell into an entirely different category. Sal half-walked, half-flew along the empty hallway. Either she was developing tunnel vision or the walls were closing in. That rolled-up piece of paper in her clarinet case couldn't possibly be a scroll from Shadow Council, it just couldn't. There were fifteen hundred students at S.C. — the odds of her winning the lottery were worse than managing a perfectly pitched B flat during one of Pavvie's deadly pre-concert warm-ups.

Turning left, she took the hallway past the gym. It was 8:10; shouts echoed from the basketball court but no one was out wandering the halls. Even so, she headed for a washroom that saw little traffic, a two-stall unit tucked behind the library. Pushing through the door, she set the clarinet case on the counter next to the sink, cautiously unsnapped the latches, and opened the lid.

It was still there, the black bow slightly squished, the scroll crumpled-looking. How had Shadow Council known she played clarinet #19? Brief relief erupted as she considered the statistical possibility of error. Maybe they'd intended to finger someone else, a *first*-clarinet player — one who mattered. But no, Shadow Council was rumored to be divine. More to the point, it had a plant in every club and student organization. Concert Band was especially well planted — Willis Cass, Shadow Council president, played first trumpet — but the guy who did their dirty work was probably drummer Pete McFurley. Percussion players were always on the lookout for attention.

Sal slid the scroll carefully off the clarinet joint and tugged at the bow. Panic snagged her heart as the ribbon caught. Swearing softly, she yanked and the bow slid free, revealing the blob of red candle wax that sealed the scroll.

*He who opens this is forever bound by the contents* was scribbled along the outside.

*Ha!* Sal thought shakily. *I'm not a he.* She tore it open.

The scroll was blank. Sal turned it every which way, but could find nothing written on the inside. The bastards! Whoever had set her up for this had a few things coming. With a hiss, she tore the scroll in half and stuffed it deep into the garbage pail, then added a few paper towels to cover the evidence.

A toilet stall opened and a girl emerged. Startled, Sal shoved her clarinet case over the rumpled black ribbon sprawled along the countertop. "Uh, hi," she stammered, the words too fast, foolish and trapped-sounding, but the girl didn't seem to notice. Her pale blue eyes flicked toward Sal, slightly unfocused, and her mouth twisted in on itself, a black slash of lipstick. Thin arms clasped a book to her chest. Quickly Sal scanned the cover in search of an easy comment, anything to fake casual.

"*Nobody Nowhere*, what an interesting title," she blurted, but the girl turned without a word and walked out the door. Gusting a sigh of relief, Sal swept the black ribbon into the garbage pail, then dug it out and flushed it down a toilet. Had the girl seen? Did it matter? She was a weird kid, a loner who always sat at the back of a classroom, her eyes in a strange stare out the window. *Nobody Nowhere* was a perfect two-word character sketch. Who knew what got through to her, but one thing was certain — she wouldn't say anything to anyone.

Sal did a rapid mirror check and gave herself a basic pass: long brown hair basically combed, glasses basically clean, buttons and zippers basically closed. She had the look assassins longed for, melting so thoroughly into a crowd, no one remembered she'd been there. Even Fate got bored looking at her. She'd never been singled out for anything — there wasn't a chance she'd win a lottery. The blank scroll was just a stupid joke. Probably Brydan's — she'd get him back with so much nonchalance, he'd start wondering if all he'd actually left in clarinet case #19 was his sanity quota for the day.

*But what if it was Shadow Council that had put the scroll in there?*

Taking out her 3½ reed, Sal stuck it in her mouth, wincing as spittle began to work its way into the wood and stale air bubbled onto her tongue. It was a moment she dreaded every time. Closing the case, she pushed her way out the washroom door and pondered all the way back to band practice, masticating heavily.

The second scroll showed up in English. Sal might not have noticed it — English was her last class for the day, her brain was set on Anticipation, and she'd managed to claim butt rights to the back corner desk next to an open window. Obviously, she was not destined for A+ status in English. Accepting her fate, she'd been investing heavily in the Pony Express, a system of note-passing that extended from one end of the classroom to the other, detouring the academic snobs who refused to participate in such petty pastimes. Many of these notes were intended as collective salutations, and most became chain letters en route, but those addressed to individual recipients were generally respected, especially if marked *Open and You Die*. It was a matter of honor to all Pony Express members to get each note to its intended destination. If caught, it was understood that your execution was your personal problem — the best solution was to drop dead and keep your mouth shut.

The note that spun whirlybird-style onto Sal's desk was heart-shaped with white lace glued around the edges, and *Sally Hanson* written across the front. Lunging to prevent the valentine from sliding off her desk, she glanced up to see if Ms. Demko had noticed. Fortunately, the teacher's back was turned, the flesh on her arm jiggling as she wrote furiously on the chalkboard — something about plot development. Synchronicity was in the air as Sal scanned the valentine suspiciously for signs of plot development. Heart-shaped notes were rare on the Pony Express — you'd have to be several dimensions past crazy to advertise romantic intentions on this party line. So far, she'd received a few skull and crossbones, and one lovely drawing of bats exiting a belfry. Sketches of Ms. Demko were frequent. Yesterday, someone had sent her a yellow sucker. It had been anonymous but unpoisoned, and she'd masticated it all the way home.

Was the heart a sequel to the sucker, or had some bozo gotten the steps reversed? Carefully, Sal flipped the valentine and read the back, skipping the chain-letter comments that had grown lewder as the note progressed across the classroom. The original message was printed in capital letters: LOOK INSIDE YOUR DESK. She sat staring at it, her face on pause while her brain made various quantum leaps. Eleven years of classroom espionage had not gone to waste — without looking up, she knew there were approximately twenty faces gawking surreptitiously in her direction, waiting for her enthusiastic dive into her desk. This had to be done right. Last year, a girl had found a dead rat stuffed behind her books. Packages of condoms and sanitary pads were common gifts. And there was that ancient rumor about a kid who'd found a finger in his pencil case.

Keeping her face poker straight, Sal slid down in her seat and peered into the desk's shadowy storage compartment ... and there it was — a white oblong shape tied with a black ribbon. Her heart thudded, deep and painful, digging its own grave. Slowly she inched the scroll toward herself. Both hands deep inside the desk, she untied the ribbon, broke the red candle-wax seal, and unrolled the scroll. The guy across the aisle kept faking a stretch, trying to gain a better perspective, but Sal casually slid her desk backward until she came up against the wall. This placed her in a small nook between a floor-to-ceiling bookshelf and the window, giving her a tiny pocket of privacy. Slumping in his seat, Mr. Yawn-and-Stretch gave up.

The scroll was blank. Sal took her time, examining it centimeter by centimeter inside the shadowy cave of her desk, but there wasn't a word, not even a mysterious hieroglyph or symbol.

*Give me a break*, she thought. *At least make this nervous breakdown worthwhile.*

If anyone saw this, she was done for. At S.C., a scroll with a black ribbon meant one thing only, regardless of what was written or not written on it. Lottery winners became lepers, social outcasts. No one remained their friend for long. Sal had to get rid of the evidence. If she picked off the red wax, the scroll could be flattened and slid into her duotang — it would pass for normal paper — but the black ribbon was a dead giveaway. She couldn't leave it in the desk, and she couldn't let it be found on her person.

Could she swallow it? When she was in grade four, her older brother Dusty had dared her to swallow a green licorice string lengthwise, and she'd tried. Halfway through, she'd started to choke and he'd yanked it back up. Then he'd chug-a-lugged the entire licorice string himself. He was an efficient garbage can. If he'd just materialize next to her right now, mouth stretched to greatest capacity, she'd happily drop in the ribbon of doom.

Was it possible these scrolls were from Shadow Council? *Anyone* could win that goddam lottery.

Balling the ribbon tight in her fist, she worked up a good spit, gagged, and got it down.


She didn't go to her locker after school but headed straight for her bike, tucked her books under her left arm, and rode home one-handed. The house was empty, her mother still at work, Dusty at the U of S, supposedly studying. Somehow Sal doubted it. Traveling the stairs to her room two at a time, she chucked her books in the general direction of the floor and took a dead man's fall onto the bed. Her aim was perfect — one wriggle and the body-shaped hollow at the center of the mattress shifted to cradle her like a hand, like sleep, a comfortable wrap-around dream. As silence settled into its customary places, she lay staring at the dust motes she'd set whirling in the window light. At certain angles, they became sparkle dust — purple, green, gold. The clock on the dresser ticked with manic precision, filling the quiet with tiny even sounds, slowing Sal's breathing until her eyes began to glaze. Sometimes, after moments like these, she'd wake to find herself sucking her thumb, or there'd be a large drool mark on her pillowcase and she'd be sleeping in it. People did disgusting things while they slept. She was never getting married. She'd have a boyfriend, he could come over and they'd have mad passionate sex, and then he could go home again. No way was she sleeping in a bed with two mouths slobbering away all night. Guys were probably ten times worse than girls if her brother was any example of what could be expected.

She lay for over an hour, wrapped in silence and the interminable ticking of her clock. Nobody knew she did this — spaced out, complete zombie zone. She had a way of stretching the tiny pocket of space between each tick of the clock and crawling into it, depositing part of her mind there, then crawling out again and letting the next tick come. It took a lot of concentration, digging the invisible hole, then stuffing it full of the parts of herself she didn't like. If the house was empty and quiet, with just the ticking of the clock and herself, she could get rid of a lot of junk. After twenty minutes she'd feel better, full of energy, the broken glass that had been scraping at her brain completely gone.

the lottery    11

Of course, there was always that large drool spot hanging around on her pillowcase afterward. Sitting up, Sal flipped her pillow and patted the dry surface. There, there — another crisis averted, and she'd handled it on her own. No one else knew, no one needed to know. Just give her an hour a day alone in her bed, and she could be her own psychiatrist. It was cheap, effective, with a little private drooling on the side. Who could ask for less?

Grabbing the half-eaten bag of Doritos on her dresser, Sal headed for the backyard and stretched out under a poplar. Above her, restless leaves pattered like rain. The tree was deep in the throes of September yellow, and spinning leaves settled with small touches onto her throat, chest and ankles. Sal licked a Dorito, then sucked it to a pasty mess in her mouth. The poplar was giving off a thick scent that came at her in waves, almost as if the tree was breathing, or thinking. Did trees send out scent waves instead of brain waves?

Sal patted the poplar's trunk. "You're a genius, tree."

The backyard, with its solid pine fence, patio swing and endlessly rustling trees, seemed far removed from scrolls, black ribbons, or any of your basic doom scenarios. Sucking on another Dorito, Sal worked it with her tongue until it caved and began to dissolve. Two blank pieces of paper tied with black ribbons — as far as she knew, Shadow Council delivered one scroll and one scroll only, and *that* scroll had fate spelled out in very clear English. Shadow Council had a reputation of getting straight to the point. She'd never heard of them jerking anyone around like this. No, the source of the blank scrolls had to be someone with a brain of the lowest reptilian order, which eliminated Brydan — and he wasn't in her English class anyway.

*Maybe* Shadow Council had started sending out decoy scrolls to keep everyone guessing. The true lottery winner had probably already received the real message, and several others were being strung along for some psycho's entertainment. Yeah, that made sense. Sal breathed in slowly, following the poplar's dreamy scent deep into her lungs. There, she had her head on straight again. No more panic grenades or gagging down unsanitary black ribbons. Whatever had possessed her to swallow it anyway? Why hadn't she shoved the ribbon into her pocket like an average normal sane person instead of being microwaved with fear, her brain dissolving into tiny white-hot waves?

Well, it wasn't going to happen again. She couldn't make a habit of losing her mind like that. But more importantly, what was the identity of the idiot who'd tied the ribbon onto that scroll? How long had it been since he'd washed his hands? Her brother never washed his hands. She would never, *ever*, consider getting into a handshake with him — he was always confusing his orifices. Not a pretty picture.

# Chapter Two

"We'll burn her," hissed Kimmie Busatto, hunched forward on her knees. "I cut every one of her pictures out of the yearbook. We're going to pass all her dark and evil molecules symbolically through the flame and watch her go up in smoke."

"Too bad it's just symbolic." Sprawled on the floor, Sal took in the details of her best friend's darkened bedroom — the closed curtains, the ravaged S.C. yearbook on the bed, the gleaming rectangle of tinfoil spread across the floor with the lit candle at its center. A terse phone call had summoned her partway through washing supper dishes with her mother, and she'd biked the four blocks to the Busatto's house to find Kimmie kneeling beside her tiny carpet of tinfoil and staring into a candle flame, a pair of scissors in one hand and a pile of jagged-edged clippings at her knee.

"We're not, uh, going to sic demons on her or any-

thing like that, are we, Kimbo?" Sal asked carefully, studying her friend's face. Kimmie's makeup was smudged, her
eyes puffy and heavy-lidded. "Summer's over, what can she
do to you now?"

Kimmie's chubby face contorted. "She's a vampire
queen, she's constantly sucking blood out of everyone.
Maybe she had problems with toilet training when she was
a kid. Heck, maybe she's still having problems with toilets
and that's why she's so vicious, but she went after me again
today. I'm telling you, it's this or physical violence." Raising the scissors above the candle flame, she made a few
ominous snaps.

"Okay, let's get this burn on the road." Dragging herself out of her sprawl, Sal mirrored her friend's position
facing the candle flame. "But we've got to make it quick
— I have a driving lesson with Dusty at 7:30."

"Fire's quick," Kimmie said grimly. "1,500° Celsius quick."
Pulling a pair of tweezers from her shirt pocket, she clamped
the top clipping and held it dramatically over the flame.

"Want to chant something?" Sal asked. "Deep and spec-
tral?"

"Just watch," Kimmie said. "Enjoy."

The edge of the clipping blackened and curled, whispering under a hot rush of flame. "Yessss," Kimmie crooned
as she picked up another clipping and extended it toward
the candle.

"Too bad it's too dark to see her face," Sal mused.

"We know what she looks like," muttered Kimmie as
the second clipping flared. "Everyone knows Linda Paboni's
malicious face. She's crawled deep into my psyche. I feel
like she watches me from the inside out. This is a soul-
cleansing ritual for me. My soul feels dark and heavy-laden."

"Linda Paboni, bitch supreme," Sal murmured sympathetically. Never having experienced a direct encounter with the vampire queen, she knew her only as one of the elite, popular, senior, S.C. students. Very popular — Linda Paboni had sucked the blood out of so many student clubs and social groups that her face appeared on every other page of last year's yearbook. The pile of clippings beside Kimmie's left knee was a sizable, if extremely vulnerable, monument to success.

"Why did I have to work with her this summer?" Kimmie rubbed soot across her face, giving herself a black eye. "Why would Sunshine Happy Day Camp hire someone like her?"

Kimmie had just completed a two-month job working as a counselor at a Saskatoon day camp where Linda Paboni had been the assistant supervisor. This meant Sal had put in the same two months listening to her best friend's hissed and tearful stories about Linda's split personality. By now, she had as much invested in a soul-cleansing ritual as Kimmie.

"Remember when Linda made me clean up Frankie Penner's vomit on the bus," Kimmie muttered through clenched teeth, "even though I had to clean up Rita Yahyahkeekoot's vomit the day before?"

"I remember," Sal said in her best supportive voice.

"Remember when she invited me to that Brad Pitt movie, then sent dweebie Ron Josephson to meet me instead of coming herself? I would *never* go out with Ron Josephson! He's got velcro hands. I can still feel them stuck to my boobs." Kimmie's chest heaved.

"We'll burn him too," Sal murmured comfortingly.

"And remember that song she taught the kids? There was a verse about each counselor." Kimmie warbled, choking out the words. "We're from happy Camp Sunshine, we love all our counselors, Kimmie Bufatso, we'll eat her for supper."

"How did she ever get away with it?" Sal said wonderingly, repeating the question she'd asked the first time Kimmie had told this story.

"Oh, it's just a mispronunciation." Kimmie pitched her voice high, mimicking Linda's mocking voice. "That's what she'd say if anyone asked, but she *taught* it to the kids that way. She'd grin at me every time they sang it, and those little buggers loved to sing it. This afternoon I passed her in the hall at school, and she sang the whole verse to me. Real loud — everyone heard it."

Kimmie's lips tightened, and she gazed stonily into the candle flame. A quick anger grabbed Sal's throat. Kimmie was always on some kind of diet and looking for a pair of jeans that would make her look thinner. She'd try on four or five outfits every morning before she left for school, moaning her way through each one. She wasn't that chubby, but nothing Sal said made any difference. Kimmie believed she looked like the Michelin Tire Man, and the slightest comment about her figure sent her into a funk for days.

"Allow me," said Sal, reaching for one of the Linda Paboni cutouts.

"No," said Kimmie, chewing fiercely on her ponytail. "It's my karma, I want to do it."

"Why don't you burn the whole pile at once?" suggested Sal, sinking back into her sprawl. "Blow her sky-high."

"Genius thinking, Sal." Clamping the pile of clippings with her tweezers, Kimmie fed them to the flame, and an entire school year of Linda Paboni's acid comments and dirty tricks went up in a brilliant whoosh. Lying on her back, Sal watched the airborne embers with a kind of awe.

Fragments of Linda Paboni's demise swirled above the candle on aimless demon wings.

"That felt so good," sighed Kimmie, rubbing more soot into her tear-smudged makeup. "If she sings that damn song again, can I borrow your yearbook for another burn?"

"My yearbook is your yearbook," promised Sal. "But I think we should write a Sunshine Happy Day camper verse about her and sing it the next time we pass her in the hall."

"Can't," said Kimmie immediately. "It'd be instant death. She made Shadow this year, didn't you know?"

"No," Sal faltered, a sudden ooze opening in her brain. "I didn't."

"She made Shadow, so she's untouchable." Scooping Linda Paboni's ashes into a neat pile, Kimmie scattered them again with a vengeful breath. "But I feel better. I thought about doing this alone, but I wanted you to be here. Just because ... well, y'know."

"Don't worry." Sal traced her fingers through the ashes, sketching the meaningless pattern of her thoughts. "She's toast now, and your psyche has been completely reborn."

"Maybe." Leaning forward, Kimmie blew out the candle with a sharp hard gust.


Dusty was at the wheel, the cassette deck blasting AC/DC, while his best friend Lizard hung out the passenger window, giving a running commentary on what he called the "sidewalk scenery." Sandwiched between them, Sal braced her knees against the dash in a vain attempt to avoid anything remotely resembling a hairy, jitterbugging, male leg. It was 7:45, the evening yet young, all three of them sucking down Slurpees as Dusty tooled along Broadway Avenue, headed for the suburbs and slower-moving life forms. Sal's birthday was in the spring, but Dusty had decided she needed a lot of practice well ahead of her driver's exam to work up her confidence. Although this also had their mother's overwhelming approval, Sal figured her confidence was already well-worked. She intended to ace that exam mid-afternoon on the day of her birth. Sweet sixteen and she'd be sweet behind the wheel, cruising every available millimeter of asphalt — she'd know Saskatoon like the back of her hand.

Suddenly curious, Sal held up the back of her hand and squinted at it. She could see nothing of interest, just a plethora of small blond hairs, another plethora of small brown freckles, and three or four bumpy blue veins. It was actually quite a dumb saying — no one ever bothered to look at the back of their hand. Now, if she was going to invent a cliché, she'd come up with one that made sense, something like "She knew Saskatoon like the tip of her nose." *Everyone* carried around a detailed soul-destroying map of the nose-zone blackheads and zits they'd groaned over that morning in the mirror.

Noting Sal's intense interest in her hand, Lizard grabbed her wrist and mashed his face into her palm. "Yup," he proclaimed loudly. "Definitely not human. Definitely the body part of an alien."

"Dusty!" Sal shrieked. Lizard was busily rubbing his oily greasy nose into her palm, infecting her with several deadly viruses. Talk about aliens — the guy acted as if he came from the planet of reverse social functions, where "please" and "thank you" were swear words.

Dusty whooped and turned down a side street. "Release the alien, Liz," he ordered. "She's about to take us into deep space."

Sticking out his meaty tongue, Lizard swiped it all over Sal's hand before leaning back with a satisfied smirk. Horrified, she stared at the gob glimmering on her skin. Talk about germ warfare. She hated it when her brother's friends treated her like a fifteen-year-old doormat, somebody's pet.

"Hey, Sal!" Dusty was standing outside the car, holding the driver's door open. "Earth to Sal."

Climbing out, she grabbed the front of his t-shirt and used it to wipe all foreign body fluids from her hand. "Where do you get your friends?" she hissed. "The mirror?"

Dusty parked his butt in the middle of the front seat and drained the last of his Slurpee. "Okay, this is major clutch time, got it? We're gonna let Sal lurch and jerk and whiplash our brains until she's slipping gears like a well-oiled machine."

The car was at least a decade older than Sal, an ancient Volvo with an insane muffler their mother was always ordering Dusty to get fixed. Dusty liked noise. With the kind of parties he attended, he said no one would hear him coming unless he ran a sonic boom off his muffler that could be heard at least a kilometer in advance of his arrival. Winters, he stored his hockey equipment in the back seat. Summers, it was basketballs, soccer balls, frisbees, and all the laundry he hadn't gotten around to "doing something about" yet. The car was an armpit. Sal wouldn't go near it unless he opened all the windows and drove up and down the block first, airing it out. Or unless she needed a driving lesson.

Sliding behind the wheel, she slurped the last of her drink and tossed the empty container onto the floor beside Lizard's feet. Technically, she and Dusty were family — they had the same last name, blood type, narrow face and brown hair, even a similar style of gold-rimmed glasses.

Everyone seeing them together for the first time commented on how much they looked alike, but still Dusty could be counted on to side with his rat-fink friends every time. She'd just have to deal with this one herself. Cautiously, Sal slid Lizard a sideways glance. Brush cut, baseball cap on backwards, smug grin all over his broad tanned face. *Hmm.* White t-shirt, three-quarters of a Slurpee to go. The world was his oyster. Sal looked around quickly, but no traffic could be seen coming down this side of Taylor Street. Unsuspecting, Lizard lifted the 7-Eleven cup to his lips.

Grinding into first, Sal stalled with a mighty lurch, and Lizard was snorting Pepsi ice crystals, spilling them all over his snow-white shirt.

"Sal!" Dusty howled. "I do NOT like that sound."

Sal collapsed against the driver's door, convulsed with helpless giggles.

"Get her!" Lizard choked, lunging toward her. His face streamed Pepsi rivulets. Ice crystals decorated his hair.

"Don't be such a nit, Liz." Leaning forward, Dusty effectively blocked Lizard's access to Sal's throat. "You know Sal and first gear. It was an accident."

"Ah!" cried Lizard, lifting both hands in a gesture of defeat. "An accident. Of course." He slumped against the seat, tugging disgustedly at his soaked t-shirt. Sal's giggles accelerated into the hyperventilation stage.

"Not too subtle, sis," Dusty hissed, then turned down AC/DC and announced loudly, "Okay, let's get this show on the road. How 'bout you turn in there, Sal?"

Crunching into first gear, Sal turned into the indicated parking lot and surveyed the possibilities. It was the teachers' parking area at Walter Murray Collegiate, which meant she was on enemy turf. Year after year, Walter Murray wiped their feet on S.C. in sports events. Maybe she could take out the parking lot barrier fence, or leave a skid mark as her signature. She'd watched Dusty spin enough donuts — all it took was a quick turn of the wheel. And Lizard still had a third of his Slurpee to go ...

Dusty's firm hand came down on the wheel. "Whoa, Sal. Whatever it is you're thinking about doing, you can stop thinking about doing it right now!"

Sal put on a very docile look. So, it was to be yet another boring driving lesson. Moping visibly, she drove back and forth across the asphalt as per Dusty's instructions, approximately one hundred kilometers per second behind her imagination.

"That's good," purred Dusty, locking his hands behind his head and stretching. "Now, shift second into third. So good, Sal, soooo good. Now, slow it down. Beeeautiful. Put it in reverse. Gooood. I like that sound, Sal, I like it just fine. Now, first to second ..."

"So, S.C. found out who this year's lottery winner is yet?"

They were driving back across the city, Dusty at the wheel, AC/DC once again ruling the ionosphere. Lizard had asked the question. Trapped in his lap, Sal was wrapped tightly in his arms. When she and Dusty had switched places, Lizard had come in for the kill, pouring the rest of his Slurpee down the front of her t-shirt and pressing his own soaked t-shirt to her back. Obviously, he'd missed the point — his t-shirt was white, hers was black — but she didn't bother explaining. Or struggling. Lizard loved a victim.

"No," Sal replied, ignoring a sudden scattering of heartbeats.

"Shadow's late this year," Lizard commented.

"They still pulling that crap?" asked Dusty.

Sal shot him a glance. His mouth had tightened, two lines pulling down the right corner. She knew the signs — this one was the prelude to a gigantic mood switch.

"Hey, it's a tradition," Lizard said shortly. "Goes back over thirty years, to the early 70s."

"So do the Bee Gees," scoffed Dusty. "Garbage can of history, man."

"The lotto winner gets perks." Lizard's left knee started jiggling.

"Kiss-my-ass perks." Dusty's fingers slapped erratically against the steering wheel. Abruptly, he leaned over and turned up the volume on the cassette deck. Lizard said nothing, his left knee manic. The sudden tension in the car made AC/DC sound like an understatement. Lizard's profile was fixed in a rigid glare out the side window, every part of his face mirroring Dusty's frowning stare out the front. Why would a casual reference to the lottery winner set them off like this? Sal gave a tentative wriggle to see if the change in mood meant she'd escaped Lizard's reptilian consciousness, but his arms tightened immediately. If he didn't forgive her soon, their clothes would dry, pasting them together for life.

"Uh, Liz?" This had to be done real casual — so smooth, the question would seem to be asking itself.

"Huh?"

She could feel the word form in his stomach. No surprise — that was where his brain usually hung out. "You were on Shadow Council, weren't you?"

"How'd you know that?"

"You're in the Celts' yearbook picture."

"Oh yeah." Lizard started rolling down the rim of his Slurpee cup. "What were you doing looking that far back?"

She was keeping it cool, her voice careful as a creeping cat. Leave no obvious tracks. "You guys graduated two years ago. It's not ancient history."

"Guess not," said Lizard. Dusty's fingers continued to slap the steering wheel, a short hard staccato, full of the unspoken. "Yeah," Lizard muttered uneasily. "I was on Shadow during my grad year."

"So," hedged Sal. "Exactly *how* does the lottery winner get informed? There's a scroll, right?"

"Black ribbon, red seal," Lizard said promptly. "Delivered directly to the lottery winner, and then the good times begin."

Dusty snorted and Sal shot him a runaway glance. This was getting really interesting, but she knew her brother — if she asked him anything straight out, he'd slam the lid on everything.

"So, uh, what does the scroll say?"

"That's a secret between Shadow and the lottery winner," Lizard said immediately. "Internal security. Dead secret or I'm dead, even two years after I graduated."

"But the scroll *does* say something, doesn't it?" Sal probed carefully.

"Yeah, sure it does. Otherwise, why send it?"

"And there's only one?" Sal's heart was picking up the pace.

"Yeah, there's only one scroll." Lizard was beginning to sound confused. "One scroll, secret message, black ribbon, red seal. It's legend, everyone knows it."

"What're you asking for, Sal?" Dusty shut off AC/DC. They were stopped for a red light, his face turned toward hers, holding the intense scrutiny he reserved for her. They both had their father's eyes — large, greenish-hazel. Sometimes, when Dusty looked directly at her, it was like staring straight into her own mind, the eyes of someone who could see deep inside, someone who *knew*. She'd choke, the air suddenly dark, the ground going into a swerve beneath her feet.

"Just wondering," Sal said coolly, leaning against Lizard's sticky chest and bracing her knees against the dash. "Everyone wonders, y'know. That sucker could be anyone."

"One lucky bastard a year," Lizard said evenly, still staring out the side window.

"Just so long as it wasn't you, eh, Liz?" Dusty asked quietly. The light turned green and he ground the gears into first, lurching the car across the intersection.

# Chapter Three

Overnight it rained, turning the house into a fragile membrane of sound. Sal dreamed of water sluicing through shadowy yellow trees, rushing down eaves and along gutters, carrying away old thoughts, ugly pain, everything that needed to be forgotten. In the morning she woke to a world heavy and water-soaked, dripping like a glad song, the sky stretching into a clear faraway blue. *The kind that takes your eyes and runs away with them*, she thought, standing by the garage with her bike and gulping the deep fresh air — it swooped into her as if it had wings, as if she could ride it anywhere and belong there.

A sudden breeze scattered the circle of raindrops dangling from the basketball hoop above her head, and she had to remove her glasses to dry them off. The hoop was ancient — the netting sagged and rust spots flecked the rim. Her father had nailed that hoop above the garage door for Dusty way back when Sal was still crawling around in diapers. The year he'd died, she'd been eight and Dusty twelve. That time was a vague gray smudge in her mind. She couldn't remember much of it, just the pale blur of her mother's face and the constant dull bounce of the basketball out back as Dusty played Terminator basketball nonstop through rain, fog, sun and snow. He'd spun pirouettes, bounced the ball backward, run at the basket for stuff after stuff until he'd dropped, gasping, to the pavement, but he'd never tried out for school teams, had dropped phys ed as soon as it was no longer a required course.

He could still swish jump shots from incredible angles up and down the alley, but right now he was splayed in bed, Snoresville. Second year university, and Dusty never got up before nine, regardless of his class schedule. Sal thought university sounded like a great improvement on high school — no one taking class attendance, responsibility that could be abused in an endless variety of ways. She could hardly wait.

Mounting her bike, she rode the clean wet streets toward Wilson Park, a route she often used as a short cut to school. Her hair lifted easily into the breeze and she raised her chin so she couldn't see the ground, even her handlebars — an old game where she pretended she flew above the earth like the wind. This morning she wasn't going to think about scrolls, tasteless jokes, or the jerks who played them. From what Lizard had said, it couldn't have been Shadow Council who'd sent her the two scrolls, and anyone else was relatively irrelevant. Reaching the park, she jumped the curb, then veered through an opening in the hedge that ran around the perimeter, getting a soaker when her knee brushed the foliage. The grass was a sparkling film of droplets, broken by footprints and one double set of wheel tracks that curved in a long sinewy wave pattern. Looking up, she spotted Brydan cruising across the park. The sine wave pattern was his signature. He said he was practicing logarithms.

"Hey, brown-noser," Sal hollered. "Getting your Trig done early?"

Brydan spun a one-eighty and waited for her to catch up. As usual he was smoking, jigging his shoulders as he listened to his diskman. Brydan was a big jazz fan — Keith Jarrett, Oscar Peterson, Cecil Taylor. He used a manual wheelchair and wore gloves most of the time, his upper body taut with muscle from working out in the small gym his parents had set up for him in their rec room. When he'd told Sal about the car crash, there were things he didn't have to describe — she was already there, spinning into the darkness with him. His older sister Cheryl had been driving, fourteen-year-old Brydan beside her in the front seat, both of them wearing seat belts, both high on acid. The icy patch had surfaced just before the railway crossing; they'd slid screaming through the barrier and struck the passing train. It had been an old car with a long front end. The train had crumpled the engine like Kleenex, right to the windshield, then carried the car for two hundred meters before dropping it and roaring off into the night. Brydan had lost both legs below the knees. Cheryl had survived with black eyes, a few scrapes, and recurring migraines that had her begging for the world to end.

Sal's father had hit the windshield with such force, his brains had been smeared from one end of the glass to the other. She'd been sitting next to him in the front seat, buckled firmly into her seat belt, and that moment of impact had ingrained itself deep into her consciousness where it lurked, hidden and waiting. If she tried to think about the accident, she couldn't remember a thing. Then, suddenly, memory would surface while she was staring out a window, fly right past her and disappear before she realized what had hit her. Sometimes it happened when she ran into Brydan unexpectedly — her brain would open, there'd be the mad screaming rush of memory, then a thud like a door slamming, and darkness. She'd learned to squeeze these moments thin and tiny, like the ticks of a clock, and let them pass into the deep dark nothingness of her mind.

"No way!" Putting on a loud smile, she skidded to a stop in the wet grass beside Brydan. "You took your clarinet home already?"

Clarinet case #12 poked out of the large pocket attached to the back of Brydan's chair. "My little sis wanted a go at it," he shrugged. "I had to warm up the reed for her, so I must confess my lips did make body contact."

He returned to his sine wave pattern and Sal coasted along behind him, converting his tracks into a double helix. "Your sister thinking of following in your musical footsteps?"

"Musical wheel tracks. I'm the footless wonder, remember?"

Brydan said it casually, but Sal flushed. To cover, she leaned over and gently whacked the back of his head. "Lucky this isn't one of your phantom limbs."

Brydan grinned. "Actually, it's an apparition. There I was, car smashed to smithereens, me missing both my legs and my head. How was I supposed to become a world-class clarinetist, *decapitario*? So I did this deep-six new-age visualization thing where I tapped into cosmic consciousness, and presto — I visualized a new head! Lucky everyone else can see it too."

"Too bad you didn't visualize one that worked," said Sal. "And did you have to visualize a muffler sticking out of your forehead? All that blood gushing out the back?"

Brydan was the only person she could joke with about car crashes. She hadn't told him about her father, but there was an understanding between them, like shared air. Concentrating on the double helix she was creating, she matched Brydan curve for curve. It was hypnotic, made her brain go stupid. The bike wobbled, she took a sharp swerve and had to put on the brakes.

"You wouldn't get anywhere in Special Olympics," Brydan smirked.

She opened her mouth, about to make a quick comeback when a series of shrill short screams started up close by, as if someone was being turned on and off. Making a quick U-turn, Sal saw a small group of kids at the other end of the park, pushing and shoving somebody in their midst. Instinctively she looked toward Brydan, who'd already dumped his sine wave pattern and was making a beeline toward them. Sal put on a burst of speed to catch up, then braked as she recognized the circling toughs — five grade nine boys reputed to be collecting bonus points for their frequent trips through youth court. A girl stood hunched between them as one boy pulled her hair and another grabbed her diskman. In spite of the pushing shoving bodies, Sal knew the victim immediately — the girl from the washroom, the strange loner who'd seen her in the washroom with the first scroll.

"Losers!" Brydan screamed, running his wheelchair full tilt into the back of the nearest boy. The domino effect took over, bodies falling everywhere, Brydan careening off his chair onto the top of the heap. Swerving to miss the group, Sal landed on her knees in the wet grass. The shock was jarring but she dragged herself to her feet, wanting to help Brydan off the heap before too many others got moving. He seemed all right, his glasses lopsided, his eyes fiercely bright.

"You need a seat belt for this kind of thing, Bry." As the groaning heap of bodies began to disentangle, she shoved the wheelchair toward him and extended an awkward hand. How was she supposed to get him from the ground into his wheelchair? What was the etiquette for this kind of situation?

"I've got it," Brydan muttered, grabbing the arms of the wheelchair and swinging himself easily into the seat. "My diskman fell off. It's in that pile somewhere."

As the heap erupted, Sal braced herself for another attack, but the five boys took off, waving the two diskmans and hooting loudly. Brydan stared after them grimly, hands jerking the wheels of his chair back and forth as he pounded after the thieves on phantom feet. Sal knew how tight his family's finances were — they'd never be able to replace a stolen diskman. Heart in a dull thud, she reached for her bike, but Brydan's voice stopped her.

"Leave it. They'd take your face off."

Popping a wheelie, he let out a string of swear words. Unsure of his mood, Sal squatted and began picking up the books that had fallen out of his wheelchair pocket. Then a quiet whimpering made her look up. Forgotten by them both, the girl who'd been attacked was sitting nearby, hunched in the wet grass, her arms around her knees, rocking. Odd cries came out of her.

"Hey." Tentatively, Sal touched her shoulder. "You all right?"

With a harsh scream, the girl swung at Sal's hand, knocking it from her shoulder. Sal jerked back in surprise and the girl began pounding her own head with both fists — whack, whack, whack — quick and frantic, directly on each temple.

"Oh my god!" Sal tried to grab the girl's hands.

"Sal, don't." Brydan pulled at her arm. "Back off."

"What do we do then?" demanded Sal. "Watch her hit herself?"

"I dunno."

They watched in silence as the girl continued to pound her temples, rocking and moaning. Sal couldn't help glancing at her watch. Twenty to nine — they were going to be late. Uneasily, she picked up the rest of Brydan's scattered books, drying them with her sleeve before sliding them into the pocket on the back of his chair. The girl kept rocking and hitting herself, Brydan watching her dully. Then, as Sal picked up his clarinet case, the girl's voice changed into tiny sliding cries, as if she felt helpless in her own throat.

Sal's throat locked, she forced a swallow that went endlessly down. The way the girl was crying, that voice — she hadn't heard it for so long she barely recognized it, but there it was, her own voice coming out of the other girl's mouth. Suddenly she was deep in memory, her bedroom quilt twisted tight around herself, the same wild cries coming up her throat. There had been no one to help her then, her mother and brother locked into their own pain. Alone in her room, completely alone, she remembered burrowing into the inner darkness, going down, way down — past the sound of her heartbeat, past thinking, down to where there was nothing but silence. At first she'd thought she was dead, but then she'd realized she was waiting — for what, she didn't know, just that she'd reached the end of everything she had and something had to come to her, touch her, give her what she needed to go on.

What had come to her, alone in that darkness, had been a voice, a deep blue voice that sang without words. It had come to her as if it knew her, as if it had always known her, as if it knew exactly the way her heart had once sung and the melodies it needed to hear again. For months after her father died, Sal had gone into her room, curled up alone, and waited for the blue voice to find her. Then, for some reason, she'd stopped — stopped so completely that for seven years she'd forgotten about the voice and its aching beauty until now.

If she could somehow reach into herself, find the deep peace of that voice and share it with the whimpering girl in front of her . . . But how? The voice had come to her only in dreams and daydreams, inside her head — Sal knew her physical singing voice was nothing anyone would choose to listen to. Still, there was Brydan's clarinet. As the hunched girl continued her wavering cries, Sal dropped to her knees and fumbled with the clarinet case, suddenly feverish to get the instrument unpacked.

"Here." She shoved the reed at Brydan. No way was she putting herself through a first-degree mastication of someone else's germs. "Suck on this."

Quickly she joined the clarinet's parts, then took the moistened reed from Brydan and slid it onto the mouthpiece. His eyebrows rose and she shrugged. Neither of them were virtuosos — that went without saying. How could she explain a phantom blue voice to him, except to say she probably felt it the way he felt his missing feet.

The girl's forehead was red with hit marks. Tentatively, Sal blew into the clarinet. It squeaked, no surprise. Then a low C caught and held. Not bad — no trembles or cracks. She thought of the blue singing voice, the way it had come to her, and sent herself into the C like a search. Then she descended into sound — B, A, G, the notes peaceful, long and even, shadows at dusk. Swinging upward, she shifted into minor intervals, the notes growing stronger, deeper into themselves — thoughts rising out of her body, a sweet blue voice stroking her mind: *You'll be okay, honey, just you wait and see. You're a sweet child, a good child, you never meant any harm. Your daddy knew you loved him …*

Eyes closed, Sal knew when the girl slowed her hitting by the way the air unclenched and loosened into easier breathing. Opening her eyes, she saw the girl still striking at her own head but slowly, like a toy winding down. Although her eyes were closed, the girl had shifted so that she now sat facing Sal. Gradually, as Sal continued to play, the girl's fists stopped connecting with her head and she rocked with her hands upheld and loosely clenched. When she finally opened her eyes, she stared about herself as if confused, her pale blue gaze not quite focused, returning again and again to Sal's general direction as if asking a question. Sal didn't know what the question was, much less how to answer it. Heck, from the look in those unfocused eyes, Sal wasn't sure the girl even *saw* her. Resting the clarinet bell on her knees, she watched the girl rock, more gently now, both hands limp in her lap. She was thin, her coal-black hair obviously dyed and cut in ragged chunks, as if she'd done it herself. Once again, she was wearing black lipstick, but the rest of her clothes were gray. Why the black lipstick and hair if she wasn't after the usual image? She didn't look tough.

The girl sighed heavily, something leaving her. Then, without speaking, without even glancing in Sal's direction, she climbed clumsily to her feet and walked away.

"Whew!" said Brydan. "Music tames the savage beast, eh?"

Startled, Sal felt his voice pull her back into the reality of Wilson Park, the scuff marks left by the grade nine toughs in the grass, and the raw throb the clarinet had imprinted into her lower lip. Everything felt dreamy and indistinct, as if she was halfway between worlds, still riding the effortless blue voice. Without replying she dismantled the clarinet, placing each piece carefully into the velour-lined case. Something deep and beautiful floated within her body, changing shape like clouds — a deep singing peace, slowly fading.

"Since exactly *when* have you been able to play actual *music*, Sally Hanson?" Brydan demanded.

Sal shrugged and slid the clarinet case into his wheel-chair pocket.

"I swear you've been possessed by the ghost of Benny Goodman!" Brydan sat, openly staring. "No, worse, you actually practiced all summer!"

"I just visualized it." Sal picked up her bike.

"Visualized what — a phantom embouchure? Pavvie hears you playing like that, he'll stick you on first."

"Then he won't hear me." Mounting her bike, Sal pedaled off quickly. "Firsts have to *practice*."

Brydan caught up with her, arms pumping. She slowed her pace.

"Who was that girl?" she asked. "D'you think she'll be all right?"

"Tauni Morrison?" asked Brydan. "She's always been weird. Freaks easy, but she should be okay if people leave her alone for a while."

Sal could relate. "I think we're going to be late."

"No kidding. It's twenty after nine."

"It is?" She gaped in astonishment.

"You were playing for half an hour." Brydan gave her an odd look. "Didn't you notice?"

A delicate fear winged through Sal. How could something rise out of her and change everything, just like that? Where had that beautiful playing come from, those lovely sounds that had trickled through her like willow trees stroking water? They were gone now, lost, like everything else in her life that had blessed her, then disappeared. Grinding her foot hard against the pedal, Sal put on a burst of speed.

"Hey!" hollered Brydan.

"Oh, sorry." She braked and waited for him to catch up. "You got any condoms?"

A slight flush hit Brydan's face as he coasted past. "What is this, an invitation?"

She did this to him sometimes, talked to Brydan as if he was Dusty, Lizard or another of her brother's uncouth friends. It never failed to take Brydan into the red zone, as if he thought she'd somehow managed to deke his civil pretenses and zoom straight into his thought life. Why did guys think they were so different from girls when it came to thinking about sex? "I just thought, in case the office secretary asks us what we were doing, we could show them to her. Put her mind at ease."

Brydan laughed drily. "Sal, did anyone ever tell you that your grasp on reality let go a long time ago?"

"Hey, I'm holding on with my phantom limbs."

He liked the joke. Everyone liked a joke. Tell enough jokes and no one looked past the surface, down to where the strange wailing cries were hidden. Putting on an easy grin, Sal pedaled through the clean wet morning toward the sunlit walls of Saskatoon Collegiate.

# Chapter Four

The third scroll was dropped onto her binder as she rushed between classes at mid-morning break. The halls were crowded, she hadn't seen anyone of note beside her — the scroll hadn't been there, then suddenly it was. Instinctively, she pulled the binder to her chest, crushing the scroll to invisibility. A mad screaming started in her head: *No, it can't be, it can't, why is this happening to me?* To her left, she spotted an open maintenance closet, full of cleaning solutions and wet mops. Stepping in, she closed the door and fumbled for the light switch. The air gave off the usual slight crinkling sensation as the electricity cut in, and the small room grew sharp-edged with light. Frantically she tore at the ribbon and the wax seal, not caring if the paper ripped. Things often came in threes, it was the number of finality. This had to be the last scroll, the last *blank* scroll, and the end of a tasteless joke that just didn't know when to quit.

The crushed paper opened uneasily. Sal's eyes skimmed the contents, then darted to the bare bulb above her, its vivid electric wire. In the stillness her breath repeated itself, harsh in her throat. Thick chemical odors closed in like a cage. As her eyes reluctantly returned to the black message scrawled across the page, the lightbulb's electric afterimage danced across her retinas, confusing her vision, but the third scroll's contents had already been seared deep into her memory.

*Congratulations! You are this year's lottery winner. Report high noon, you know where. Tardiness will not be tolerated.*

She was on her bike, pedaling furiously. She burrowed deep into her bed, sucking her thumb. She huddled in a bean-bag chair under the giant Winnie-the-Pooh at the downtown library branch, nose buried in *Miss Pickerell Goes to Mars* and shaking uncontrollably. Endless escape scenarios flashed through Sal's head as she slouched near the back of her French class, each granting a brief virtual-reality burst of freedom before returning her to the late-morning classroom, the desk with the cracked seat that pinched her butt, and the clock at the front of the room sweeping its hands around the final fateful arc toward twelve o'clock.

She sucked at her tongue, swallowing and swallowing the sour taste of fear. There was no way to avoid this meeting. All over S.C., Shadow Council members were slouched in similar desks, faking interest in quadratic equations and the dissection of dead rats while they plotted her doom. Her name hadn't yet been released to the general student population — no one had started treating her as if she'd contracted rabies — but the important students knew. She could feel their minds, like lasers in an electronic network, closing in on her from all over the school. In thirty minutes ... in fifteen ... in ten, the twelve o'clock bell would ring and those minds would materialize into bodies. Someone was probably already standing guard, waiting for her outside in the hall. They'd have her class schedule; Shadow Council always took care of details like that. Hell, they probably had a plant sitting somewhere in this very classroom, watching her right now.

"Sally Hanson, lisez le commencement du chapitre trois, s'il vous plaît." The teacher's voice, its crisp concise accent, was a sudden missile winging through Sal's brain.

"Huh?" As Sal straightened, her hand slipped on her notebook, leaving a sweaty imprint on the blue-lined page.

"Frère Jacques, Frère Jacques, dormez-vous?" sing-songed the teacher. The class laughed, a sound defined by its ordinariness. Over by the window, Kimmie faked a coma, then flashed a sympathetic grin. Swallowing hard, Sal stared at the friendly neutral expressions that surrounded her. In approximately one hour, her first meeting with Shadow Council would be over, the invisible all-important X marked permanently on her forehead, and her name released like oxygen into the bloodstream of S.C.'s rumor-mill. At that time, she would be set finally and ultimately apart. Never again would anyone look at her with generic friendliness or indifference. This ordinary moment, this classroom of grinning faces was like a banished prisoner's last glimpse of a familiar homeland as the king's ship took him to the deserted island where he'd been condemned to live alone, forever in exile.

It was a door like any other, in a hallway shared with classrooms and a girls' washroom. Bare and nondescript, there was nothing to announce its purpose, unlike the insignia that appeared on the school store, yearbook, and darkroom doors. No sign had been tacked to it announcing *Enter With Trepidation*, no neon skull and crossbones glowed above the doorknob, but there wasn't a single S.C. student who approached its threshold without having achieved the elite rank of membership or a direct summons. Teachers, even Mr. Wroblewski, the school principal, knocked before entering.

Officially, Shadow Council fronted as the Celts, a club that had been established decades earlier to assist with school events. Members helped the maintenance department with various tasks such as setting up for school assemblies and sports meets, and they frequently did odd jobs for other clubs, such as distributing publicity posters throughout Saskatoon. In return for these services, they'd been given the use of a small clubroom. Applications from students who wished to join the club were voted on by the current membership. Over the years the Celts had gained an elite status as an exclusive, all-male club, until a female principal had forced the gender issue. Now it was an elite, gender-inclusive, exclusive club that put in its required muscle-time stacking chairs, distributing posters, and posing for its annual yearbook photo surrounded by cartons of Molson Canadian — a club that, on the surface, looked as ordinary as the door that closed it off from the rest of the school.

As Sal approached the door she could hear muffled voices punctuated by bursts of laughter. To either side the hallway stretched into an echoing emptiness, the early noon-hour rush over, only the occasional student ambling past. For the past ten minutes, she'd been drifting in and out of the girls' washroom across the hall, disguising herself as a weak bladder, but none of the glances thrown her way had been remotely speculative. Even after receiving the third scroll, there was nothing to set her apart — she continued to fade into the masses as seamlessly as she'd always done.

No one had been waiting outside her French class. Shadow Council must have assumed, in its arrogance, that she'd show as expected, no matter what kind of blood, sweat and dissolving entrails she dragged in her wake. Another burst of laughter erupted inside the room, inverting her stomach, and Sal groped for the doorknob. The cool metal slipped under her hand, and she had to try a second time. Then, suddenly, the door was swinging toward her, panic opening wide, as if someone had torn the ribs from her chest and now there was nothing to stand between herself and the sheer fear of her heart.

For a moment she saw them as they were without her — nine senior students in jeans and rugby shirts, sprawled across an old couch and several armchairs, and laughing over cans of Pepsi and cafeteria lunch trays. Linda Paboni, vampire queen, perched on a guy's lap. Others sat, feet dangling, along a row of cupboards. They could have been a group of popular students from any public high school. There was nothing to distinguish them in any way except the presence of Sal Hanson herself, standing in the doorway with the third scroll clutched in her right hand.

A face turned toward her, then another. Like a chalkboard eraser, silence moved across the group, erasing conversation. A gleam seemed to hover over them and they radiated an invisible menace, their layered eyes looking out from behind secrets. Even though Sal was the only one standing, it felt as if they were all looking down at her. Someone snickered.

"Come in, come in," called a soft voice. "Don't let the grass grow beneath your feet."

The speaker sat in a burgundy armchair, a shaggy, dark-haired guy with long sideburns — Willis Cass, trumpet player, Student Council vice president, and one of the school's top athletes. Not once, during all of last year's Concert Band practices, performances and parties, had Sal spoken to him. Now, as she stepped slowly into the doom of that room, she felt his eyes watching her speculatively, as if she was some kind of conversation piece, curious and oddly shaped. Settling onto the arm of his chair, a bleach-haired girl giggled and slapped his shoulder.

"Close the door behind you, if you don't mind." Willis's voice seemed to lean toward Sal, encircle her with concern. Turning too quickly to comply, she knocked her hand against the doorframe and felt nothing. She'd gone completely numb. The door clicked quietly as it slid into place, closing her in, and she stood staring at the doorknob as if she'd never seen one before.

"We've saved a chair for you. Come and sit down," Willis continued, his voice gentle and insistent. Sal watched her hand slide off the doorknob as if it belonged to a stranger. It did belong to a stranger — *she* was a stranger, she'd never met the person she was becoming, walking woodenly toward the foot-stool Willis was indicating at the center of the group.

"Sit down," he said and she sat facing him, her eyes on his sloppily laced Reeboks.

"Give me the scroll."

Automatically, she handed it to him, his voice the key that unlocked her movements.

"Thank you," he said and a silence ensued, a silence of eyes and breathing. All about her she felt it — a soft-breathing circle of watching eyes. She wasn't looking up, no way was she making eye contact with the horde of predators that pressed so close, she could have touched any one of them without stretching. She might have to be here, trapped in this room, there might be no physical escape, but she knew how to squeeze her mind small and run off into cracks and crannies. They could stare at her body for as long as they wanted, she was already gone, crawled into a hole in the baseboard or deep into the wall — *The Wall Live*, her favorite CD, *the* classic album of all time and the one she and Dusty pumped to top volume in the rec room when their mother wasn't home. "Don't be a brick!" they would yell at each other, twitching and convulsing to Gilmour's achingly gorgeous guitar chords and Waters' heartbeat bass, throbbing at the core of the universe. "Don't be a brick!"

"You know why you're here," Willis said after a long pause.

Eyes fixed on the double knots in his shoelaces, Sal jerked out a nod.

"Tell us why you're here," said Willis.

"The scroll," Sal croaked faintly. The girl beside Willis giggled and Sal fumbled for her name — Ellen Petric, a girl who had mixed success with Nice'n Easy. One day she'd be honey-blonde, the next, a vibrant carroty sheen.

"The scroll?" probed Willis.

"... told me to come," faltered Sal.

"And why did it tell you to come?"

"Because I won the lottery."

"That's right," Willis said approvingly. "Tell me, Sally Hanson — what does it mean to win the lottery?"

The words were automatic, unthinking, her brain dulled by fear. "It means I'm your dud for the year."

Willis's eyebrows rippled. A look of amusement crossed his face.

"Demerit," said a voice directly behind Sal.

"Reason for the demerit?" asked Willis mildly, looking past Sal to the girl who'd spoken.

"Victim showing disrespect to Shadow Council president," replied the girl, her voice clipped and flat.

"Rolf, record one demerit," said Willis, nodding at a lanky blond guy on the couch.

"Sally Hanson, one demerit," murmured Rolf, marking an X in the binder on his lap.

Not even five minutes had passed, and there was already an X beside her name. "What's a demerit mean?" Sal blurted, her voice a small explosion in her throat, scaring her.

"Second demerit," snapped the girl.

"Reason for demerit?" asked Willis, his face expressionless.

"Victim speaking without permission," said the girl.

"Record second demerit," said Willis, and Rolf's hand marked another X.

Sal's lips parted slightly, as if trying to speak without sound. Jagged waves skittered across her brain, coming and going — nothing that made sense, nothing to hang onto.

"If you wish to ask a question," Willis said softly, "raise your hand and wait until you're given permission to speak."

Slowly Sal's hand rose.

"Yes?" asked Willis.

"I'm not a victim," said Sal.

"Demerit," the girl behind her snapped again. "That's not a question."

"Record demerit," said Willis.

Fear was a large dry tongue, filling Sal's mouth. Again, her hand went up.

"Yes?" prompted Willis.

"Do I get to give demerits?" she asked.

For a moment, Willis's face seemed about to break into a laugh. Then he leaned forward and took her chin in his hand. Sal stopped breathing. Touched — she hadn't expected to be touched.

"Listen to me, little sis," Willis Cass said quietly. "We know you better than you think. In fact, we knew you before you entered this school. We were waiting for you to start S.C., and we've been watching you since you got here. Maybe it's a coincidence you won this year's lottery, and maybe it isn't. Whatever — your name got drawn, and you're the lottery victim. You know what that means. Everyone knows what that means."

He paused, letting the silence gloat. Sal stared at the network of blue veins on his upturned wrist.

"You ever talk to last year's victim?" he asked finally.

Knowing descended upon her. Motionless, she sat without speaking.

"I asked you — did you talk to last year's victim?"

Sal shook her head.

"So, you know how it works. Everyone cooperates. Everyone wants a victim, Sally — even you. So how can you complain? Did you protest when it was someone else? No, you watched, you enjoyed, and now it's your turn. Now you're Shadow's victim, Shadow's dud for the year. We'll assign you duties, and you'll perform them. When we pull your leash, you'll come. We whistle the tune, and you dance. Listen up now while we introduce ourselves, so you won't confuse us with the masses that dwell under our guiding light.

"I'm Willis Cass, Shadow Council president." Releasing Sal's chin, Willis raised his right hand, the middle three fingers pointed upward, the fifth and the thumb tucked in.

"Ellen Petric," smirked the carrot-blonde beside him, also raising the middle three fingers of her right hand.

"Rolf de Regt, Shadow Council secretary," said the guy with the binder, giving her the same hand signal.

"Fern O'Brien," said the girl next to him, and so it went, the circle introducing itself one by one, pausing longest at Linda Paboni, Shadow Council vice president and demerit enthusiast sitting directly opposite Willis Cass. *Jesus*, thought Sal, *I left my back wide open*. Several runaway glances were enough to match the girl in front of her to Kimmie's vampire queen stories — the power smirk, the knowing eyebrows, the direct hazel gaze sharpened to a killing edge. Slightly giddy, Sal continued to rotate on the footstool, obediently receiving each name and three-fingered salute until she found herself once again facing Willis, another lengthy pause, and a long swallowing silence.

"Four demerits," Willis mused, stroking his chin. "Punishment begins at five, Sally. You're lucky I didn't give you two for your last indiscretion, but we're going easy on you today. We're not brutes, we know you're learning the ropes, but we have to follow the traditions that were set in place long before any of us started at this school. We all have our parts to play. You play yours, and you'll find out we're really on the same side. Friends."

Sal's stomach lurched, and she fought the neon urge to throw up all over his double-knotted Reeboks.

"In fact, we're the only friends you've got now." Willis's voice faded to a whisper and the circle around Sal sighed and rustled as if some kind of epiphany had been achieved, something beautiful released.

Straightening in his burgundy throne, Willis's

demeanor changed. "Okay, listen up, folks. Wroblewski and McCormick are dropping by in five to give us the run-down on our prospective duties. Everyone tighten your asses. Fake respectable." His glance trailed across Sal as if he'd forgotten her presence. "Victim dismissed," he said. "When we want you, you'll know."

She stumbled to her feet, muscles stiff from gripping panic in one position for so long. Ellen Petric snickered and the circle parted, defining her escape route. At the door she fumbled for the knob, breath locked in her lungs until she reached the hallway, until she was free.

"One more thing," said Willis, as her hand tightened on the doorknob. "Shadow business is dead secret. No one outside hears about it. Ever."

She felt the leash about her throat, tightening like the silence in the room. Then someone coughed, the doorknob turned, and she was stepping into a hallway that echoed with a long, indifferent emptiness.

# Chapter Five

When she walked into English, she knew the word was out. Her first class after lunch had been Music — there'd been the usual grimaces and sideways glances as instruments squeaked and lips grew puffy and raw, but nothing conspicuous, nothing that loomed out of people's eyes and said they knew. Now, as Sal walked into English, the clue was the sudden silence that followed her across the room, a force field turning faces down and away as she blundered along the aisle toward her desk. Collapsing into her seat, she banged a thigh and felt again the absence of pain, though her joints were disintegrating and cold waves traveled her gut. Then, suddenly, sensations loomed, her cheeks throbbing with heat, her skin a slow gloating fire. With a loud sucking sound, her sweaty hand slid across the varnished surface of her desk. Biting her lower lip, she swiveled to face the window.

Outside, the sky was a flawless blue, arcing up and

away. She stared at it, part of her rising into its blueness, a part that no longer belonged to her because it couldn't live within anyone as trapped as she was. For she was well and truly trapped. There was no way out. She remembered last year's winner — Jenny Weaver, a grade eleven student. Brainy, popular, Jenny had decided the whole thing was bogus and hadn't responded to the summons. Instead, she'd gone on with her life as if nothing had happened. Rather, she'd tried to go on with her life, and some of her friends had initially gone along with the charade, pretending right along with her. Shadow Council had left Jenny alone — completely alone — focusing instead on her friends, applying their quiet, behind-the-scenes, persuasive tactics. One by one, Jenny's friends had dropped off her phone-call list. No one would sit with her in the cafeteria, and as long as she defied Shadow Council, nobody had signed out books when she'd worked at the library checkout counter. Sal remembered Jenny's face, how she'd refused to give in, keeping her chin up, her smile bright and hard, and meeting everyone's eyes, giving each person she encountered the chance to redeem themselves by returning her smile.

No one had smiled back. By Thanksgiving Jenny's smile had begun to waver, but her face had continued to fight off doubt. Sal could still feel the weight of the other girl's eyes sliding across her own one afternoon in late October — desperately sure of herself, resolutely carrying a flag for the possibilities of human nature — and the way her own gaze had dribbled away, leaving the lottery winner to stumble on to the next pair of eyes. By Hallowe'en, Jenny Weaver had given up her mask of hope, and on the Day of the Dead had finally presented herself at Shadow Council's door.

Her term as lottery winner was now over. People were

talking to her again, she sat with a circle of friends at lunch time, Jenny Weaver was as popular as she'd ever been. Last year, and the hell it had brought her, seemed to have dropped off the face of the earth, unless you looked directly into her eyes. Just this afternoon on her way to English, Sal had passed the former lottery winner in the hall with two of her friends. Jenny had been talking a mile a minute, her eyes darting like a dragonfly, here, there, landing nowhere, as if everything she saw was an illusion, a shifting hologram of smiles and laughter, and beyond this stretched the long ache of a truth she'd have to carry alone for the rest of her life.

At the front of the classroom, Ms. Demko began to write the day's assignment on the chalkboard. As usual, the Pony Express broke into a wild gallop as soon as her back turned. Out of the corner of her eye, Sal saw a note progressing along the back row, hand to hand. As it approached, something fierce and painful fluttered in her chest. She dug her teeth savagely into the inside of her lower lip, telling herself she didn't care and if she did, it was of no consequence — emotions were trash, should be firebombed and tossed into the dustbin of history. The note slid into the hand of the guy to her right. He read the name written on the front, then slowly, deliberately, leaned across the aisle and tapped the shoulder of the girl sitting ahead of Sal. Slipping the note up her sleeve, the girl waited as Ms. Demko fussed through some papers on her desk, before passing it to the student in front of her.

The note should have come through Sal. The Pony Express followed an established route of dependable couriers, and Sal was definitely on it. She'd taken a giddy pride in her elaborate note-passing skills, riding the communal current that sang through the network of note-passers as each message reached its intended destination. It was a small pleasure, a silly one, something so ordinary she'd never noticed the assumption in it.

*Everyone loves a victim.* There was no arguing with the words of Willis Cass. Ask the Pony Express. Ask Jenny Weaver, or any one of her so-called friends. Sucking a steady flow of blood from the tear in her bottom lip, Sal realized that if she tried to catch Jenny's eyes at any point during the rest of this year, the other girl would look away.

She didn't know whether to show for her after-school rendezvous with Kimmie. They were supposed to meet Tina Wong at the bike racks, then head downtown and cruise Midtown Plaza for Tori Amos CDs. But those plans had been made at mid-morning break, just before Sal had received the third scroll and the world had turned its face inside out, displaying the other side of its mask. Since then, everyone's eyes had been sliding over and around her as if she was made of Teflon, and no one had spoken to her. Which side of the mask did Kimmie belong on? What would her true face reveal?

*The same as always*, Sal told herself, shoving her books hard into her locker and trying to force back the panic. They'd been friends since grade two, no high-school boycott could interfere with that. Or could it? Kimmie wasn't all that strong. She might act tough while putting the match to a pile of yearbook pictures, but one glance at the vampire queen in the flesh would have her in tears, running for cover. She'd never be able to resist all of Shadow Council.

How would it happen? What would the moment be

like? Sal fought off the knowing that descended upon her, the images flashing through her mind. Would there be words, would they fumble through sentences, trying to get the explanations just right? Or would Kimmie just walk past ...

No, no, she wouldn't. They'd been friends forever and they would stay friends. Closing her locker firmly, Sal turned toward the exit that would take her out to the bike racks, but found she couldn't make herself take the necessary first step. Maybe she'd just hang around the front entrance at the other side of the school for a while. That would give Kimmie and Tina extra time to arrive at the bike racks so she wouldn't have to stand around, fidgeting moronically while everyone stared. Then, when she did make her appearance — just a little late — Kimmie and Tina would already be there waiting. She'd be able to see them as soon as she came around the southeast corner of the school. Immediately, she'd know.

Emerging from the front exit, Sal descended the stairs in a rush of students, then stood hesitating at the bottom. Normally she would have made a beeline for one of the nearby groups, grabbed a swig from someone's Pepsi and dived laughing into the next available joke. But today she found herself edging inexplicably to the right, in among a row of fir trees that ran along the south side of the building. Not too far in, just enough to take her out of casual observation — all things considered, a practical solution to an unbearable present tense.

To her left, students poured down the stairwell, a constant stream of words and laughter. No one noticed as she stood among the fir trees, an impervious breeze lifting the tiny hairs on her arms. Five minutes passed, and she decided to give it five more. Sometimes Kimmie was late but she was dependable, she always showed. Then, as if some inner signal had been given, Sal looked up to see two girls coming down the stairs. Pressed to the outer rail, they were so close she could have reached out and touched the short chubby girl with the long dark ponytail and the slightly smudged makeup. Kimmie's eyeliner was always smudged; she was forever rubbing her eyes with the heel of her hand and giving herself a distinctive sunset look. But she had 20/20 vision, and as she came down the stairs that 20/20 gaze kept flicking toward the right, toward the row of fir trees camouflaging the school wall, as if she'd seen ...

Had she seen? Had she? Kimmie paused, head down and gripping the handrail. Sal jammed herself back through the fir trees so fiercely that she collided with the school wall. Branches scraped her face and arms, snapping into place as she fought the wild harsh rhythm of her breathing. Cautiously she peeked out and withdrew with a hiss. Kimmie was still standing motionless, halfway down the stairs, trapped inside a decision she couldn't force herself to make. Then someone bumped into her from behind and she stumbled forward, gaining momentum. By the time she reached the bottom of the stairs, she was in a full-out run, headed across the lawn.

"Hey, wait up!" called Tina, racing after her. "What's the rush?"

So that had been it — the moment come and gone. Watching her best friend disappear into the crowd, Sal methodically chewed the inside of her lower lip to a bloody pulp. It hadn't been that bad, not really. They hadn't had to fake their way through explanations, hadn't even had to choke out a single word. It was simply, suddenly, all over — decided, just like that.

Waiting until the stairs cleared, she fought her way out of the fir trees' manic embrace.

The bike racks were half-empty, a few kids standing around chatting. As she bent to unlock her bike, she could feel the glances, but no one commented or acknowledged her in any way. Straightening, she felt the sky like an enormous boulder pressing down on her back. This, then, was the size and weight of loneliness — everything outside herself. Backing her bike slowly out of the rack, she considered swinging onto the seat but felt too exhausted to do anything but walk.

"Sal!"

For a moment it didn't register — the wheelchair coasting toward her, the guy with the glasses, goofy grin and oversized ears cruising both sides of his head. Then meaning broke through the numbness, and relief hit her so violently she felt torn open, end to end. Brydan Wallace was speaking to her. She wasn't alone. Shadow Council didn't rule.

"Hey Bry — where's the clarinet? Shirking your musical fate yet again?" Biting down on the tremble in her mouth, she looped her chain-lock around her bike seat.

"Don't want to overdo things." Popping a dramatic wheelie, Brydan came to a halt beside her. "Strain these talented lips."

"Got big plans for those lips?"

"Big plans," he said, flushing slightly. "Monumental plans."

They started off down the sidewalk, the flow of students parting to make room for Brydan's wheelchair. Keeping her head down, Sal coasted through the heavy thud of her heart. It was only a matter of time before someone turned and commented, Brydan realized his mistake, and absolute loneliness descended upon her again.

"This way," he said, heading down a driveway to avoid the upcoming curb. His map of Saskatoon looked very different from most people's. Large Xs popped up everywhere: *don't go here, don't even think about going there.* Before meeting him, Sal had never considered the height of the average curb — just one step up from the base of the average wheel.

"Y'know," said Brydan, veering around a parked car. "I used to have a girlfriend who could put her entire hand in her mouth. She could even get half her foot in."

"Now that's using your lips." In spite of everything, Sal grinned. Turning at the corner, they left the stream of students behind. A car passed slowly, the girl at the wheel belting out an enthusiastic monotone to a song on the radio.

"She's really good at that note," commented Brydan. "If she and I got together, we could sing a great minor third."

"That'd be a great future for your lips."

"Mmm," said Brydan, and Sal drifted on the thinking sound of his voice, trying to decipher his thoughts. Would he bring it up? Would he want to talk about it? He was probably wondering the same thing about her, but what if he hadn't heard? How could she face the moment his face turned inside out and his friendliness vanished?

Coasting to a stop, Brydan pulled a package of DuMaurier from his shirt pocket and lit up. "Want one?" he asked, quirking an eyebrow.

"No thanks."

"You a nicotine virgin?"

"I tried it once," Sal said. "Way back in grade five. I stole one of my brother Dusty's cigarettes and went into the bathroom on the first floor. I thought I had it all worked out so I wouldn't get caught — I even blew the smoke out the window so Mom wouldn't smell it."

"Did you inhale?"

"Nope. My lungs are still virginal," Sal confessed. "But our neighbor, Mrs. Hume, just happened to be outside, raking her lawn. When she saw smoke coming out our bathroom window, she called the fire department. I think they sent every fire truck in the city — sirens, flashing lights, police, the whole works."

"Your first cigarette." Brydan said it with awe. "Now that could really put a person off."

"Yeah," said Sal. "Big Brother never takes his eyes off me."

It was a hint, coded but obvious. Would he pick up on it? She was sworn to silence — as Willis had said, all Shadow Council business was dead secret, and as of today, she was official Shadow Council business. But Brydan wasn't sworn to anything, and it was entirely possible that by wheelchairing her home he was declaring a full-fledged revolt against the lottery winner boycott. He had guts. She'd known this, but the awareness had never before opened within her like a gift.

"Big Brother," said Brydan, turning into Wilson Park, "can go take a boo."

Sal grinned at the back of his head, the stuck-out bill-board quality of his ears. She had the sudden urge to lean forward and grab hold of them, let him carry them both toward the monumental future of his lips.

"Want to come to Shoppers Drug Mart with me?"

Brydan balanced his cigarette in one corner of his mouth and gave the park a speculative look. Sal knew that expression — he was about to hunch down and go all out, blood, sweat and speed, toward the horizon.

"What's the big attraction at Shoppers?" she asked. "Big sale on aftershave?"

Brydan patted his neck thoughtfully. "Yes, I do smell irresistible, don't I?"

"The flies are swarming."

Brydan pulled a pout. "Actually," he said, brightening, "I've got a few lottery tickets to cash in. See if my numbers came up."

*Lottery tickets*. He was talking in code, letting her know he knew.

"If I win," he added, grinning broadly, "I'll buy you whatever your little heart desires. Anything you want in Shoppers will be yours."

"A lottery winner," Sal said deliberately, tasting each word, watching him as she spoke. "Must be fate."

Brydan didn't blink. "Fate can go take a boo, too." Then, crouched in his wheelchair, he was off, hands pumping furiously as he careened, a low-flying god, across the park.

# Chapter Six

That evening, Sal rocked. Descending into the basement rec room, she slid *The Wall Live* into the CD player, donned headphones, and blew her mind so far out she drifted among stars and small floating bits of rock. The stereo was a good one — Dusty had invested most of a part-time job into it — and the headphones had a ten-meter cord, leaving her free to travel in wicked twisting convulsions from one end of the room to the other. She kept pumping the volume up and up, wanting sound to pound through her, slam her with guitar chords and electrocute her brain. Upstairs, her mother puttered heedlessly about the kitchen. To either side, families in other houses went about their routines, putting another mundane day to rest, while down in the bowels of the earth Sal whirled, a vortex of rage, rhythm and pulse.

Shadow Council wasn't going to get her down. No way

were they running her life. Sure, they'd gotten through to
Jenny Weaver, but Jenny hadn't had any real friends. Okay,
so maybe Shadow had also gotten through to Kimmie and
Tina and a whole host of other decent kids, but there was
still one basic difference between this and last year's lottery
winner — she, Sal Hanson, had a friend, a true-blue gut-
real friend who'd decided to stick by her. Earlier that afternoon, his numbers had come up at Shoppers Drug Mart —
he'd won five dollars and bought her a Sprite and some
Cheezies. The empty Cheezies bag was now pinned to her
bedroom bulletin board, proof of Shadow Council's impend-
ing demise and the fabulous school year that awaited her.

If Brydan Wallace could give the finger to Shadow
Council, so could she.

"Go take a boo!" Sal shouted at the shadows dragging
at her heels as she whipped herself around the room. Ah,
the air felt good, full of invisible crumbling walls. "Go take
a fucking boo!"

Tears streamed down her face, her body throbbed with
guitar riffs, she floated on their long shimmering ache. *The
Wall Live* ended and she put on Deep Purple's *Come Hell or
High Water*, poised to whip herself through "Child In Time"
and Ian Gillan's wordless screams. The song was another of
the great classics, introduced to her by her brother, esteemed
connoisseur of big loud sound. By the time the connoisseur
came home from his evening class, Sal was shuffling about
in a stupor, hair plastered to her head, body soaked with
sweat. With a wave, Dusty dropped into the beanbag chair
across the room and worked his way into a half-eaten bag of
Doritos. It was their unspoken agreement — the person
wearing the headphones had ascended into an alternate
dimension. You didn't invade. You waited to be invited in.

"Smoke on the Water" faded and Sal removed the headset, returning to her body, the thick posts of her legs, and the bright cramps that threaded her arms and chest. With a groan, she sank to the floor and splayed herself, face down.

"What you listening to?" asked Dusty.

"The screaming in my head." Exhaustion was a drug, small pools of peace that lapped through her body. If only she never had to move again.

"Screaming anything in particular?" Dusty chomped casually on a Dorito.

"Just screaming."

"Screaming's best when there are no words," agreed her brother. "You got Mom worried though. She heard you and came downstairs to inquire after your emotional health, but you wouldn't answer her."

"Huh?" Sal rolled over to face him. She couldn't remember her mother coming into the room.

"Your eyes were closed," Dusty shrugged. "You were screaming, and you had the headphones pumped to what level?"

"Seven," said Sal, putting on her glasses and checking.

Dusty's eyebrows skittered. "I explained scream therapy to her. Showed her a few paragraphs from one of my psych textbooks. Told her not to take it personally."

"I didn't know she was there," muttered Sal. "I thought she had another board meeting."

"Don't worry about it." Dusty crumpled the Doritos bag and bounced it off her head, then retreated into silence, watching the corner lava lamp ooze through itself — a relic from their mother's adolescence. Sal knew he wouldn't come right out and ask her why she'd been seven-level screaming. All the demons in hell couldn't drag such a question from his lips. No one in their family took the direct approach, preferring to flutter in wordless sympathy about a sufferer, like a moth around a candle flame, getting its wings singed. It was as if they'd all signed a contract to keep things calm and even-paced, to never look beneath the surface where the bad things lurked. Unfortunately, no one had explained the consequences of this kind of contract, the way it left you alone with the things that mattered most, carrying them like a cupped handful of water.

Maybe that was why she went underground to let the wildness out. One crazy afternoon when she was ten, she'd watched Dusty and Lizard cover the rec room's ceiling, walls and floor with orange shag carpet. Lizard had dubbed the result "Retro-Whatever" and the room had become the ac- knowledged domain of the Hanson offspring, fervently avoided by their mother. Down here in Retro-Whatever no one poked, prodded, or asked for emotional status reports. Down here, you put on "Child In Time" and let Ian Gillan scream.

"My period's coming." Sitting up, Sal traced the shag carpet imprints on her forearms. "It's a woman thing."

Dusty nodded, expressionless.

"Well, have you ever been a woman?" Sal demanded, suddenly on the defensive.

"Have you?" deadpanned her brother.

"Getting there." She tossed a throw cushion at his head. "Faster than you'll reach macho manhood, Tarzan."

"Granted." Dusty's eyes skimmed her face, hesitant. With a sigh he flopped back in the beanbag chair, his eyes fixed on the ceiling as if something of all-consuming impor- tance had summoned his attention upward. Watching him, Sal felt a rush of affection that was almost pain. How she loved his skinny, intelligent face, the shy vigil he maintained over her and the great lengths he went to hide it. But she couldn't tell him any of this — it would mean dipping beneath the surface, and it was crowded down there. Who knew what she'd come up against? In silence, the two of them splayed at opposite ends of Retro-Whatever, the stereo shut off, the glory vanished. Quietly, the air rebuilt itself, brick by brick. *The Wall* — in this family they lived it, breathed it, ate it.

"Hey Sally-Sis, just tell Mom goodnight before you go to bed, okay?" Dusty asked softly, counting orange shag threads above his head. *One, two, yum yum goo. Three, four, I want more. Five, six, grunt, smack, lick.* She could almost hear his thoughts, a feeding rhyme he'd taught her when she was still in diapers. His lips moved soundlessly as he chanted — her brother was also an expert at vanishing inside his head. And if he wanted her to, well, she would track down the eternal clicking of her mother's laptop keyboard and interrupt those whizzing fingers long enough to deliver a perfunctory goodnight kiss. It shouldn't be too stressful. It wasn't like her mother to do much more than sigh when anyone tried to lure her attention temporarily from her computer screen. And for Dusty — well, for Dusty, Sal would do anything.

"Your wish is my command." Grunting to her feet, she stumbled stiffly toward the door.


She woke to the last warmth of autumn. Outside her bedroom window, leaves glowed cranberry and gold. Opening the screen, Sal breathed in their heavy wet scent and stroked the raindrops that slid, still dreaming, across their glistening surfaces. In the early morning light, the ornamental crab tree that guarded her window was an impossible scarlet, a myriad of tiny stained-glass windows. She plucked a single radiant leaf, ducking the immediate reverberation of water droplets. Then she pinned the leaf to her bulletin board beside the empty Cheezies bag and headed downstairs for breakfast.

Her mother was in the kitchen, inserting Tupperware containers into her briefcase. Sal knew the sandwiches sealed inside one of those containers were layered with meat, cheese and lettuce, their crusts carefully trimmed. Carrot and celery sticks were lying in the other container, crisp in a pool of water, and the accompanying bottle of kiwi juice would go straight into the office fridge upon her mother's arrival. Ms. Hanson had prepared the same lunch every workday for the past decade. Last fall, Sal had had to work herself into an emotional cyclone before convincing her mother that she really *really* would absolutely and terminally die if she ever had to ingest a similar lunch in front of her high-school friends.

"And just what do you think you're going to eat?" her mother had demanded.

"The four major food groups," Sal had replied. "French fries, gravy, hamburgers and pop."

"Smart ass," her mother had said. "It'll give you zits." Then, too tired to argue, she'd handed over the lunch money, and Sal had realized she had her mother in the palm of her hand. Unfortunately, it had nothing to do with being doted upon. Rather, it was the fatigue factor — since her mother had been promoted to supervisor at work, she no longer had any residual energy to deal with her sprouting adolescent offspring. Other than a very well-intentioned chat about vaginas and penises, tampons and condoms, a definite NO! to body piercing and tattoos, Ms. Hanson had left Sal to clamber into maturity on her own. It wasn't a formula for bosom buddies. Every now and then, Sal caught her mother giving her quick confused glances as if unsure from which orifice her daughter had originally emerged. Other than this, they were supersonic jets, occasionally crossing each other's tailwinds.

"Did you finish studying for your math quiz?" Picking up her briefcase, her mother turned toward the door.

Math quiz? Faking composure, Sal frantically scanned her brain for data regarding her first-period math class, but *The Wall Live* must have blown it somewhere past Pluto. Then she remembered.

"That was Tuesday, Mom." A perfect circle of bran muffins sat awaiting her and Dusty on a plate — everything her mother did was so geometric. Snagging the biggest one, Sal stuffed half of it into her mouth. She loved the way raisins exploded softly onto her tongue. "Don't give me a heart attack."

"Just asking. Don't *you* take a heart attack." Her mother retreated into her customary wounded stance and the air sagged the way it usually did between them, weary and bruised. "It's a mother's *job* to ask these things, y'know."

"Hey, why not quit and apply for employment insurance?" Sal spoke without thinking, the joke an exuberant flash passing through her brain.

"Parents don't get insurance," snapped her mother, jamming on her sunglasses. "No matter what happens, they're stuck with it."

The screen door slammed behind her, and Ms. Hanson's heels descended the outside steps in sharp precise clicks. Open-mouthed, Sal stood in the empty room, staring at the door. Suddenly, the kitchen shifted into a dark swerve around her. There was the familiar ooze of her brain into memory, and she could feel the tight line of the seat belt once again trapping her against the seat. Then someone began screaming as the car left the road and jolted in and out of the ditch, headlights fixed on a large aspen, the dead-ahead brilliant trunk.

"Mom!" She had to get back, back to the place her mind had been before ... before what? A dark dizziness lifted, and Sal found herself swaying in the sunlit kitchen, the screen door still quivering in its frame. She remembered ... something about Mom being angry, leaving the house angry. Terror ascended on huge wings. Not angry — her mother couldn't leave angry. It was a really bad idea to get into a car feeling angry.

Bursting through the screen door, Sal stumbled on the steps and had to grab the railing for balance. "Mom!" Her ankle gave off a sharp twinge but she ignored it, running alongside the car, hanging onto the doorhandle as her mother backed down the driveway.

"What?" Unrolling the window halfway, Ms. Hanson glared balefully over her sunglasses.

"I think I passed," Sal panted, scooping words off the surface — this word, that word, any word that might change the expression on her mother's face.

"Passed what?"

"My math test!"

"Oh." The tired intricate lines on her mother's face softened. So many, Sal thought. Why hadn't she noticed them before? "That's good, honey."

"And Mom ..."

"Yes?"

"Drive careful, okay?"

Her mother's eyes reddened. She blinked rapidly, then looked away. "You have a good day, sweetie," she said huskily. "Take care of yourself, too."

"I will, Mom, I promise." Catastrophe averted, Sal stood in the middle of the street, waving her mother to the corner and out of sight. When she turned back to the house, the sudden dark swerve in the kitchen had been forgotten and the memory tucked back in its place, safely underground with the darkness and the dead where it belonged.

She was late for band practice as usual, everyone else seated, their fingers skimming casually through various warm-up scales. As she came through the door, her eyes darted instinctively to the back row of risers where the brass section ruled. Directly at their midpoint sat Willis Cass, trumpet raised to his lips, ascending a gleaming line of notes. He hadn't noticed her enter, his wolfish gaze prowling the ceiling, floating with the sound of his trumpet. After yesterday's session with Shadow Council, encountering him in the middle of something as normal as a Concert Band practice felt like receiving a jolt of electric shock. Sal's eyes leapt guiltily away, she grabbed clarinet #19 from the wall cabinet and maneuvered through the hedge of front-row music stands. But in the moment before she sat down, she felt her gaze pulled again toward the trumpet section. This time, she found Willis watching her, one eyebrow raised and a smile puckering his lips. A flush hit her hard, leaving her charbroiled and helpless. Hastily she sat down and began joining the joints of her clarinet, ducking her head to avoid Pavvie's pointed glance as he stepped onto the podium. The conductor rapped his baton and lifted it, the room inhaling a brief four-second silence as he gave the introductory beats to "In the Mood."

"Earth to Planet Marduk, cover your ears," Sal hissed at Brydan, just beating the cacophony that erupted on all sides. Sticking her reed into her mouth, she masticated furiously, then slid the reed onto the mouthpiece and tightened the ligature. Settling her fingers onto the holes, she pretended to play along.

"Hey, where are we?" she whispered, elbowing Brydan slightly.

Beside her there was no change, no finger shooting toward the page and jabbing at a specific bar. Turning toward Brydan, Sal quirked an eyebrow expectantly but he continued to sit, his eyes riveted to the page, tooting through a series of whole notes as if the entire future of the S.C. Concert Band depended on his getting each and every one correct ... as if his own existence depended upon it.

A sick brilliance twisted Sal's gut. It couldn't be. It couldn't. Elbowing Brydan again, she willed him to turn toward her, but he kept his gaze rigidly on the page, a third-degree blush mounting his neck. Panic began picking up different parts of Sal's brain and walking off with them. Brydan hadn't acted like this yesterday afternoon, and the word had been out then. He'd known, surely he'd known. This had to be some kind of joke, or maybe he'd gone into temporary malfunction and was experiencing vertigo. It happened — people lost their minds for seconds, here and there, then regained them. Didn't she lose hers several times a day? And didn't she also have an empty Cheezies bag pinned to her bedroom bulletin board, concrete evidence that her friendship with Brydan Wallace was going to continue against all

odds, *proof* that what was happening here at this very moment was a fluke, a five-second fling with insanity? Brydan's
current actions were impossible. She was going to make
them impossible. Fiercely, she elbowed him a third time.
Swaying slightly in his wheelchair, he kept his eyes fixed
straight ahead.

The jerk had choked halfway through the first page
and here she was, elbowing a corpse with flyaway ears and
a clarinet glued between his lips. What a way to die. Reck-
lessly, Sal launched into the second page. It was a miserably incorrect guess and she was caught flat out in a burst
of angry eighth notes when the rest of the band suddenly
finished several bars ahead of her. Normally Brydan would
have offered his grinning congratulations, but today he sat
beet red and ramrod straight, staring dead ahead.

"You shit," she hissed in full-hearted panic.

"Talking, talking!" Lurching forward, Pavvie rapped
the top of their music stand. "Always talking!"

The conductor's dark mustache bristled and his eyes
were pale green accusations. Shrinking into her seat, Sal
counted heartbeats until Pavvie once again retreated behind the podium and began a series of clipped instructions
to the lead saxophone player.

With a slight cough Brydan cleared his throat and Sal's
eyes darted wildly toward him, begging for a sign, any
discreet gesture of friendship. As she watched, his right
hand lifted from the clarinet. Slowly, deliberately, his three
middle fingers straightened while his thumb and pinkie
tucked themselves in.

The air peeled back on itself then, tearing away the
surface reality Sal had always known and leaving her with
something entirely different. Everything still looked the

same, the surface appeared intact, but she knew it was gone, completely gone. What she was left with was a world of strangers who looked like friends — friends she used to believe in, friends with whom she'd tossed small jokes and confidences back and forth, not realizing these carefree disclosures had been small parts of her body, and the joke had always been on her.

Rapping his music stand, Pavvie lifted his baton. "Again, from the beginning!"

Without a sound, scream or whimper, the world continued on, Brydan's right hand returning to the clarinet and positioning itself for the first note. *Everyone loves a victim.* Two rows behind her, Sal felt Willis Cass raise his trumpet, his eyes drilling softly into the back of her head.

# Chapter Seven

For the rest of the week, they left her alone. No scrolls appeared in her desks and no one flashed mysterious hand signals at her in the halls. In fact, Shadow Council demonstrated such a complete lack of interest in her existence, Sal might have dismissed the entire ordeal except for one minor detail — every student at Saskatoon Collegiate now treated her as if she didn't exist. Eyes blanked as they crossed her face, voices talked around her, she felt unsubstantial as a breath of air. Former friends were the worst, their eyes glazing with dread whenever they accidentally bumped into her. Brydan had it easiest — he simply ducked his head and treated her as part of his regular hallway obstacle course — but the rest of her friends were eye level and had to keep inventing a sudden interest in their watches or turning in the opposite direction. Feeling in some way responsible for their discomfort, Sal avoided her favorite haunts and used out-of-the-way washrooms, but it was impossible to predict every encounter. Thursday afternoon, two days after she'd received the third scroll, she entered the girls' washroom in the tech wing to find Kimmie Busatto coming out of a toilet stall, zipping her jeans.

"Oh my god!" Kimmie cried, her chubby face collapsing as she caught sight of Sal standing, equally stunned, in the doorway. Then her zipper caught and she refocused on it with manic relief, yanking and swearing.

The second day of classes, Sal had already memorized Kimmie's schedule and she knew it better than her own. Kimmie had just gotten out of History and her next class was English, halfway across the school. Any other girls' washroom in the entire building would have been more convenient than this one. "What're you doing in *this* can?" she whispered, cold realization settling in.

The zipper remained static, caught on a thread and refusing to budge. Keeping her eyes down, Kimmie worked it frantically while Sal counted nuclear butterflies in her stomach. Until that zipper moved, the two of them were trapped in a washroom both of them had chosen in order to avoid encountering each other on the opposite side of the school.

"I hate this place." Kimmie's voice was muffled, directed into her chest. "I hate what they do to people here, I hate what they're doing to my *friend*." The thread gave, and she quickly zipped up her jeans. "I hate," she continued softly, staring at the floor, "myself." Without looking up, she sidled quickly and carefully around Sal's motionless body and out the door.

Sal endured the long ache of her next class, wondering what she could have said to change the situation. Should she have challenged Kimmie and begged her to dig into some hidden reserve of courage? But wasn't that something that happened only in novels and war movies? Who kept hidden reserves of anything for daily living, unless it was a few bucks to invest in the next lottery ticket? And after the way she herself had treated Jenny Weaver last year, did she have the right to say anything to anyone else?

Somewhere deep within, a calm voice kept repeating, *You don't deserve this. Keep your chin up and it'll pass. They're idiots, don't waste your time on them.* But the fact was she did care, and it was the small ridiculous things she cared about — like drawing Bic tattoos on someone's arm while waiting for french fries and gravy in the cafeteria lineup, or joining the rest of a class in shooting paper airplanes at a preselected human target every time a teacher's back was turned. She longed to add her comments to the colloquial archives of the Pony Express. A lightning-bright pain ripped through her each time she was bypassed by a note, as if the hands passing that note had also reached into her chest and torn out her heart — and then the damn thing grew back again, fresh, naive, and ready for the next death.

Friday noon found her standing at her locker, putting off the desolation of yet another solitary lunch as students standing on either side of her bantered back and forth.

"Yeah, I got suspended," said the guy opening the locker to her left. "For four days. It was like a vacation. I watched the soaps with Mom. She took me grocery shopping. You should see her at the baked goods section, man." His voice arced, false and high, imitating his mother. "'Oh, look at these donuts. Doesn't this one look good?' And then," he continued, his voice returning to normal, "she poked her finger right through the jelly filling, licked it off, smiled at me and walked away."

"No way, man." The guy pawing through the locker to Sal's right straightened and grinned. "That's your mom?"

"My mom," said the first guy, "never took mom lessons."

Sal laughed. Forgetting the invisible barrier that had been constructed around her, she turned to the guy on her left and said, "That is *so* cool. I wish my mom was like that."

The guy looked like Dusty, with his long thin hair, Pink Floyd t-shirt, and scattered constellations of forehead zits. For the briefest of seconds their eyes connected and she was alive among other humans as an answering grin started across his face. Then his expression went blank and his eyes shifted away. Behind her, the second guy cleared his throat.

"What say we go check out McDonald's?" he said and they slammed their lockers, catching Sal in a vise of sound. Stunned, she had to fight the urge to dive into her own locker as the two guys walked away. The body did such strange things when it was afraid. There was no arguing with it — weakness hijacked every joint and all it wanted was to go fetal, crawl into the nearest bed and suck its thumb.

Head down, she traveled the labyrinth of school halls, veering to avoid oncoming students as if the briefest body contact would send her up in smoke. The crowd thinned as she entered the tech wing where music classes were held. Junior Band practices took place every Monday and Wednesday at noon, and the music room was always open for extra practice, but only the most dedicated could be found, lips pressed to a mouthpiece, on a Friday lunch hour. Turning into the hall that led to the music room, Sal watched the linoleum pattern swirl beneath her feet. This corridor showed no signs of life, no oncoming rabbity eyes or hastily averted faces to avoid. Still, she didn't look up. Over the past few days, she'd been developing a hefty visual preference for floors. They were a comforting architectural structure, always there when you needed them. In fact, the floor was a great friend that never betrayed you or suddenly took off, leaving you standing on thin air.

Further down the hall a door opened and two figures emerged from a tech classroom. With a brief comment the teacher headed in the opposite direction, while the guy in the wheelchair popped a graceful 90° turn and came coasting rapidly toward Sal. Focused on a metalwork object in his lap, Brydan didn't look up until he was approximately ten meters away. When he did, she was close enough to watch his next thoughts flash across his face — he could make a quick one-eighty and take off the other way, or continue grimly toward her, blanking the inside of his head until he was safely past and escaping around the corner.

He continued to approach. They were seven meters apart, then five. Each spoke in Brydan's wheels whispered into the enormous silence. Would he speak to her? Would he? Brydan was an unpredictable guy, sidestepping all stereotypes and at the same time fitting in everywhere. You were as likely to see him smoking with the metalheads as grabbing a quick game of chess with the brown-nosers. Wasn't this what she'd always liked about him — he wasn't locked into any particular way of seeing things, turning every situation instead into an opportunity?

Head lowered, his hands traced his wheels slowly, as if reading his options there in braille. Then, two meters from her, he began to arc to the left and she realized he was going to do it, he was going to pass her like a stranger. No, less than a stranger — simply a hallway object to avoid.

With a moan, she stepped in front of him. Caught by surprise, he ran into her. She lost her balance and had to brace herself against his shoulder. For a moment, everything was the scent of her hair tangled with his, the sound of quick warm breathing. Then he backed up and veered to the right. Again, she stepped in front of him, her eyes narrowed to slits, her body shuddering with deep breaths. It was crazy, she knew she couldn't win, but some raw mad fist was squeezing her brain and she couldn't think. Again, Brydan veered to the right and again she rammed herself, a stubborn desperate wall, into his path.

"Sal," he said finally, his voice gusty and frightened. "Let me past, *please.*"

She hadn't meant to frighten him. Stepping aside, she let her hair swing across her face and listened to Brydan's wheelchair take him slowly down the hall.

The music room was empty except for a disheveled-looking Pavvie who sat huddled at his desk, marking papers. He was wearing her favorite outfit — a yellow-and-black checked blazer and the infamous yellow pants. At her entry, he looked up with a pleased nod as if he'd been expecting her, had been secretly waiting for her to discover her hidden reserve of talent.

"I thought I'd get some extra practice in," Sal mumbled, suddenly exhausted at the prospect of another human interaction, no matter how brief. "Is a practice room free?"

"Sure, sure." Pavvie nodded approvingly. "Room B."

"Thanks." Grabbing clarinet #19, she headed into one

of the two soundproofed rooms that had been built onto the music room's west side. In the small enclosed space, several chairs and music stands stood at various angles. Through the adjoining wall came the muffled sounds of a brass player warming up in Room A. Slumping into the nearest chair, Sal let the full weight of solitude press down upon her.

It wasn't going to change. Forty-eight hours had gone by, two full days of living inside a transparent tomb and staring out at the living. Nine and a half months of invisible exile remained before her sentence would be lifted — at least 270 days. Sal's mind buckled at the thought. And after that? How was she going to feel when the year ended and everyone started talking to her, pretending none of this had taken place? Would she and Brydan be able to ignore what just happened in the hall? Could she pick up again with Kimmie without ever mentioning a full year of torment as the lottery winner? Wouldn't that just make the whole thing worse?

Dully, Sal opened the clarinet case and began to fit the instrument together. Pavvie had looked at her with such hope. She should at least spew forth a few squawks and toots. Flipping through her music folder, she pulled out "Dixieland Jamboree" and putted through it half-heartedly. She gave it her best, trying to focus, but she sounded like a pair of copulating dachshunds. Bleary notes rose and fell, disintegrating into a wave of sadness. Who was she trying to kid? Since when had she given a hoot about "Dixieland Jamboree"? Why should she? No one ever noticed if she actually played or not. She could sit through next Tuesday's practice faking it, playing silence as she often did, and no one would catch on. Wasn't this exactly what she'd been doing for the past forty-eight hours — performing a role of silence, except this one had been assigned?

The door to Room B opened and her eyes instinctively dropped, seeking to avoid the incoming face that would go blank upon seeing her and begin backing out. But as she stared at the floor, there came the soft sounds of someone settling into the chair beside her, placing a music folder onto a stand and opening it. Darting sideways, her eyes fixed on a pair of sloppy Reeboks and flew upward into the careful wolfish face of Willis Cass.

"I wondered who was in here," he said casually, fiddling with a valve on his trumpet. "I thought maybe we could take a run through "The Call of Fate." The second page is a bitch for first trumpets."

She stared as if expecting to see him explode into nuclear fusion, a devil-red mushroom cloud, but he continued to sit beside her, a casual grin on his face, faking humanity.

"I am *not* playing with you," she blustered. "No way!"

"Why not?" Fluid, relaxed, he leaned back in his chair and studied her. She wanted to scream and launch herself at him, shove that trumpet anywhere she could make it fit.

"Because you're despicable, that's why."

"I'm no different than you."

"Look," she spat, leaning toward him. "Maybe I didn't talk to Jenny Weaver last year, but I didn't *know* her. It wasn't like I was betraying a friend. And I am not like you — forcing this whole lottery thing on everyone."

"How could Shadow force fifteen hundred students?" shrugged Willis. "We're giving them what they want, or they wouldn't be going along with it."

"They're doing it because they're afraid!"

"Afraid of what?"

"Of you. You and your popular ... monsters."

"Are you afraid of me, Sally?"

Words dissolved in her throat and she retreated into silence, her eyes sinking to the floor.

"Not too afraid to lambast me." Willis's voice was thoughtful. "You've got more guts than most kids at this school."

Her heart leapt at the compliment, leaving her nauseous at its betrayal. Who did this guy think he was, twitching her this way and that like a piece of dental floss? "You're just saying that," she accused. "For some hidden purpose."

"Actually," he said, "I'm not. And what have you got to lose by spending one lunch hour practicing with me?"

"My self-respect."

He blinked, his mouth tightening. So she could affect him, tilt the ground slightly beneath his feet.

"I'll tell you something, Sally Hanson," he said softly. "If you want to succeed in life, you've got to be a jerk. So I've decided to be a nice jerk."

They sat watching each other, and in this odd moment of truth Sal realized that Willis Cass wanted something from her. Exactly what this was she couldn't figure out, but she could feel it — a vague insistent question that pulsed between them.

Why shouldn't she step into this new game for a while and try out whatever he was offering? It wasn't as if she'd be breaking any of Shadow Council's rules by joining Willis Cass in a brief trumpet and clarinet fling, not if their president was asking her. And if she was betraying her self-respect by associating with the highest form of scum S.C. had to offer, none of the lower scum were currently begging for her attention. Surely some scum was better than no scum at all?

"I hardly ever play real notes," she confessed. "The only reason Pavvie hasn't kicked me out is because he never actually hears me."

Willis's grin was effortless as the sky was blue. "This could be the beginning of a beau—" He paused, then lifted the trumpet to his mouth. "Well, something."

The weekend passed, a marathon of lonely rollerblading along Saskatoon's bike trails. If Dusty or her mother had asked, Sal would have been ready with a list of phantom friends she'd been spending time with, but neither did. Her mother was absent all day Saturday and half of Sunday, rushing to beat a deadline at the office, while Dusty worked late at the university, researching for a group presentation. Sal returned home both evenings, windburnt and drenched from sudden downpours, to an empty house and a silent phone.

Monday morning she once again walked her solitary exile through the crowded school halls. The walls buzzed with the early morning rush, comments and catcalls reverberated in every direction. Reaching her locker, she found students swarming the lockers to either side, their backs turned to her, their voices pitched unnaturally loud. She asked three times to be let through, but no one moved, and it wasn't until she began pushing her way into the group that a path finally opened. Eyes slid toward her, then away. Up and down the hall, no one was obviously watching but everyone tuned in as the path before her widened, displaying a white rectangular object taped to her locker. The envelope was blank, without black ribbon, red wax, or identifiable markings of any kind, but she knew immediately what it contained — her first duty from Shadow Council. She wondered briefly who'd taped it there — Willis? Rolf? Ellen? No matter. Once the envelope had gone up, word would have spread rapidly, the hall filling with students eager to watch the historic moment she walked up to her locker, accepted the duty, and her role as lottery winner began.

Every one of the watching students now thought of her as the lottery *winner*. Only the inner elite, the actual members of Shadow Council, called her what she really was. And yet it was obvious, so obvious — the lottery winner was a victim. At some level everyone knew this, so why did they call the poor sucker a winner? To make it worse for the victim? To make it easier on themselves?

Inside she was shutting down, a city of water faucets turning off one by one — a private trick she'd picked up somewhere along the line that had probably seemed meaningless at the time. Now she realized that the whole of her life had been a rehearsal for this moment. She'd been so well prepared for her fate that she could be run at top speed into a brick wall and feel nothing. Stepping up to her locker, she tugged at the envelope. The tape resisted, ripping the envelope before it gave, a flicker of muted pain as the last illusion died. Then she was tearing open the envelope and sliding a pile of plastic circles into her hand, the kind of color tabs used to identify players in a board game. On the inside of the envelope she found the word "Targets," and a list of names with a homeroom written beside each one. Across the top of the list, someone had scrawled the word "DELIVER." Obviously she was expected to deliver the tabs to the targets in their homerooms.

She had twenty minutes. Saskatoon Collegiate's classroom

doors were identified by a number and a compass direction. The closest on her list was E32 — east side of the
school, room thirty-two. Without opening her locker, Sal
turned right and headed numbly toward the east hall. The
main body of the school was laid out as a one-storey rectangle, with the auditorium in the center and the tech wing
and gym added to the north end. Room thirty-two loomed
quickly, the door open, a male teacher standing just inside,
flicking a ruler absentmindedly against his palm.

"Excuse me." She had to try several times before she got
her voice out of her mouth. "I need to talk to Peter Fleck."

"Pete?" said the teacher, scanning the class. "I don't
think he's here yet. Hey Calvin, you know where Pete is?"

Slouching deeper into his desk, a boy with long camouflage hair slid his eyes across Sal. "No sir," he said with a
small grin.

Sal felt a whiplash of fear. How was she supposed to
deliver the tabs to the targets if they weren't in their
homerooms? *Wait a minute*, she thought, sucking the tremble in her lower lip. *It doesn't say I have to put them in their
sweaty little hands.*

"Would you like me to give Pete a message?" asked
the teacher.

"Yes," said Sal, handing him a tab. "Please give him
this."

The teacher grimaced, nonplused. "From whom shall I
say it came?"

"It's not important." Backing out the door, Sal booted
it to the next room on her list. S8's door was closed, but a
peek through the window showed Ms. Ferwerda, her math
teacher, sitting at her desk. As Sal entered, she felt a current surge through the room, plugging each student into

awareness. In response her own body stiffened, fighting off the unspoken.

"Excuse me." She paused at Ms. Ferwerda's desk. "Could you tell me who Norma Lotz is?"

"Good morning, Sally," said Ms. Ferwerda. "Norma is over there — third from the back, fourth row in."

"Thanks."

Sprawled and hunched in their desks, the class surreptitiously watched Sal progress across the room. The only person who seemed oblivious to her presence was Norma Lotz. Leaned into an animated conversation with another girl, Norma looked like the kind of girl who could easily juggle being beauty queen and high-school yearbook editor — certainly not the exemplary candidate for an assassin that Sal herself had always been. Avoiding the startled eyes of the girl across the aisle, Sal placed a tab on Norma's desk, then quickly turned and walked to the front of the room, still carrying the gaze of the class.

"Have a nice day, Sally," said Ms. Ferwerda.

"You too." As Sal exited, she ran a finger lightly along the doorframe. Yes, it was solid, and her hand didn't pass through it, so that meant she was solid too. This wasn't a dream. Everything that had just taken place was unbelievably, staggeringly real.

Both the name and the face of the third target were familiar — he'd been the star of last year's spring drama production. As she approached classroom N17, Sal spotted Brent Vandermeer standing outside his homeroom, joking with friends. There didn't seem to be any way around it this time. Direct contact looked unavoidable. She was going to have to walk up to one of the most popular guys in the school and place a tiny plastic bomb in his hand.

"Excuse me," she said, lurching forward. "Brent?"

He turned toward her, his face flickering with recognition, then fear.

"I'm supposed to deliver this to you." She jabbed the tab awkwardly into the soft warmth of his palm. Slowly his fingers closed over it, his eyes staring vaguely past her right shoulder. Then, incredibly, a tiny smile crept across his mouth.

"Okay, well, bye now," she said idiotically, backing away from the dreamy statue he'd become.

Fortunately the next two targets hadn't yet reached homeroom, and she was able to leave their tabs with their teachers, but the final one had definitely arrived. No one had to point him out. She would have recognized those ears anywhere. Entering S23, she spotted Brydan immediately by the window. As she approached, his eyes lifted from a conversation with the girl seated behind him and locked with hers. For a moment she couldn't breathe, the weight too heavy, a ton of raw pain. Then she was coming to a halt in front of him and depositing the tab onto the duotang lying in his lap.

"Just don't expect me to tell you what the hell it means," she said in the voice of an utter stranger, then turned and left the room.

She saw the girl with the black lipstick ahead of her, drifting down the hall. Thin body curved protectively inward, hands empty at her sides, the girl seemed unconnected to anything she passed. Other students walked alone, but their faces turned continually to watch what went on around them — they grinned and called out to the jostling, joking throng that surrounded them as if everyone in the vicinity was tuned in to the same set of brain waves, the same basic thoughts. Only the girl with the black lipstick followed the beat of a different drummer, only she tuned in to a vibe so unique it didn't register within this reality, giving her the appearance of floating without purpose, going nowhere.

Falling into step behind her, Sal took on the same drifting gait. It was lunch hour; she'd fulfilled her Shadow Council duties and had nothing to fend off absolute loneliness but a stack of algebra homework. Ahead of her, the girl turned into the west hall, freezing as several guys charged en masse around the corner and clipped her arm. Oblivious, the guys rushed onward and the girl collapsed against the nearest wall, momentarily inert. Then she straightened and began to bounce herself gently off the wall, making contact only with her shoulder blades. Her face remained expressionless and she seemed zoned-out, with no sign of the fear she'd shown at Wilson Park.

Ten lockers down, Sal slumped against the wall, studying her. What was it with this kid? Was she on drugs? Was she an alien from another planet? Why would she plaster her mouth with black lipstick when she didn't wear any other makeup? Dressed in an oversized gray t-shirt and leggings, the girl displayed no visible body piercing or tattoos. The black lipstick and hair dye didn't fit. Nothing about the girl fit. She was the missing part of a jigsaw puzzle — the hole left by the absent piece. The girl was an absence.

Pushing out from the wall, the girl started off again, head down, arms wrapped protectively around her chest. Sal picked up the pace and slipped in close behind. There seemed no need for secrecy, the girl showed no awareness of her presence. Sal was just another absence. Together they were two girl-shaped phantoms drifting through a hallway of solid human objects.

The girl was muttering under her breath. Sal pressed closer, listening.

"Don't walk into the wall, walls hurt," the girl whispered fiercely to herself. "Walk into the door, not the wall. Doors open, walls don't." Putting out a hand, she trailed it along the nearest wall, as if using it for some kind of radar. "Don't walk into the water fountain," she mumbled, tracing the outline of the drinking fountain. "Don't walk into the garbage pail. Don't walk into the ... object." Without raising her head, the girl veered abruptly around an approaching teacher and continued on. "Okay, now find your feet, find your feet."

Turning into the library, she paused for a second as if bracing against something and pushed through the turnstile. Then she headed straight for the science fiction shelf, pulled out several paperbacks and disappeared into the non-fiction stacks. A minute later Sal found her in a study carrel, feet tucked onto her chair, chin on her knees, and reading. What had Brydan said her name was? Tauni Morrison — a weird kid, a loner. Sal paused, tasting the nervous acid of her thoughts. So, was Tauni Morrison weird enough to consider responding to a question from the lottery victim? Or was she too spaced-out to even know what a lottery victim was?

"Excuse me," said Sal, leaning over the front of the carrel.

Giving no response, the girl continued to read. Was she deaf? No, she couldn't be — she'd obviously heard Sal playing the clarinet at Wilson Park. Sal glanced at the title of the book propped open in the girl's hands: *The Space Swimmers*. A second paperback lay beside her arm: *This Alien*

*Shore*. More character sketches, Sal thought wearily.

"Excuse me," she said again, and when the girl continued to give no response, repeated it a third time, loudly.

A shudder ran through the girl. Without taking her eyes from her book, she leaned backward, away from Sal.

"Please," Sal said quietly, pulling back so that she was no longer leaning into the other girl's space. "Tauni?" She knew better, now, than to touch.

The girl gave her a quick sideways glance without the slightest hint of recognition. "Yeah?" Her voice wobbled, tight and high in her throat, as if rarely used.

"I was wondering," said Sal, "why you wear black lipstick."

Slowly the girl's face turned toward Sal, her blue eyes not quite focused as if her brain was between radio stations, picking up Sal's voice through a lot of distortion.

"For my mouth," she said vaguely. "So I know where it is."

"You wear black lipstick so you'll know where your mouth is?" Sal asked cautiously.

"So I'll know where my face is." The girl began to speak more quickly, as if gradually tuning in.

"Why don't you know where your face is?" Sal was definitely getting muddled.

"In the mirror," said the girl, watching the space above Sal's head.

Carefully, Sal added up the girl's fragmented comments. "You can't find your face in a mirror without black lipstick?"

"And black hair," the girl said slowly. "In the mirror ... it doesn't make sense. I see things ... but I don't know what they are. What's me, and what isn't me? Black helps me ... find things. The black stands out. So that's where my face must be."

"Oh," said Sal, and the girl returned to her book, outer space, other planets, wherever it was she went to escape the reality of here.

# Chapter Eight

"Ready for a higher gear?" Dangling his car keys, Dusty lounged in the bedroom doorway. "Learner's permit heaven, coming right up."

"Where's Lizard?" Sprawled on her bed, Sal regarded her brother over a Batman comic.

"Sucking Slurpees somewhere else," he replied. "C'mon, I drove all the way home with my windows open, airing out my car for your supreme nostrils."

"Mmm," said Sal. "I'll need a Slurpee."

"Slurpees are essential to a learning driver's focus," agreed her brother.

"And a bag of Doritos."

"You drive a hard bargain, fair lady." Dusty clapped a hand over his heart. "But moonlight hath no pleasure without your fair company."

"That's two 'fair's' in two sentences," Sal pointed out

severely. "You're going to have to work on your adjectives."

"And you could use some work on your gratitude." Dusty tossed her the car keys. "You're taking us on a back-alley tour to the 7-Eleven for Slurpees."

"Back alleys!" wailed Sal. "Give me Broadway Avenue, the Lawson Heights Mall!"

"Back alleys," scowled her brother, "at a top speed of ten klicks. Come along, little roadrunner."

Ten minutes later she was putt-putting up and down central Saskatoon's back-alley garbage route while Dusty lounged in the passenger seat, subjecting her to his creative instruction techniques. "Watch out for the baby crawling out from behind that garbage bin," he said casually, his head resting against the back of the seat.

"What baby?" screeched Sal, slamming on the brakes.

"Not a real baby," grumbled Dusty, peeling himself off the dash. "A metaphorical baby. Always drive past every parked car as if a baby was about to crawl out from behind it. Metaphorical babies should always be on a good driver's mind."

"I wish I had a metaphorical brother," muttered Sal, edging her foot off the brake. An uneasy silence descended as she practiced U-turns in the parking lot of a Mennonite church. Dusty was pulling at his lower lip, extending it like a wad of chewing gum. Something was definitely brewing in her brother's psych-major brain — Sal could feel him peering at her through a metaphorical hedge, trying to figure her out. Sudden understanding flared through her. This wasn't a casual off-the-cuff driving lesson, it was a setup. As she nosed the car out of the parking lot and down the alley, Dusty emitted a delicate sigh. She braced herself.

"Sally-Sis," he asked softly, "what's wrong? What's got you lower than a carpet?"

He looked deeply stressed, as if asking the question broke some cosmic privacy rule. Avoiding her pointed glance, he squinted straight ahead, his eyes rescuing metaphorical babies from every imaginable catastrophe. When Dusty was fifteen, the family dog Spot had died of overdone old age. Dusty had cried for weeks, until their mother had flat-out refused to get another pet. Dusty had a heart like a cooked beet — soft, the color of a deep bruise.

"Nothing's wrong." Sal's voice was unnecessarily loud, a thick shoulder of a voice. "You're taking too many psych courses, okay?"

Dusty cleared his throat tentatively. "Look Sal, maybe you think I don't pay attention, but I have noticed that Kimmie hasn't been around lately. I've ... been watching you, and you seem different. Quieter. It's not like —"

"I'm quieter tonight because of you and all your goddam metaphorical babies!" Sal was a capped volcano about to explode, her fury so sudden she felt dizzy. "How d'you expect me to learn to drive if I've got to worry about babies crawling out of everywhere? Don't you remember what happened to me in a car? D'you think it's easy —"

Her brain tilted and the scene in front of her changed, the back alley swerving into darkness, headlights making their fateful brilliant arc across a two-lane highway. Screaming, there was that screaming again, the sound of high-pitched terror.

"Sal. Sally-Sis, it's okay, you're okay now." Dusty's arm tightened around her shoulders and she hunched over the steering wheel, locked into dry heaves. "It's okay," he kept repeating, a soft mantra in her ear. "Everything's okay now."

"What?" she asked, groggy as if coming out of deep sleep, the right side of her brain split with pain. She wished someone would pull the axe out of her head. "What happened?"

"It's me," Dusty said softly. "I'm a stupid ass, that's all. You want me to drive?"

She noticed his foot rammed on the brake. "Did I hit something?"

"No, everything's fine. You just need a break."

"My head hurts. Right here." She touched her right temple.

"Just a headache. All those metaphorical babies, like you said."

"I guess." Sal climbed in the passenger door completely exhausted, as if she'd been swimming through mud. Giving Dusty her back, she curled into the upholstery's familiar sag — it cradled her like a friend, the kind who'd never desert her, never go wrong. Warm tears slid down her cheek and she wanted to suck her thumb. How could Dusty ask such dumb questions when it was obvious she was stressed out about a landscape teeming with crawling infants? Babies could really scoot when they got going. What if she hit one of them? Even metaphorical babies bled. Dusty should know better than to stress her out with metaphors that had anything to do with car accidents and blood.

Nuzzling the upholstery, she was asleep before the car reached the end of the alley.


"What the hell d'you think you're doing?" snapped Linda Paboni.

Sal stood before them a second time, one hand on the doorknob, half in, half out of the open doorway. Facing her was the full circle of Shadow Council's power, nine of the most influential students in the school. Members of Student

Council, Athletic Council, and the prominent clubs, they'd all been chosen for the respect they commanded from their peers. Each one maintained a B+ average or higher — there were no slackers here, no third clarinetists. Linda Paboni had been one of last year's Citizenship Cup recipients.

Sal opted for a numb silence. She had no idea what she was doing, why she'd been summoned, if she could answer this question without demerits, or if her stomach would survive its current battery-acid state.

"Come in," said Willis, his voice picking up her feet and moving her into the room. Somehow the door closed behind her.

It was Tuesday morning, 8:10. Five minutes late for band practice, she'd arrived to find Rolf waiting outside the music room. Raising the three fingers on his right hand, he'd said, "Follow," then turned and started off down the empty hall.

She'd followed.

"Come sit down," said Willis, and she walked the tight-rope of his voice toward the footstool at the center of the circle. Seated, she watched his long hypnotic fingers stroke his chin.

"Yesterday," said Willis, "you received your first duty."

Sal hesitated. It wasn't exactly a question, but he seemed to expect a reply. Keeping her eyes on his chin, she nodded.

"And what was this duty?"

"To deliver the plastic tabs."

"Deliver them where?" asked Willis.

She was beginning to get it. One side of her brain took a sickening lurch into the other. "To the names on the list."

"Exactly!" snapped Linda Paboni.

An electric current was lifting tiny hairs up and down the length of Sal's back, but she fought the urge to swivel around and face the vampire queen. So this was the reason she'd been placed at the center of a circle — no matter which direction she faced, she was in a position of weakness.

"Then why the *hell* did you give three tabs to teachers?" This voice came from Sal's left. If she turned her head slightly, she could just see the guy. He looked jockish. What was his name — Mark? No, Marvin Fissett.

"But they weren't in their homerooms," Sal protested faintly. "How was I supposed to find them? I didn't even know who most of them were."

"Ask around," hissed the girl seated beside Willis. Not, Sal noted, Ellen Petric. Today it was Judy Sinclair — another drama star.

"But no one will talk to me," said Sal. "No one's allowed to talk to the lottery winner."

"That doesn't mean you go handing Shadow business to teachers," snapped Linda. "You never, *ever*, involve teachers."

Sal swallowed acid and took a chance. "But how do I find out who a target is if I can't ask anyone for help?"

The room settled into a pause as everyone digested her question.

"She *is* in grade ten," Rolf said finally, doodling in his secretary's binder. "Jenny was in grade eleven — she knew just about everyone."

"What did they do other years when the victim was in grade nine or ten?" asked Judy.

"Before Jenny, the victim was Carlos Ferraro. He was in grade twelve. Before that it was Ian Ecott, grade eleven." Rolf shrugged. "Before that was before my time. Anyone else remember?"

"There was a grade nine victim five years ago," said Willis.

"Oh yeah." Linda sounded thoughtful. "How did Shadow handle that one?"

"Before my time," Willis shrugged.

"We'll have to give her the sign," Rolf said suddenly.

"I don't think so." Linda's tone made her distaste for the suggestion obvious.

"Why not?" asked Rolf.

"We shouldn't be handing out signs to victims," said Linda.

"It's just one victim," said Willis, "and one sign."

"I don't like it," said Linda.

"Got any other suggestions?" Willis asked softly.

"No," said Linda huffily. "I don't."

"Rolf, teach her the sign," said Willis.

"Victim, turn to receive the sign," said Rolf.

Sal's stomach was about to give up the biscuit big time. She swung a dizzy quarter circle toward Rolf, and Linda Paboni came into view, her long red hair scooped into a utilitarian ponytail, her thin body hunched like a ferret's. If anyone was typecast for Shadow Council, it was Linda. She was on the yearbook and cafeteria committees as well as Athletic Council, and had joined various teams and clubs, even Masks and Selves, the creative writing group. The entire school cringed before her presence. Wherever she went she left a trail of blood.

"This is the Sign of the Inside," said Rolf, raising his left index finger and rubbing the left side of his nose. "When you use this sign, anyone who knows it will offer you assistance."

Sal raised her hand.

"Victim may speak," said Rolf.

"How will I know who knows the sign?" asked Sal.

"Use it and you'll find out," snapped Linda.

Sal raised her hand again.

"Victim may speak," said Rolf.

"What if no one around me knows the sign?"

"Someone will," said Rolf. "Like Linda said, you'll find out."

"But you use it only for Shadow business," Linda said sharply. "If we find out you've been using it for anything else, there'll be retribution. Just like there should be for delivering those tabs to teachers. One demerit, at least."

"No demerit," said Willis.

All eyes swung toward Willis, Sal traveling her footstool until she once again faced Shadow Council's president.

"Her instructions were unclear," said Willis. "They didn't say deliver directly to the names on the list, it just said deliver. If we're unclear, this is what happens."

"But to a teacher?" demanded Linda.

"She won't do it again," said Willis. "Who was responsible for the instructions?"

"I was," said Ellen Petric miserably. "But I didn't know she was that stupid."

"Ellen gets one demerit," said Willis casually. "Victim dismissed."

The air vibrated with frank astonishment as Shadow Council's eight other members stared at their president. Rocked by a wave of nausea, Sal clutched her seat. She'd definitely been on one too many rotations around the footstool.

"Victim dismissed," Willis repeated, looking directly at her, his face devoid of friendliness.

The invisible leash tightened around Sal's throat, jerking her to her feet and dragging her to the door. Hand on the knob, she paused, waiting for a last set of instructions, but none came. Then she was through the door and beyond it, bent double in the empty hallway, gasping and gasping as if she'd never before breathed free air.


The line to the till inched forward. A package of tampons in her hand, Sal shifted her weight to the other foot and heaved an enormous sigh. It was a busy day at Shoppers Drug Mart. Everyone seemed to be buying cigarettes and lottery tickets, and paying for them with their bank cards. If only there was a separate line for emergency purchases like tampons. She always tried to mark her period due date on her bedroom calendar, but there'd been so much on her mind this month that she'd forgotten it. Actually, she usually forgot it. Anything that had to do with blood freaked her out, even that kind of blood, the kind that gave life.

Miserably she recounted heads — still eight people in the line ahead of her. In the past five minutes, the clerk had processed two customers. Today *everyone* was buying lottery tickets. It had to be a big jackpot. Curious, Sal watched the lottery hotline and there it came, the neon letters splitting, then rejoining and flashing. This week the Super 7 was worth fifteen million bucks. No wonder so many Saskatooners were lining up to buy tickets. All across the country, there were probably millions standing in lines like this one, waiting to invest in their lucky numbers. Out of all those dreamers would emerge several fluke winners, their numbers selected by chance. It was a weird system, Sal thought. All those guaranteed losers paying for the dreams of a few winners, yet everyone seemed feverishly eager to fork over their last dollar. Why would so many people invest in a system with such lousy odds, instead of going out and creating their own happiness?

And what about the opposite situation? What about the scenario in which everyone got to be a winner except for the one poor suck whose name got drawn? What if the prize for *not* getting your name drawn was continued relative social security, the guarantee that for now, at least, you weren't on the bottom rung, that for one school year you got to step on someone else's fingers because destiny had selected her name instead of yours? There was so much strength in numbers. Who would risk stepping outside the safety of a crowd the size of the S.C. student body to stand beside a single fated lottery victim?

Sal hadn't done it for Jenny Weaver. She knew there was no one to point the finger at but herself. Up at the till another customer pocketed several Super 7 tickets, the line took a collective step forward, and the jackpot swelled another million dollars, a silent mouth swallowing them all.

Slouched in the passenger seat, Sal slurped Shreddies from a plastic cereal bowl while Dusty tooled through the evening streets. She liked it this way, sunk below the windshield, cradled within AC/DC's pounding vibrations and watching the overhead trees whirl by — everything rhythm and motion, a gold-amber pulse. Spooning another mouthful of sugary milk and soggy Shreddies, she worked the conglomeration to mush on her tongue. How she loved the disintegrating grid of each soaked Shreddie, the silky texture of brown-sugar milk. For years her mother's breakfast litany had been "Sal, not so much brown sugar! NOT SO

MUCH BROWN SUGAR!" But the point of eating cereal was working your way down to the treasure trove of sugar hidden at the bottom of the bowl and scooping those sweet loaded spoonfuls into your mouth. Shreddies and milk were just the necessary camouflage.

Dusty made a casual one-handed turn into the recycling depot. "Finished your sugar fix?"

"You can't have any," mumbled Sal, spooning the golden dregs.

"You'd say that to your own gene pool?" demanded her brother.

"You got the Y chromosome, I got the X," Sal replied complacently, tipping the last sugary remains down her throat.

"I am crushed." Getting out, Dusty began hauling boxes of newspapers and bottles from the back seat. The recycling depot was at one end of a strip mall parking lot, a fenced-in drive-through area with two rows of large green bins. At the opposite end a car was pulling out, leaving them alone in the depot.

"I'll handle the newspapers, you do the milk jugs," called Dusty.

"You think I'm a suck?" Grunting, Sal hefted a box of newspapers, then set it back down and slung a garbage bag of plastic milk jugs over one shoulder. "Okay, so I'm a suck."

"Think of what we're doing for planet earth," sang Dusty, lifting the lid to the bin marked *Newspapers Only* and dumping his load. "I feel one with the universe."

"I feel one with plastic," muttered Sal, approaching a bin marked *Plastic Drink Jugs Only*. As she reached to lift the lid, it popped open and a man's head appeared.

"Can I help you?" the head asked.

With a shriek, Sal dropped her bag. The twist tie gave and jugs scattered with hollow rolling thuds. Hovering above the bin of milk jugs, the severed head regarded her patiently. Blood erupted from its crushed forehead, bits of brain oozed down its face. Transfixed, Sal stood staring until the man straightened and a *Green Earth Recycling* uniform materialized beneath his head. The blood faded, the crushed forehead closed over and healed.

"Nice place to hang out, bud." Coming up beside Sal, Dusty began picking up milk jugs and firing them into the bin. His first few tosses narrowly missed the man, the next found their mark. "Scaring the lady?" Dusty hissed, scooping up jug after jug, firing fast and hard.

"Hey, watch it!" said the man, raising an arm to protect his face.

"Oh, sorry," said Dusty. "I thought this was where the *jugs* belonged."

"I was checking to see which ones were clean," the man said irritably, "and the bin lid closed. It's my job."

"Yeah, well make sure the lid stays open next time." Breathing hard, Dusty angled another jug off the open bin lid.

"Cut that out or I'll call the cops!" yelled the man.

"Dusty," shouted Sal, tugging at his arm. "Stop it. Please."

"Idiot." Without another word, her brother stalked to the car and began pulling out a box of newspapers.

"My brother," said Sal apologetically, "is very protective."

"Someone should put him on a leash," snapped the man. "Explain the basics of civilization to him."

A single milk jug lay on the pavement. Picking it up,

Sal fired it into the bin.

"Hey!" the man yelled as the jug clattered past him, but Sal spun on her heel. Heading back to the car, she hauled out a box of empty pop cans. After they finished unloading the back seat, there was a full trunk waiting. It had been half a year since their last trip, and their mother had been nagging Dusty to make this one for several months. Dusty wasn't intentionally lazy. Some things just didn't connect with him, like household chores and his university class schedule.

A van drove into the far end of the depot and parked. The side door opened and a small platform was lowered slowly to the ground. Out of the corner of her eye, Sal noted a blurry wheelchair occupant start off at a quick pace toward the milk jug bin, dragging a large plastic bag.

"Hey Brydan!" Dusty called enthusiastically, waving an arm over his head. "Over here."

Sal's eyes flew toward the wheelchair just as Brydan popped a wheelie to see who was calling. Frozen, she watched as his eyes met Dusty's and alarm exploded across his face. Turning toward the car, she dove through the open passenger door and flattened herself along the front seat. *Shit,* she thought, chewing the mangled inside of her lower lip. *Shit, shit, shit.*

The driver's door opened. "Hey, that's Brydan," said Dusty. "Don't you want to talk to him?"

"I want to go home." Sliding off the seat, Sal huddled on the floor and covered her face with her arm. If she could shrink the world down to the still small place inside the crook of her elbow, everything would be all right, everything would be fine.

"But we have the trunk to unload."

"You unload it."

"All right," said Dusty tiredly, "but I thought you two were friends. Isn't he your clarinet partner?"

Tightening her arm over her face, Sal said nothing. After a pause, she heard Dusty shuffle to the car trunk. Voices called back and forth, she made out a few of Brydan's comments, careful and monosyllabic. A short while later, her brother got in and closed the door. "You're going to have to put on your seat belt," he said. "I'm not driving anywhere with you like that."

"Drive around the corner and I will."

Dusty gave an elaborate sigh. "I really want to take a run at that milk jug bin before we leave, give it a nudge with my fender. That bastard's still in it, and the lid's down again. But you'd have to put on your seat belt if we were going to have that kind of fun."

"Not until we're around the corner."

"Sally-Sis," Dusty sighed, "what's wrong?"

"JUST DRIVE AROUND THE CORNER!"

"Thank God you got the X chromosome and I got common sense." Dusty jammed the key into the ignition and AC/DC and the muffler erupted simultaneously, demolishing all hopes of further communication.

# Chapter Nine

The following morning she discovered a second envelope taped to her locker with six more tabs and the message: *Deliver directly to the names on this list*. "Directly" was underlined twice. Someone on Shadow Council was taking obvious pains to avoid getting a demerit.

Once again she trekked from homeroom to homeroom, tracking down targets and handing out small plastic circles. This morning luck was with her. Four of the targets were already at their desks, and three were familiar— two were in her own grade, and the third was a cheerleader. The fourth name she recognized, but couldn't match to a face. Lurking in the doorway to classroom W5, she scanned heads and pondered. Jamie Shute, Jamie Shute ... something to do with sports. He had to be one of the guys in the back corner, but she didn't want to walk past the teacher's desk without being certain. Better not to invite questions to which she didn't have ready answers.

A group of students had formed to her left, their lively conversation erupting into frequent bursts of laughter. Sal studied them, considering. They looked older, at least grade eleven, possibly twelve. Should she try the sign on them? They seemed pretty average — no cheerleaders, no Student Council Exec members — but then Brydan had given her the three-finger signal, and he wasn't exactly in line for any achievement awards.

No one in the group appeared to have noticed her; she had the element of surprise on her side. Without being told, Sal knew she had to be subtle, this had to be done right. Taking a step toward the group, she dropped her binder and pretended to stumble into the nearest girl. "Oh sorry," she said, stooping to pick up the binder. The group scattered to accommodate her, placing her at the center of a jagged circle. As she straightened, Sal rubbed the left side of her nose.

A throat cleared and Sal glanced toward the sound.

"Can I help you?" asked a girl wearing a Britney Spears t-shirt.

"I'm looking for Jamie Shute," said Sal.

"He sits by the window," said the girl. "Back corner seat. Dark curly hair and something he thinks is a mustache."

"Thanks." Entering the classroom, Sal skirted the teacher, who was talking to several students at her desk, and traveled the window aisle toward the curly-haired guy in the back corner. The dark fuzz shadowing his upper lip was definitely fantasy material. "Jamie Shute?"

The guy swiveled out of his conversation, turning a wide grin toward her. As she watched, shock widened his

eyes, then something else — contempt — tightened his
face. Contempt? For Shadow Council, or for her? A blush
hit Sal, deep, like a wound.

"I'm supposed to deliver this to you." Depositing a tab
on his desk, she headed up the aisle, then paused. Did Jamie
Shute know the meaning of the tab? Had Brydan? Or were
all the targets left wondering in the dark as she was?

Looking back, she watched Jamie pick up the tab and
spin it between his fingers. Around him the group of guys
had also fallen silent, their eyes fixed on him, waiting for his
reaction. Suddenly Jamie tossed the tab into the air and
caught it, then high-fived the guy across the aisle. Laughing, his friends leaned toward him, and the tab traveled hand
to hand around the group. Someone slapped Jamie's back as
if he'd just received a promotion, but no one even glanced
after Sal, erasing her from the situation as effectively as if the
tab had appeared out of thin air.

Two targets weren't in their homerooms, but the Sign
of the Inside helped Sal track one to the Get-It-Now Shop,
the student-run school concession store, where he worked.
The last homeroom on the list was two doors over from her
own. She glanced at her watch. It was five to nine, she had
to act quickly. Stepping inside classroom S17, she brushed
the left side of her nose. Nothing happened. The floor tilted
slightly, and she fought off a wave of panic. Shuffling down
the side aisle, she repeated the gesture. Immediately, a student sitting at a nearby desk stood and came toward her.

"You need help?"

"I need Sarah Crawford," said Sal.

Obligingly, the guy led her to one of the school side
entrances and pointed out a group of smokers lounging in
the student parking lot.

"She's the one with the pierced lip," he said.

"They've all got pierced lips."

"She's double-pierced."

"Is that so she can find her mouth in her face?" asked Sal.

The guy gave her a weird look and disappeared into the school. Walking up to the girl with the double-studded lower lip, Sal handed her a plastic tab.

"Oooo," the girl singsonged, flipping it into the air. "The gods are calling." Then, setting it on her tongue, she swallowed it. Deliberately turning her back to Sal, she reached for the nearest guy's cigarette. "C'mon Jocko," she purred. "Give me a drag."

Erased yet again, Sal backed away from the group. One minute she was everyone's worst nightmare, distributing messages she didn't understand, and the next she didn't exist, wandering numbed and helpless on the other side of everything she knew.


He seemed to be everywhere — playing riotous games of euchre in the cafeteria, ramming himself into sandbags on the football practice field, or hurrying out of the music room after school with trumpet #4. Time after time she looked up to see Willis Cass bantering with someone in a classroom doorway or coming toward her surrounded by an entourage of laughing friends. Not a joke passed him by, he never seemed to miss an opportunity for a little social repartee. Willis was like the Cheshire Cat — after he was gone, all you remembered was his dazzling smile. Everything about Saskatoon Collegiate, its academic and social structures, seemed to have been designed for someone like him. Thursday lunch hour, as she wandered past the auditorium, Sal glanced in to see the weekly Student Council meeting in progress, and there was Willis yet again, seated with the rest of the Executive, facing the sprawled mass of homeroom reps and casual onlookers.

Off to one side she spotted Brydan, also watching the proceedings. She'd forgotten that he'd been elected homeroom rep by acclamation the one day he'd stayed home with a cold earlier that month. He'd thought it such a good joke, he'd accepted the position upon his return. Now, watching him from the door, Sal was hit by such an ache she almost whimpered. That morning at band practice neither of them had spoken a word, had sat instead in parallel misery, tooting off-key and out-of-synch as usual. Their devil-may-care act had never been very good, Sal realized. Shadow Council had read it like a book and called their bluff, and here the two of them were, toeing the line, as frightened and obedient as the next guy.

If Brydan had stood by her, if just one person, *anyone,* would smile at her and include her in the human race, the whole situation would be invalidated. But that was the point, wasn't it? The lottery ruled. No matter who you were, once your name was selected, fate took over your life. You were no longer an individual with specific quirks — say an affinity for tuna-and-alfalfa sprout sandwiches, or such an abhorrence for disco music that you broke out in hives — you were no longer even an individual with specific friends. Winning the lottery wiped out all idiosyncracies, reducing the victim to a simple equation — the person no one wanted to be. To look at the lottery victim, to consciously acknowledge what was happening to Sal Hanson, third clarinetist and Pony Express courier extraordinaire, would mean having to come up against your deepest fear, the realization that when everything was stripped away — all those personal quirks and peculiarities — you as an individual had no meaning, were nothing more than a face in a crowd with needs that could be completely and absolutely denied.

She wanted to run screaming into the auditorium, claw her face until it bled, and yell, "Look at me, I'm human too. Can't you see I need you?" But would anyone look? And if they did, would they see the blood? You couldn't make choices for other people — wasn't that how a democracy worked?

At the front of the room, Willis Cass stood and read out a proposal concerning student dances. When he finished, Brydan's hand shot up, seconding the motion. Turning from the doorway, Sal stumbled down the emptiness of another hall.

Friday noon found her once again in the almost-deserted music room, nodding to Pavvie's approving smile as she pulled clarinet #19 from the shelf. At the door to Room B she paused, flooded by a wave of unexpected hope that left her breathless and panicky. Biting her lip, she tugged open the door to find the room empty, nothing but a half circle of chairs and music stands. She entered, the wave of hope turning ugly, a wall of acid crashing in on itself. What had she expected, a weekly event? Some kind of mutual attraction? And what kind of attraction would that be, between a tyrant and his victim? What exactly had she come here looking for, anyway?

Behind her the door swung open and Willis entered,

carrying trumpet #4. "Good, you're here," he grinned. "I signed the room out, so we won't be disturbed."

She was suddenly shaky, her mouth stretched into a stupid grin. Parking her butt, she began fumbling with her clarinet.

"So what kind of practice rituals d'you have?" asked Willis, sitting beside her and snapping the latches to his case.

"Practice rituals? As in practice *often*?" Sal asked carefully, slipping her reed into her mouth.

"As in scales, arpeggios, warm-up drills."

"Never heard of them."

"Okay," said Willis, not blinking. "We'll start with C major scale. Quarter notes. One, two, three, four." Launching into the scale, he left Sal openly staring, her reed dangling from her lips. "C'mon," he said, lowering the trumpet. "I'm lonely here."

Slowly Sal tightened the ligature around the reed, then slid the clarinet into her mouth. C major scale — no sharps, no flats. It shouldn't be too bad, if she played real quiet.

"You use cigarette papers?" asked Willis.

"Huh?" What was he on about now? Here she'd just psyched herself up for a wavering run at middle C, and he wanted to talk about smoking?

"Your lower lip gets sore from biting on it while you play, n'est-ce pas?" Willis asked mildly.

"You got that right," she said emphatically.

Willis grinned. "My sister plays clarinet in a chamber orchestra. She folds roll-your-own cigarette papers over her bottom teeth for padding. That way she can play for hours."

"For hours," Sal said slowly.

"C major scale," said Willis. "One, two, three ..."

He led them through various warm-up drills until Sal's

bottom lip ached and she was blowing air out of both cor-
ners of her mouth. Pleading mush mouth, she sat and
watched him sail effortlessly through several more keys.
Trumpet to his lips, eyes closed, he lost some of his wolfish
look. Notes poured out of him, fluid as thought. Listening,
Sal felt the jagged gears of her mind begin to dissolve.

"That's more like it," he said, clearing his drain valve.
"Now we're ready to start playing."

"Have you had the nerves pulled from your lips?" Sal
asked suspiciously.

"Never," crooned Willis. "I've got other uses for these
lips. How about we have a go at Choppin' Ettood?" Pulling the music from his folder, he set it on his stand.

"How about first you tell me why I'm handing out
those plastic tabs?" Sal countered, leaving her own folder
closed.

She held her breath while he held his. The room went
into a long pause, Willis staring into the middle distance
while she watched the pulse beat in his throat.

"Recruits," he said finally. "For next year. The tabs indicate who we're considering."

"I thought anyone could apply," she said, confused.

"Three or four positions open a year." Willis fiddled
with his valves, not looking at her. "Anyone can apply, but
we decide who gets in. The tabs are just to let certain kids
know we're watching them. They're possibilities."

"Do they know the tabs mean that?"

"They might, they might not. Not knowing keeps them
on their toes. If we like what we see in them this year,
they'll get a more direct invitation to apply later on." He
gave her a quick glance. "You'll deliver it."

Sal thought of the sick twist in Brydan's expression

and the double-studded girl's moody laughter. There had been fear in that laugh, though she'd covered it well.

"How come so many kids know the Sign of the Inside?" she asked slowly.

"It's built up over the years," Willis said easily. "Shadow has its buddy system, but if you abuse it once, the next time you use it you'll be left to drown."

Sal stared, wordless, at her clarinet. How was it possible things had gotten this complex? Last year she'd been aware of Shadow Council's reach — who wasn't? — but only as an ugly kind of vibe, vague and undefinable. The closer she looked, the more tangled its tentacles became, and they were everywhere. "Does the Celts' staff supervisor know what you're doing?"

"Darryl McCormick?" Willis laughed softly.

"Who?"

"Head of maintenance. He's pretty slack — lets us know when he wants a couple thousand chairs unstacked and pretty much lets us hang out otherwise."

"And no one supervises you in that room?"

Willis shrugged. "Teachers and club reps drop in with duties for us to perform. We've passed out a schedule that lets them know when the clubroom's officially open and the Celts are in business. Shadow operates around the Celts' schedule. The only club member who gets a key to the room is the president, and I call meetings for both the Celts and Shadow. Usually our meetings overlap. We keep a low profile, there's no reason for administration to get suspicious." He blew a breathy riff of notes, his eyes fixed on his musical score. "Don't worry, that room's just a place for mind games. It's all virtual reality — Shadow never gets into any actual violence."

Thoughtfully, Sal opened her music folder and pulled out the Chopin Étude. Talk about mind games — so far she'd distributed twelve tabs and only four vacancies would be opening next year. Shadow Council sure liked to jerk people around. Gingerly, she placed the clarinet in her mouth and bit down on her puffy bottom lip.

"Start signing your clarinet out on weekends," said Willis. "A month from now, you won't recognize your embouchure. Okay, Choppin' Ettood, here we come. One, two —"

He launched flawlessly into the trumpet's silvery introduction to Chopin Étude.

Dusty and her mother were both out, the house holding another empty Sunday afternoon. Sal had been practicing the clarinet in her room, but C major scale just hadn't done it for her. Now she was down in Retro-Whatever, rocking to solid sonics, *The Wall Live* pumped so loud every carpet shag vibrated in orange ecstasy. Turning the volume up, she slammed herself through a reverberating bass line, then sent her soul arcing along electric shimmering notes. The music was a shape-shifter, invading her body and transforming every movement. The jab of an arm released the fury of the unspoken, the whip snap of her body emitted wordless groans, the long drag of her torso across the floor was the snake ache of loneliness.

Whipping and spiraling around the room, she dug into her own breath and muscle, the gut-singing fear where nothing could be touched by words. At some point she looked up to see Dusty in the room with her, whipping his body in parallel contortions, his thin hair vibrating about his head. Though they didn't speak or watch each other, their movements fell into an odd synchronicity — not mirror images, but conversations. She'd twist the question of an arm, he'd spin a mad reply. He'd snap his head, she'd convulse into a long gut groan. Finally, Dusty staggered to the stereo, shut it off, and sank to his knees. Across the room, Sal echoed him. For a moment they looked like two penitents at evening prayer.

"Shit, that was good," gasped Dusty, collapsing onto the floor.

"Yeah." Crawling toward him, Sal rested her head on the rapid rise and fall of his chest. "You get your essay done?"

"Nah. Soccer with a bunch of guys. You practice your clarinet?"

"Three or four notes."

They lay, gulping long passageways of air. Sal's clothes were pasted, she ached in every possible way, felt like lying on the cradle of her brother's lungs for the rest of her life.

"Dusty?" She counted the steady body-wide thuds of his heart. "I like talking to you like this."

"Me too, Sally-Sis," he whispered, clumsily patting her sweaty head. "Nothing better than you, little sis. Nothing better."

Hours later, their mother found them in the same position, fast asleep.

The bike racks were full. Unwrapping the chain-lock from her seat, Sal locked her front wheel to the mesh fence that surrounded the school practice field. *Monday morning, back to the same old grind*, she thought, her eyes tracing the silver links that crossed and crisscrossed the length of an entire city block without a break. As she turned toward the school's east entrance, the full strength of the nearest wall hit her — thousands upon thousands of red bricks cemented firmly together. In that silence, nothing moved. The building was over a century old, and none of its bricks had shifted a millimeter. Even the windows took the morning light and threw it outward, letting nothing in.

But that was only the way it looked on the surface, Sal told herself. When you were inside, the windows let in light. It was only a trick of perspective that made it look as if the windows also functioned as a solid wall, opaque bricks of glass.

As she came down the hallway toward her locker, Marvin Fissett stepped out of the crowd, flashing the three-fingered salute. Even in the cacophony of the busy corridor, it came at her like a vivid electric current. Nodding once, Marvin continued down the hall and she followed, an obedient puppy held tight by an invisible leash. At the library he pushed through the turnstile and headed for the stacks, pausing midway into the geology section.

"Brad Carter," he said, handing her an envelope. "Homeroom S18."

"That's next to my homeroom," Sal said surprised, as if this was somehow relevant, gave the transaction some kind of meaning. Without a word, without even a shrug, Marvin walked off, leaving her standing with her mouth still holding the shape of her words.

*Speaking without permission, one demerit* — she could hear him thinking it as he exited the library. Staring down at the blank envelope, she repeated the name to herself: Brad Carter. She'd never heard of him. It looked like this one called for another nose-rubbing job.

That afternoon, envelope delivered, she filed through the crush of packed hallways toward the auditorium with the rest of the student body. Everyone, including the teachers, looked to be in sleepwalking mode — the scheduled assembly promised to be a snorer, an easily forgotten hour spent listening to the Leader of the Opposition, a federal politician touring western Canada, who'd decided to include several Saskatchewan high schools in his itinerary. Entering the auditorium, Sal joined the fifteen hundred students crowding into tight wall-to-wall rows of chairs. So, Shadow Council had been busy, contributing to the official side of its existence. Off to one side, members of the Celts could be seen lounging against the stage, watching as students filled the chairs.

Behind the podium sat the school principal, Mr. Wroblewski, and a second man who was studying the packed audience with an amused expression. Balding and double-chinned, he didn't look like a worthwhile reason to hold fifteen hundred adolescent minds hostage for an hour. Reluctantly, Sal wormed her way past a dozen jam-packed knees, sinking into a chair just as Mr. Wroblewski walked to the mike and began reciting the Leader of the Opposition's personal accomplishments in education, business, politics and charitable activities. Slouching lower in her seat, Sal wondered how much time this charitable politician intended to expend on his speech. A short speech, she figured, would be a charitable and much-appreciated donation to the frenetic lives of fifteen hundred high-school students.

*Make it ten minutes and I'll vote for you when I get old enough*, thought Sal. *Make it five and I'll vote for your party every election for the rest of my life.*

Mr. Wroblewski stepped back from the mike, and the

amused-looking Leader of the Opposition stood and approached the podium. Leaning into the mike, he opened his mouth, about to begin speaking, just as a piercing scream cut the air and a tall, skinny, naked male student with a paper bag over his head came tearing out of the wings. Running at top speed, he passed the gaping men at the podium and disappeared backstage. For two beats of a conductor's wand, there was absolute silence. Then a tidal wave of laughter engulfed the auditorium. For the next five minutes, pandemonium reigned as wave after wave of hysteria rolled over the student body. Every time a pocket of calm appeared, someone would hazard another guess.

"Eddie Langlotz?"

"He's over there, man."

"Joe Rosencrantz!"

"Impossible — Joe has too much hair on his chest."

Students collapsed onto one another. They rolled off their chairs and lay gasping on the floor. Sprawled in her seat, Sal gasped with the others until a scattering of harried-looking teachers managed to restore a relative calm. Eyes narrowed, she watched the Leader of the Opposition once again lean into the mike.

*Yeah, Mr. Politician*, she thought. *Follow that one. Follow us.*

The man wore a broad grin. Glancing toward Mr. Wroblewski, then back at the student body, he drew a deep breath and said, "Reminds me of my youth."

Sal rode the second fifteen-hundred-strong eruption of laughter. Around her, students kept forgetting who she was, turning toward her with faces that ached with mirth. Invisible bricks dissolved, the air filled with shimmering waves of light.

"Did you catch who that was?" they kept demanding. "Did you recognize him?"

"Sorry, didn't recognize that particular paper bag," Sal replied, but she had a feeling she knew the streaker's identity. Brad Carter was tall and skinny as a toothpick. Brad Carter wouldn't know chest hair if it was tattooed on. In fact, remove Brad Carter's clothes and pull a paper bag over his head, and he'd be a dead ringer for the tall skinny streaker who'd just run screaming across the stage. A massive grin waylaid Sal's face. Shadow Council had just pulled off a genius move, and she'd been part of it. She'd delivered the message that had triggered an event that would become legend to every S.C. student in succeeding years. The Pony Express was dribble compared to this — the Pony Express ate Shadow Council's dust. For one glimmering, soul-singing moment, Sal wouldn't have traded anything for the privilege of being Shadow Council's shadow.

Up at the mike, the Leader of the Opposition cleared his throat and fifteen hundred students leaned forward, ready for any details he was willing to let fly about his naked screaming youth.

*Mister, you can take all afternoon*, thought Sal. *You can take the rest of my life.*

The music door stood open, the sounds of early morning voices and warm-up drills pouring through it. Out in the hallway, Sal stood hesitating. For once, she was on time — just a fluke, it hadn't been intentional, and it meant she was going to have to sit silent and isolated as a wooden post while everyone around her exchanged morning breath and the requisite jokes. Of late, Brydan had been developing a chipper relationship with the female oboist to his right. His conversation had a desperate edge, and he turned himself in his wheelchair so that he sat at a forty-five-degree angle to the front of the room, presenting Sal with his back until Pavvie gave a preliminary rap of the baton. Sal knew there was nothing personal in this; Brydan was simply talking *at* the girl because she happened to be there. Still, a steel rake clawed her gut every time she remembered that a week ago he would have been hard-pressed to remember the oboist's last name.

Coming through the door, her eyes flicked dangerously toward the back row of risers. Most of the trumpet players were seated, a kaleidoscope of notes streaming from their instruments. At the center of the row sat Willis, trumpet on his knee, consulting with his music partner about a particular passage. As she entered, he looked up. Their eyes met, and she saw him the way he appeared to everyone else — dark shaggy hair, thick sideburns that begged to be stroked, intelligent eyes on the alert for every potential joke, and so tall that even sitting he loomed above the back row of trumpet players, drawing the Concert Band to its peak.

He saw her, and another level opened fleetingly in his face. For a second, it was there — a smile that opened inward, a window letting in light. Then his eyes dropped, and he was again consulting with his trumpet partner. Just inside the door, Sal stood alone in an uproar of saxophones, trombones, and a long unmitigated drumroll, bewildered at what had just come and gone. How could something that lasted a millisecond take her on a spin halfway around the world, its shimmering ache more real than anything she could touch with her hands?

Fetching clarinet #19, she maneuvered through the

music stands and into her seat. Beside her, Brydan stiff-ened and launched into yet another scintillating conversa-tion with the oboist. This morning, however, it hardly seemed to matter. This morning she floated above it all, caught in the ephemeral web of Willis Cass's smile.

Snapping the latches on her clarinet case, she reached for her reed. There, tucked beside her cleaning swab, was a blue package of Zig-Zag cigarette papers.

# Chapter Ten

The girl was always alone, like Sal. No one spoke to her, she drifted through the rush and shove of school hallways as if she was on an alternate plane of reality, visible only to those as lonely as she was. Tauni Morrison never looked at anyone, never began a conversation, never initiated contact in any way. Every noon hour she sat in a back corner of the cafeteria, eating her bag lunch in short quick bites, then disappeared into the library to bury herself in yet another book. *Like Color to the Blind*, Sal had seen her reading. *Sensation and Perception*. *Shadow Syndromes*. What could a kid like her possibly want with books like that?

She was a good student. When Sal racked her brains, she remembered Tauni's name being called at last year's award assembly. The MC had spoken her name several times into the mike, and polite applause had rippled across the auditorium, but no one had come forward to receive the plaque.

Whatever was going on inside that girl's head, it kept her up and out of reach, far away from the chaos that surrounded her. It was almost as if she'd divided herself into two parts, then sent her mind as far from her body as it could travel, maintaining minimal contact like a radio kept at low volume, so quiet it was only the faintest murmur in the ear.

Her next summons came Wednesday morning. Inserted into her French textbook, a black cutout of a human shadow oozed across the first page of Chapitre Quatre, that day's classwork. Flipped over, it displayed a white bell pasted on the back, bearing the message: *Twelve o'clock sharp. You know where.* Picking it up, Sal stared at its eerie distorted shape. How could Shadow Council have known which page she would turn to on that particular morning? Who could have told them?

Kimmie, of course. Though they never spoke, never even made eye contact, the two girls were still trapped in the same French class three times a week. And as the lottery victim's former best friend, Kimmie was probably high on Shadow Council's list of official suckers by now. But then, so was Sal. It wasn't as if she was in any position to lay blame. And it could have been any other member of the class. All it would have taken was a quick question slid into a casual conversation. The respondent probably hadn't had a clue she was being ransacked for information.

But how had they gotten the message into her textbook? The book had been in her locker. Supposedly no one knew the combination to her lock except front office personnel. Did Shadow Council have access to school records?

No, Sal thought, it was far more likely someone had been spying over her shoulder one day as she fiddled with her lock. It wasn't as if she was compulsively neurotic about hiding her combination. It had never crossed her mind that anyone would have the slightest interest in breaking into her locker — the only things she kept there were her school-books and compass set, the bare minimum required to keep a high-school student functional. Still, it was the only private pocket of space in the entire building that belonged to her. How many times had they been into her locker? Had they had her combination last year too? What else did they know about her? Exactly how paranoid was Shadow Council causing her to become?

From her position on the footstool, she watched them. Today she'd been placed off to one side of the room. When she'd knocked at twelve o'clock sharp, Rolf had opened the door and said, "From now on, you will give the victim's knock." He'd rapped a specific rhythm on the door — three short taps, then two long — and made her repeat it several times before leading her to the footstool in a far corner of the room.

"Sit," he'd said, and returned to his own seat. Unsure if he wanted her nose stuck to the wall, Sal had hesitated, then taken a steadying breath and faced the room. To her surprise, only Shadow Council's Executive was present. Once she was seated they ignored her, treating her as if she was nothing more than an irrelevant comatose object that had been parked in a corner until needed. Since this wasn't far from the truth, Sal settled into her coma, counted acid surges in her stomach, and waited.

They were arguing. It seemed to have something to do with two male students and a punishment. Gradually Sal

pieced together the events surrounding the original crime
— a drunken beach party and some boisterous lyrics that
hadn't been particularly respectful of Shadow Council.
Apparently one of Shadow's suckers had been lurking in
the darkness beyond the firelight, listening in.

"We have to hit fast and hard," said Linda, making a
quick chopping motion. "We can't let disrespect for Shadow
stand unanswered. And it has to be obvious, something
that rubs their noses in the dirt so no one'll dare do it again."

"Rubbing noses in the dirt can get people's backs up,"
murmured Willis, stroking his chin. "Put out one fire, start
three others."

"No one'll play with matches if they explode in their
faces," snapped Linda. "We hit hard this time, we won't
have to hit again."

Jaw jutting, she perched on a couch arm and surveyed
the two guys. Linda Paboni obviously needed work on her
group discussion skills. At the couch's other end sprawled
Willis, head back, eyes sketching a world map across the
ceiling — further territory to conquer. Seated opposite, in
one of the armchairs, was Rolf, secretary's binder open in
his lap, doodling.

"You have to understand the male ego," Willis said
slowly. "The way it works."

"Believe me, I know how it works," said Linda.

"The guys were drunk," said Willis. "When guys get
drunk, their brains are one-hundred proof. You can't expect them to behave like rational human beings."

"Can you ever?" muttered Linda.

"Their brains swell," continued Willis, still studying
his ceiling dream world. "Beerheads think big. Their
thoughts get oversized, too big for their actual brain mat-

ter. They see themselves as superheroes, the King Kong clan. They have to take on the biggest threat in their lives, prove they're the tough guys."

"That doesn't mean they can mouth off about Shadow," said Linda, making another chopping motion.

On the edge of the discussion, Rolf doodled thoughtfully.

"In a way, it's a compliment to Shadow," said Willis. "We were the biggest thing they could jaw off about."

"I hardly think being called a pig's ass is a compliment," Linda said drily.

"Labatts' poetry," shrugged Willis. "Molson Canadian sonnets. We get uptight over this, they'll be jerking our chain every time they pop a beer."

"We have to do something," said Rolf, rubbing his pencil against the bridge of his nose. "The pig's was the first of many asses we got shoved up in that song."

"But we make it work for us," said Willis, finally pulling himself down out of the ceiling. "These guys are big mouths. They want to be seen as tough guys, full of derring-do."

"We hang them out to dry." Linda was really into the chop-chop gestures today. "Show them what wimps they really are."

Slowly Willis shook his head. "We give them a duty that proves how tough they are," he said softly, "only we make it work for us. We win their loyalty *and* we come out on top. From now on, Labatts will be singing our praises every time, guaranteed."

"These guys are your friends?" Linda asked suspiciously.

Pursing his lips, Willis stared directly at her. "What d'you take me for?"

Linda's eyes dropped. "Okay, so what are you suggesting?"

"Something big," said Willis. "A sign, or a banner."

Instinctively their faces turned toward the window, growing vague with thought.

"A monument to Shadow," mused Willis.

"And they have to put it up!" said Rolf excitedly.

"Except it has to be indirect," said Willis. "Everyone will know it's Shadow, but it can't point directly to us."

Another pause fell on the three, their bodies drooping, their jaws growing slack.

"Walter Murray Collegiate," said Linda suddenly. "Right over the front entrance."

Rolf's face broke into an easy grin. "A banner to S.C., so it looks like it means Saskatoon Collegiate."

Linda was looking excited. "What about *S.C. Is The Power*. Or maybe *S.C. Is Watching You*."

"Too obvious," said Willis. "Sounds like Shadow."

"I guess," grunted Linda.

"It has to be tied to something else," said Willis. "Something S.C. is doing."

"The football game, Friday after school!" exclaimed Rolf.

Willis snapped his fingers. "That old banner we have in storage — *S.C. RULES*. It'll look like a football prank, but the word will get around. The two guys will bask in the glory, but since they were doing our bidding, we'll look good too. I guarantee you that pigs' asses will go extinct as far as Shadow's concerned."

"Yeah," said Linda, looking pleased. "Good thinking, guys."

"But how will they get the banner up on Walter

Murray?" asked Rolf. "The roof's at least two storeys high."

"Not off Taylor Street," said Linda. "My dad teaches there so I know the building. There's a side entrance that's low, just one storey high. It's covered by several trees so no one'll notice them climbing onto the roof from the outside, and there are no windows anywhere along that side of the building so no one'll see them from the inside. They'll have to haul the ladder up with them because the roof takes a hike a couple of times, but if they're quick they should be able to manage it."

The three high-fived one another.

"Okay, now for the instructions," said Willis. "Write the same thing for both of them, and don't include any names, theirs or Shadow's."

A knock sounded on the door. Instantly, Shadow Council's Executive stiffened, Linda's eyes darting toward Sal.

"We aren't officially open," she hissed.

"We're always official," Willis replied calmly. "This just so happens to be a Celts Exec meeting and we're working out our fall schedule. Go see who it is."

"What about her?" asked Linda, pointing at Sal.

"Victim, come sit over here." Willis glanced toward Sal without making direct eye contact. "We'll say you came to deliver infomation from —" He hesitated.

"— Pavvie," said Sal, sliding into the burgundy armchair. "About the fall concert publicity."

"Yeah," agreed Willis, closing his eyes, a smile sifting through the layers of his expression. "Good thinking, victim."

"Fine," snapped Linda, getting up and opening the door. In the hall stood a teacher holding a stack of posters. A quick conversation ensued — the posters concerned an upcoming mock United Nations assembly for high-school students that S.C. was hosting. Smiling, Linda accepted the armload of posters along with a list of delivery points. The satisfied teacher thanked the three Celts, and the door closed behind him.

"See?" said Willis. "No sweat. They want to believe, so they believe. No one ever looks further than what they want to see. Now, where were we?"

He was right. The teacher had seen the hard concrete evidence — Sal Hanson, lottery victim, sitting in the Celts' clubroom — and had walked off without batting an eyelash. The floor heaved uneasily and Sal gripped the arms of her chair, unsure if she was expected to remain where she was or return to the footstool. She felt illegal in the burgundy armchair, as if the soft cushion beneath her butt was too good for her, but no one had ordered her back to her corner. Better to remain silent and not attract attention by moving.

"Okay, shoot." Tearing two pages from his binder, Rolf poised his pen, awaiting Willis's dictation.

"Time, colon," dictated Willis. "Friday, October first, nine-fifteen AM. Place, colon, Walter Murray Collegiate. Duty, colon, use a ladder to get onto the roof from the Taylor Street entrance and drape the *S.C. RULES* banner across the front of the building. Note, long dash, and then write the following in capital letters, do not cover the windows, exclamation mark."

"Gotcha," said Rolf, writing it down, then copying it onto a second page.

"How will they get the banner?" asked Linda.

"It will mysteriously materialize somewhere in their vicinity," said Willis.

"Locker mania," grinned Rolf. Placing the instructions inside two envelopes, he sealed them. "Victim approach," he ordered, without looking up.

Startled, Sal stood and took two steps toward him. She was almost brushing his knees.

"Two envelopes," said Rolf brusquely, handing them to her. "And two locker combinations." He placed a small piece of paper in her hand. "Make sure you put the envelopes where they'll be seen immediately."

Sal stared at the piece of paper. On it were written two locker numbers and two corresponding lock combinations. How many student locker combinations did Shadow Council have in its possession? "Someone'll see me," she protested. "I'll get caught."

"Not my problem," shrugged Rolf.

Sal's eyes flicked toward Willis, but he stared back, his face blank as the envelopes in her hand. Numbly, she started toward the door.

From behind her came Willis's soft voice. "Pony Express."

He was right, she realized. This was another version of the Pony Express — a little more malicious toward its targets and a lot more deadly for its courier, but it operated on essentially the same principles. How had Willis known about her Pony Express expertise?

"Victim dismissed," said Rolf.

She left the room quickly. Except for 8 AM, the halls were emptiest at lunch hour. If she worked fast, she should be able to get this done before the one o'clock bell.


Friday morning at nine-fifteen, Sal stood holding her bike and watching from a nearby bus stop as two male figures wearing black balaclavas appeared on the roof of Walter Murray Collegiate. Unrolling a long red-and-gold banner, they worked quickly, draping it so that it hung across the front of the building, but not so far down that it covered the windows and could be seen from inside. Stretched to full length, the banner was an easy ten meters, the letters a brilliant gold. And upside-down, Sal realized with a flash of panic. Only it didn't look as if the balaclavaed guys had noticed. Kneeling at opposite ends of the banner, they seemed to be anchoring it. This accomplished, they would head back to the ladder and down off the roof. Once their feet touched ground, it was unlikely they would climb back up to correct their mistake.

Mounting her bike, Sal rode frantically across Taylor Street and onto the school lawn. "Hey!" She waved her arms, trying to yell quietly. "S.C., S.C.! Shadow!"

At the word "shadow," one of the guys glanced down and saw her. Placing one hand above her head and one at her waist, Sal rotated them one hundred and eighty degrees. *Upside-down*, she thought maniacally at the two watching guys. *Upside-down, beerheads.*

Leaning forward, the first guy peered over the edge of the roof, then gave her the thumbs-up signal. As she watched, the balaclavaed figures righted and anchored the banner, then retreated swiftly across the roof, leaving the banner suspended in red-and-gold glory across the front of Walter Murray Collegiate. *S.C. RULES*. Sal observed it with a mixture of pride and dread. Not until that moment had she realized she'd wanted the venture to succeed, she wanted Shadow Council to rule.

No, she didn't. She didn't want a small group of ego-terrorists running fifteen hundred students with threats and mind games. And she certainly didn't want them jerking her life around for the next nine months. Then why the brilliant thread of satisfaction — no elation — that glimmered through her as she stared up at the red-and-gold banner? Why had she skipped her first-period math class, risking detention and her mother's wrath, to watch this happen?

Suddenly she realized she was a dead giveaway, gawking gleefully upward on the front lawn of enemy turf. Mounting her bike she pedaled off furiously, glancing back several times to anchor the vision of the rebel banner firmly in her memory. Even after she turned the corner, it continued to hang gleaming across the center of her thoughts, a gorgeous claim to supremacy, a third-finger salute suspended through all that was mundane.

The luminous notes of Willis's trumpet could be heard halfway down the hall. Entering the music room, Sal returned Pavvie's quick nod, grateful for his reticence. The man rarely spoke unless absolutely necessary, the only person at S.C. who talked less than Sal herself, unless you counted Tauni Morrison. Maybe he was another person who needed a tube of black lipstick to find the mouth in his face.

As she opened the practice room door, Willis gave a dramatic flurry of notes.

"Everyone's talking about it. It's all over the school." Sal's face broke into an exuberant grin. "Did you see it?"

Eyebrows raised, Willis pointed to the open door. She closed it.

"Of course I saw it," he said immediately, lifting his trumpet and releasing several glad notes. "Snapped a few

Kodak memories while I was at it."

Sal hit the nearest chair with a thud. "You were there?"

"I had a spare, so I thought I'd watch from my car. I caught you on film, making your genius tactical move. Way to go, Sally-O. I'll make you an extra copy."

"You will?"

"You were part of it. Part of the team."

A delicate shyness winged across Sal's face. Ducking her head, she began assembling her clarinet. Willis tooted softly into the silence, something low-lying and blue.

"You practice this week?"

"Couple times," she admitted reluctantly. It wasn't easy, surrendering her perception of herself as an eternally care-free, wimp-lipped third clarinetist. "I tried those cigarette papers you put in my case. They really helped. Thanks."

"Good. I want to try out a new piece with you. Something I wrote."

"You wrote this?" She stared in astonishment as he slid a sheet of composition paper onto the music stand in front of her, full of penciled-in notes and treble clefs.

"It was originally for two trumpets," Willis said, settling back again, "but clarinet and trumpet play in the same key so I didn't have to transpose."

She could feel him watching her as she scanned the piece. It was in the key of G, mostly half and quarter notes, with a few eighth notes scattered throughout. She should be able to handle it, unless he wanted it in cut time.

"Willis?" She was frightened at the question that loomed through her, terrified she was about to lose the only good thing she had going in her life, but she had to ask. She *had* to. "Why are you doing this?"

"Doing what?"

"Meeting me here. Practicing with me." She kept her eyes down as she spoke, watching her fingers fiddle with the clarinet keys.

He shrugged. "Because I want to."

"But you're not supposed to. You never act like this at Shadow meetings."

"It's our secret," he grinned.

Still staring down, she swallowed the slimy balloon in her throat. "You've got friends. You don't ... need me."

Willis shifted, suddenly uncomfortable. "I don't have friends."

Sal snorted, choking on astonishment.

"You think Shadow's my friends?" Willis asked. "Would you pick them for friends?"

She waved a hand vaguely. "Everywhere you go, you're surrounded. Everyone wants to be your buddy."

"Even you?"

"You took away all my friends. What else have I got?"

Willis's eyes narrowed. Sal felt the danger rushing her blood.

"Were they your friends?" he asked softly. "Really?"

"They were enough," Sal said bitterly.

"Enough for *then*," said Willis, "but now? They'll never be enough again."

Sal thought of Kimmie's whispered washroom confession, of Brydan sitting stiff and miserable beside her, practice after practice. She thought of Jenny Weaver's eyes, the way they never rested within the safety of anyone's gaze.

"What are you saying?" she asked. "Relationships are all illusions, there are no real friends? If your name had been drawn instead of mine, d'you think everyone would be shunning you?"

"Shadow members' names don't go into the lottery," said Willis. "Why d'you think I joined?"

"That's why you joined?" Sal demanded. "So you could do to other people what you couldn't face yourself?"

Willis stiffened, then nodded. Staring into the blunt reality of his face, she realized that he was staring back into the harsh mirror of her own, that he wanted this kind of truth.

"You still haven't answered my question," she said. "Why are you meeting me here? Why would you want to?"

"You figure it out," he said softly.

"Is this another one of Shadow's games?"

"No one knows about this except you and me. Our secret."

She watched his careful narrowed gaze. Was this friendship he was offering her? No, friendship didn't hide inside secrets and Friday lunch-hour practice rooms. Then what was it?

"Warm-up scale?" asked Willis. "C major?"

Did she have to have all the answers right now? Did anyone ever have all the answers? Slowly she raised the clarinet to her lips.

"What d'you think of the title of my piece?" Willis asked.

She glanced at the page in front of her. Across the top was written *Inside the Question*.

"Story of my life," she said slowly.

"Me too," said Willis. "Okay, warm-up time. C major scale, quarter notes. One, two, three, four ..."

# Chapter Eleven

Voices clamored through the open doorway. It was Friday after classes, and the few students who hadn't taken off for the S.C.-Walter Murray football game had collected in the drama room. Standing in the hallway, Sal shifted her feet hesitantly. The PA announcement had said all volunteers were welcome, and experience wasn't necessary for building props. But did this include the lottery victim? What would happen if she walked into that room? How long would it take for silence to eat its slow acid through every conversation as head after head turned in her direction? Which one of the students in that room wouldn't go into paranoid convulsions if she sat next to them? She would have to sit beside someone, and teachers were always big on assigning group activities. How could she request to work on a stage prop by herself? What excuse could she invent — syphilis? Insanity? An allergic reaction to being treated like a normal human being?

She *wanted* to work backstage on the fall drama production. *A Midsummer Night's Dream* and Shakespeare were definitely beyond her, but she liked the idea of building things. The lottery victim had a right to *want* something, didn't she?

Edging up to the doorway, Sal scanned the approximately twenty students in the room. Divided into small groups, they laughed and chatted animatedly. Was there anyone she knew well, anyone that mattered? Yes, she realized, as a chubby ponytailed girl sitting with a circle of friends rose to her knees and threw a wadded paper ball at someone across the room. Heart sinking, Sal backed away from the door. She couldn't go in there and make Kimmie suffer. Not again. Thirty seconds trapped in Sal's presence had been enough to send her former best friend fleeing from a washroom in tears.

"Great, another volunteer!" exclaimed Mr. Tyrrell, the drama teacher, coming up behind her. "Come on in. We're just about to start."

"No thanks," said Sal quickly. "I was looking for something, but I guess I lost it somewhere else. Have a really great time."

Turning, she faded down the hall.

Retro-Whatever was a wall of sound, a reverberating force field of sonics. Every nerve in Sal's body throbbed like a guitar string. She lay vibrating in a web of sound so loud she became *The Wall Live*, rose and fell on deafening waves of guitar and keyboard. *Take me*, she thought, pushing deeper and deeper into the gigantic pulse. Something lay beyond it, something she needed to smash her way through to. Maybe then she would understand. *Crush my skull,* she thought. *Smear my brains, take me away from this shit I call myself.*

Suddenly the headphones lifted from her ears, and she opened her eyes to see Dusty leaning over her. Rocked by the roar in her head, she watched the blur of his lips, waiting for normal hearing and vision to kick back in. "No, Sally-Sis," she finally heard him say. "This isn't the way to do it. This isn't the way."

Then he was holding her, rocking her slowly back and forth, ignoring the sweat that soaked her body and pasted her clothes. A huge sigh shuddered through her, then another. Wordless, she leaned into his thin chest, feeling the world solidify around him. Things looked so different, smaller and mundane, when she returned from blasting her head, as if sound itself was an alternate reality, a place where the mind took its truest forms.

Over by the stereo, Lizard stood gawking at the volume setting. With an awed whistle, he flipped it off.

"C'mon Sal," said Dusty. "I'll make you a cup of hot chocolate."

Numbly, she allowed her brother to lead her upstairs. Sitting at the kitchen table, she watched him bustle about the kitchen, nuking a mug of milk, stirring in the Nestlé's, and adding a quarter cup of miniature marshmallows. Bright tears stabbed her eyes, and such an intense wave of love engulfed her that her throat ached. What would she do if Dusty finally decided to grow up and move away from Saskatoon? There would be no one left, no one at all.

"Hey, what about me?" demanded Lizard as Dusty set the steaming mug of chocolate in front of Sal.

"Ladies first." Dusty edged into the breakfast nook beside Sal. "I made it warm, not hot, so you wouldn't burn your mouth," he said encouragingly.

She wanted to blubber, open her mouth and wail. Cautiously she raised the mug, her hand shaking visibly.

"We were going to take you driving," said Dusty. "Lizard even promised to behave and sit in the back seat. But you look kind of tired."

"I'm not tired," Sal mumbled into the marshmallow froth.

"You look wasted," said Lizard. "Roadkill."

Her hand jerked, and hot chocolate slopped onto the table.

"I'll get it," said Dusty, reaching for a stack of paper napkins on the counter.

"I can drive." Sal stared, dumb with exhaustion, into the soft crinkle of melting marshmallows.

"You can drive yourself to bed," said her brother. "Deep sleep, where you belong."

"No," Sal whimpered. She ached to tell Dusty about being the lottery victim — the urge threw itself around inside her like a prisoner in a cage. But there was also so much ... *crap* ... pushing, shoving, ranting and raving within. If she opened just a crack to let out the truth about the lottery, all the other ugliness would come with it. She would explode, bits of ugliness flying everywhere. Who would she be after something like that? Weren't there enough problems while she was still in one piece?

But if she couldn't tell her brother what was really going on, she still needed him right beside her. She couldn't go to bed — sleep would take her too far away from him. "I want my driving lesson. I want to drive," she mumbled, rubbing at the tears sliding down her face. Beside her, Dusty dissolved into sympathetic agony. Even Lizard looked anxious.

"Here, give me some of those," he said gruffly, grabbing most of the napkins Dusty had left on the counter. Seconds later, Sal's face was being patted with a giant wad of primrose-patterned napkins. Lizard seemed to think she'd metamorphosized into Niagara Falls. Helplessly, she began to giggle.

"That's not crying." The napkins vanished and Lizard shoved his face into hers. "Hey, Dusty — I think she's feeling better."

Sal shoved his friendly grin back to the other side of the table. "Please can I have a driving lesson?" she pleaded sleepily. "Pretty please?"

"Tomorrow, Sal. You're too tired now. I'm putting you to bed." Sliding off the bench, Dusty took her arm. "I'll walk you upstairs."

"I don't want to." Sal's lower lip swelled into a pout. She felt grumpy and eight years old.

"Sal." Fear sharpened her brother's voice. "This is getting silly. You're so tired you can't hold that mug properly."

"Yes I can." Sal stood, bracing against her own surge of fear. "I'm fine. I'm fine as you are." Stepping out from the table, she felt the room go into a sudden lean. The mug slipped from her hand and crashed to the floor.

"Take her legs, Liz." Dusty hooked his hands under Sal's shoulders, and they lugged her firmly out of the kitchen and down the hall. Swinging helplessly between their bodies, she caught a pendulum view of the front door opening as her mother came in from an evening meeting.

"What's going on here?" Ms. Hanson asked, shaking out her umbrella.

"Just putting the kid to bed, Mom." Grinning, Dusty turned up the stairs and into Sal's room. Still trapped in her brother's arms, Sal watched as Lizard confiscated the bags of chips and cookies scattered across her bed. Then they both force-tucked her under the covers and held her down until she stopped struggling.

Immediately she was sinking into a swoon of sleep. "Dusty, I love you," she mumbled, turning into her pillow and burrowing into its familiar scent. "I love you better than no one else."

"I know, Sally-Sis," he whispered, hovering above her.

"Something's really bugging her, man," said Lizard, his voice floating in the far nearby.

"Shh," said Dusty. "She's so smart she can hear you in her sleep."

"Myra Hurgett's been pissing me off." Linda scowled from her position at the center of the couch. "I want something done about her."

"Pissing you off how?" Willis was seated in his usual throne, at right angles to the couch and vague mental angles to everyone in the room, refusing direct contact. Lethargically, he picked at a zit on his chin.

"Swaggering around the court, grabbing the ball when it isn't going to her, blocking my moves." Linda's hands sliced the air, execution style. "It's only her first year on the senior team and she's getting too big for her britches. I want a terror campaign."

"Myra Hurgett?" Ellen asked doubtfully.

Linda sent her a machete glance. "She steps on my toes, she's stepping on Shadow's toes."

Sal watched from her footstool in the far corner, tracing the surface of the wall behind her. The Celts' clubroom was small, one step up from a maintenance closet. The dull yellow walls seemed to lean inward, the outline of each brick visible beneath the paint. Gently, robotically, she traced the brick beside her right hip, shrinking herself into its small rectangular shape. She had nothing to do with this, she was just a brick in a wall. She wasn't here, really. She was just a brick ...

Seven Shadow Council members were present at Monday's lunch-hour session, swilling Pepsi and leaning conspiratorially into their circle. The mood was dour — Walter Murray Collegiate's football team had dragged S.C.'s butt through the mud at Friday's game, then made a big show of slashing the *S.C. RULES* banner with a pair of gardening shears. Everyone in the room was carefully avoiding the subject. The United Nations posters sat on a nearby table, ready for distribution, and Willis had started the meeting by handing out the fall schedule for chair-stacking duties at school assemblies. Then they'd switched gears and begun foraging for ideas, tossing out suggestions for targets. Sal recognized some of the names — Myra Hurgett was a well-known grade eleven member of the elite Nikes set. Half the people in this room were supposedly her friends.

"A terror campaign involves a lot of targets," Willis said slowly. "It's usually a defense of someone's honor."

"This is about my honor," snapped Linda, "my honor as volleyball team captain. My honor is Shadow's honor. I want that message rubbed in her face."

"More noses in the dirt," murmured Willis.

"It doesn't have to be that obvious," said Marvin. "Trip her up in the hall, steal her stuff off her desk when she's not looking, send her a few Pony Express notes. Small crap. See how fast she folds. It'll be a practice run for us, so we know how to machinate the big moves."

Willis nodded, pursing his lips. "Practice run, flexing our muscles. How about we use, say, three or four targets?"

"Ten," said Linda. "I want her tripped, I want her shoved, I want her locker broken —"

"Too obvious," said Willis. "We want to break her morale, not have her complaining to front office."

"Fine," glared Linda. "But here's what I want the Pony Express notes to say."

"Uh uh." Willis shook his head. "Let the targets figure out their own messages. That way it'll be more generic. You want a terror campaign to be grassroots, coming from everywhere. If it all comes directly from us, it'll look like it's coming from one source — us."

The discussion continued, suggestions being volleyed by various members of the group.

"She wears this stupid charm bracelet," said Judy. "She's really attached to it — I think it belonged to her dead grandmother. Steal that charm bracelet and you'd really get to her."

"Fill her gym shoes with Javex," shrugged Marvin.

"Give her a new nickname," said Fern. "Get everyone calling her Flab Butt or Cellulite Queen."

Rolf nodded, scribbling furiously as the group grew more animated.

"Throw a balloon filled with Aqua Velva at her in the hall," gloated Ellen.

"Spread a rumor she's having an affair with Diane Kruisselbrink," grunted Marvin.

The entire group dissolved into snorts of laughter. Diane Kruisselbrink was easily 250 pounds. Then there was the additional weight of the chorus line of comments that followed her daily as she swayed through the halls.

"Diane Kruisselbrink!" cried Linda gleefully. "Have you ever seen the inside of her gym locker? She keeps a month's worth of used underwear in it. She must change after each class and leave the dirty pair in there. It reeks."

"Diane Kruisselbrink takes gym?" Rolf asked in awe.

"She has to," said Linda. "She's in grade ten."

"How'd you get her locker combo?" asked Willis.

Linda waggled her eyebrows. "I have my sources."

"So what's your suggestion?" asked Willis.

"I suggest," purred Linda, looking blissful, "that a target be given the duty of taking all Diane's used underwear and taping them to the outside of Myra Hurgett's hall locker."

"Oh yeah," said someone softly. The circle sat silently, contemplating inner visions.

"Overkill," said Willis after a moment. "One pair would do it."

"One of Diane Kruisselbrink's gotch would cover three lockers," Rolf said speculatively.

"Okay." Willis tugged at an earlobe. "So who's the target for this one?"

"Has to be a girl," said Linda immediately. "Preferably in Diane's gym class."

Over in her corner, Sal went into red alert. She was in Diane Kruisselbrink's gym class. Shadow Council must have this information somewhere in their possession — certainly they would have checked out the lottery victim's class schedule — but would they have bothered to memorize it? Blanking her face, she tried to fade into the wall behind her.

"Grade ten," mused Linda, her eyes sweeping past Sal, then swinging back, suddenly focused. "Victim!"

Warily, Sal straightened.

"When do you get gym?"

"Period five," Sal said faintly.

Linda stroked her chin. "Four demerits," she purred. "Should be seven or eight by my reckoning."

"She's not due for punishment yet," Willis said quickly.

Linda's eyes narrowed. "Getting a bit friendly with the victim, Willis?"

"Just following the rules," said Willis easily.

"I say we vote on it," said Linda. "How many think the victim should get this duty?"

Six hands went up.

"Passed." Linda settled back, her eyes on Willis. "Victim, bring your footstool into the circle."

"The Celts are officially open," said Willis. "Someone might come in and see her there."

"They'll knock first," Linda countered.

"You know best." Willis lifted his hands in a gesture of defeat, and Sal carried the footstool into the center of the circle.

"Face me, victim." As Sal rotated toward her, Linda flipped through a notebook. Copying three locker numbers and one lock combination onto a small piece of paper, she handed it to Sal. "This afternoon, period five, your duty will be to remove two pairs of Diane Kruisselbrink's filthy bloomers from her gym locker," she sneered. "Tape one of them to Myra Hurgett's hall locker and the other to Diane Kruisselbrink's hall locker."

Shadow Council broke into a collective grin as Sal folded herself in around her molten stomach. For the past five weeks, she'd been watching Diane Kruisselbrink grunt through the required calisthenics and weave her thunderous way up and down the gym holding a field hockey stick. Every gym class, she'd caught herself secretly marveling at those pale mounds of flesh, the bleak girl's heaving stamina.

*Not Diane Kruisselbrink*, she wanted to whisper. *I can't. I won't.*

Seated in his armchair throne, Willis remained as silent as she did.

"Victim dismissed," smirked Linda.


Standing in the cold drafty gym, Sal waited as Ms. Simms took a quick attendance. Then, as the teacher bent to pick up a volleyball, she slipped out of the cluster of girls and through the door that led into the locker room. Pulling the slip of paper with Diane Kruisselbrink's locker combination from her pocket, she headed for the wall next to the showers. Diane's locker stood seven from the end. Ten minutes earlier Sal had watched, carefully counting and recounting locker doors as the huge soft-gasping girl had bent to pull on her gym shorts and tie her running shoes. Now it took three spins of the dial, and the lock clicked in her hand. The locker rasped startlingly loud in the empty room as it opened to reveal the hidden contents of one girl's life: a rank pile of crumpled polyester underwear, a pair of street shoes worn severely on the instep, a huge pair of jeans, and a white blouse — nothing extraordinary but private nonetheless, almost holy, as if the locker contained a sad tenderness that couldn't be carried into the actual activities of living.

There really was quite a stench. Quickly, Sal pulled out two pairs of stretched, stained underwear and stuffed them into her binder. Easing the locker shut, she leaned her body around the lock to muffle the click as it closed.

Even so, the sound ricocheted through her like a bowling ball. Her heart kept taking runs up her throat. Guilt crawled out of her palms. She felt a terrible urgency to wash and rewash her hands.

She came out of the locker room into a hall that stretched into a long begging loneliness. Walls loomed, every brick in place, every other student in class — only she stood outside the perimeters of life as it was supposed to be. Walking quickly down the north hall, she progressed along a row of endless locker doors. Quiet and unassuming, #772 appeared on her right, without any insignia of shame or self-loathing to identify its current occupant. Slowly, Sal pulled the first pair of underwear from her binder. Even in the drafty hallway, there was an immediate reek. Diane Kruisselbrink obviously didn't invest much in personal hygiene. She certainly never showered after gym.

Also inside Sal's binder was the tube of Krazy Glue that Rolf had handed her as she'd left the Celts' clubroom. Holding a panty seam to the left side of Diane's locker, Sal squirted Krazy Glue under it and pressed firmly. One of her fingers stuck and she panicked, visualizing herself eternally glued to locker #772 as an expressionless Diane Kruisselbrink trudged remorselessly toward her. Then her finger pulled free, minus a small patch of skin, and she carefully glued the panty's other seam to the opposite side of the locker. Stepping back, she tugged once to make sure the gotch was hanging securely in place before taking off pell-mell for the west hall and Myra Hurgett's locker.

When she slipped back into class, Ms. Simms was on the phone in the office, the girls running laps around the gym. The tube of Krazy Glue had been ditched in a nearby washroom garbage pail, and no one seemed to have noticed her leave or return. In fact, the only evidence that anything out of the ordinary had taken place was the tiny patch of missing skin on her left index finger.

*Were you real if nobody noticed you?*

Tucking her wounded finger into her palm, Sal waited as a drawn-faced Diane Kruisselbrink puffed past, then joined the line of girls twenty on down.

After class she changed quickly, one eye fixed on the row of lockers by the shower door. Diane didn't undress in front of everyone else, retreating instead to the privacy of a toilet stall, but when she returned, Sal watched her hang up her t-shirt and gym shorts, then drop one pair of used underwear into the bottom of her locker.

Drawn by a magnet of guilt, Sal slid into the small slipstream Diane carried in her wake as she left the gym. The usual comments followed the girl as she headed down the hall: *Hey Tubbo, wanna come talk dirty to my pet elephant? Why don't you try out for the Saskatchewan Roughriders — you could be their practice field.* Diane was a monument slipping through the masses, tall, silent, and obdurate as the Statue of Liberty. Turning into the north hall, she shuffled unsuspectingly toward her locker, her eyes lifting from the floor only as she encountered the packed throng of bodies around #772. As the crowd parted to let her through, Diane's gaze didn't rise above their knees — no doubt the faces around her were rarely worth looking into. Shifting her books to her left arm, she reached for her lock, her eyes finally settling on the stained panty crotch that dangled just above it.

A ripple crossed her face, nothing more. Blinking twice

she turned, stumbling over someone's foot. The jeers began, the crowd fencing her in, Diane staring without expression at their vicious yapping mouths. She couldn't hear them, Sal realized suddenly. Somewhere inside herself, Diane had found the switch that cut off the torment of sound entering her brain. The world had been disconnected, and the faces that surrounded her sneered and leered without meaning.

Twice she lumbered forward and was pressed back. The third time her face lifted, but the only change in her expression was a slight corner tuck of the mouth as her arms shoved out. Bodies went flying. Diane stepped through the gap and made her slow painstaking way down the hall.

"You're a monster," someone yelled after her silently retreating figure. "A genetic defect. They should exterminate fat cells like you."

Diane didn't look back.

# Chapter Twelve

Headed along the north corridor toward the bike racks, Sal kept her eyes down, counting feet. *One, two, who are you? Three, four, think some more.* As she passed each classroom she stiffened, her body braced against the possibility of Diane Kruisselbrink's sudden emergence from an open doorway. Everything around her — the floor, walls, especially the doorways — radiated with the guilt that had been building through her last class. *Five, six, you're derelict. Seven, eight ...*

One open doorway from the end of the hall, Sal looked in and saw her. Alone in a classroom, Tauni Morrison sat with her back to Sal, facing the chalkboard. Books lay open on her desk. She'd obviously been kept in to catch up on her work. Instead, she was staring out of the classroom's row of windows, watching the wind tear long streams of yellow from the trees.

She was singing. As Sal huddled in the open doorway at

the back of the room, low wordless notes unfolded in Tauni's throat and floated from her mouth, directionless as the leaves that blew past the windows. Pressed against the doorframe, Sal listened open-mouthed to the sound drifting from the solitary girl — it was the voice that had come to her after her father's death, the low blue voice of dreams and day-dreams that had touched her when she'd reached the end of things, giving her what she needed to continue on.

How could the same voice come to them both? Why did it sing so completely through Tauni Morrison and not through her? Creeping into a back-row desk, Sal hugged her clarinet case to her chest and watched the other girl sing. Tauni's eyes were closed, her face and body shifted with each note like a gauze curtain on a breeze. Closing her own eyes, Sal entered the same beauty, the voice that knew everything — every small, hidden, twisted shame — the voice that knew, yet returned time and time again to bless with wonder, its slow deep waves of peace.

Abruptly, Tauni stopped singing. The sound left her and she opened her eyes, staring around herself as if the classroom and its meaning were utterly incomprehensible. With a sigh, she laid her head on her arms and turned her face to the windows, taking no notice of the notebooks and pens, the copy of *Nobody Nowhere* she'd knocked to the floor. Huddled at the back of the room, Sal wondered if Tauni could still hear the blue voice in her head, or if it had just vanished into the silent depths as it did when it left her.

She wanted to lean forward and ask, *Did you hear me coming down the hall? Do you know what I did to Diane Kruisselbrink this afternoon, the stinking ugliness I carry inside? Were you singing for me?*

But Tauni Morrison freaked at the slightest sound or

touch, and Sal's voice, after such beauty, could only bring more ugliness into the world. Slipping from the room, Sal left the girl staring, silent and listless, at her own loneliness.

That evening she sat on her bed, cigarette papers wrapped over her bottom front teeth, descending note by note into the clarinet's sound. She'd been practicing for over an hour, had gone over the basic scales and warm-up drills, then plodded through most of her Concert Band pieces, but it had been nothing more than going through the motions, obediently following a line of black specks across a page. Scales just didn't do it for her and neither did the third clarinet's part to Chopin's Étude — no inner doors of wonder opened, she was left floating at the surface of herself like a scrap of driftwood. Now she was trying to do what Tauni Morrison had done, sending herself into sound note by note, making small slides and climbing minor intervals, calling to the deep blue voice with her miserable squawking melodies, the only sound she had.

But it wasn't happening. Sal's head ached, white static filled her brain, and Diane Kruisselbrink's face kept flashing in front of her — the complete lack of expression like a no-man's-land and then those arms lashing out, solid with determination and strength. Diane had fought back, had pushed her way through a wall of contempt and walked away. She might have been targeted, but she wasn't a victim. Anyone who thought Shadow Council had won that afternoon's encounter at locker #772 was an utter fool.

It probably didn't look that way to Diane though. Sure, she'd experienced a moment of bitter triumph, but what about tomorrow? The janitors would remove the offending underwear, but no one could eliminate the smirks and sneers in a school full of eyes. Diane would never live this one down, not if she lost a hundred pounds, and Sal had been the one who'd done it to her — she'd taken the handful of salt Shadow Council had given her and rubbed it directly into Diane's gaping wound. She was now an inextricable part of Shadow, a direct accomplice to their malice and filth. No wonder the blue voice didn't touch her the way it touched Tauni Morrison — she was contaminated. The voice had far more deserving souls to visit.

Moaning, Sal bent forward on the bed. This time she could feel it coming — the swerving darkness, the arcing headlights, the screaming. And she also knew what would follow next. It was so awful, why didn't someone stop it for her, why didn't the blue voice sing it all away? Dropping the clarinet onto the bed, Sal raced into the hall and down the stairs to the first floor, her mother's closed office door an eyeblink, there and gone.

"Sal!"

She ignored Dusty's call as she stumbled down the basement stairs, gripping the bannister to keep herself from going into a swerve — that was where the memory began, where it caught and locked her in. Flicking on the lava lamp, she headed for the stereo. What she needed was headphones, *The Wall Live* pumped to catastrophic glory, bigger than anything that could come at her. Volume jammed to full, she dived into the oblivion of crashing guitar chords. The headphones vibrated against her head, kicking noticeably with the bass line. This was good, waves of sound were flattening her brain, nothing would be able to get through. But there it came again, the sound of screaming, the eight-year-old girl's voice. Shaking, Sal reached for the stereo. Pump up *The Wall Live*, pump it up. But it was already on full and the eight-year-old's voice was growing stronger, the scream shaping itself into words: *I hate you, I hate you.*

*No*, thought Sal, pushing helplessly against the volume control. *No.*

A hand came down on hers, flicking off the stereo. For a moment, a chasm of silence engulfed her brain. Then she felt Dusty's hands take her face, his voice saying, "Sal, look at me. Can you hear me? It's Dusty."

She couldn't pull out of it, the process was inevitable, nothing could change history. As the room darkened into memory and the car went into its swerve, Sal knew she couldn't bear it, couldn't bear to watch her father's head hit the windshield yet again. What she needed was a bigger force to dull the impact and absorb the shock. She needed *The Wall Live* to smash, crush and annihilate memory, but there was Dusty standing between her and the stereo, holding the headphones. Desperation sent her lunging at him, shoving the way Diane Kruisselbrink had shoved her tormenters that afternoon in the school corridor. Ditching the headphones, Dusty tackled her and the two of them went down on the floor, Sal kicking and screaming as memory went off in her head with nothing to block it, nothing to prevent the full horror from opening up, that long-ago moment when her world had shattered to absolute smithereens.

She went limp, Dusty rolled off her and they lay on their backs, gasping at the orange shag ceiling.

"What's wrong?" Dusty panted miserably. "Sally-Sis, just tell me what's wrong."

But she couldn't. He wasn't the blue voice, he wouldn't love her when he heard what she'd done. Besides, he already knew that she'd been in the front seat when their father had crashed the family car into the tree. He'd seen the closed coffin at the funeral and read the coroner's report.

"Fuck off," she said, struggling to her feet. "Just fuck the hell off and leave me alone."

She woke to a tumultuous rain, wind sweeping the house, the roof a drenched, pounded shell. Beyond her bedroom window, Tuesday morning was a smear of colors, one ache dribbling into the next. She was cold. Why hadn't her mother turned up the heat last night? Muttering her way to her closet, Sal pulled on her housecoat and shuffled grumpily down the hall.

"Good, you're up," said her mother, coming out of the washroom. "If you're ready in twenty minutes, I can give you a ride to school."

"For eight o'clock?"

"It's Tuesday. Don't you have band practice?"

"Oh yeah." Too many aches had run together, she was beginning to lose track of the basics.

"I'll pack you a breakfast to eat in the car," said her mother. "C'mon now — skedaddle."

She skedaddled through her hair and face, avoiding her eyes in the mirror as she brushed her teeth. It was with her constantly now, a pale sick feeling that clung like a half-peeled skin. Washing didn't do anything, and getting her sugar high or flying the streets on her bike was nothing but a temporary fix. The sick feeling had attached to her like a phantom understanding, the kind that told her things about people she didn't want to know.

"For Pete's sake, go back into the house and get an

umbrella!" hollered Ms. Hanson as Sal ducked, soaked to the skin, into the passenger seat.

"I'm already wet." Sal set her clarinet case on the floor and accepted the muffin her mother handed her.

"But you have to walk home."

"This isn't Noah and the ark, Mom. I'll survive."

With a long involved sigh, her mother put the car into gear and backed down the driveway. The hood thrummed with rain. Everywhere Sal looked, water poured in long, blurred streams, the outside world putting in a brief appearance with each swipe of the windshield wipers. Settling into the damp give of her clothes, Sal worked her way through the oatmeal muffin, tunneling her tongue into the coarse grainy texture, chasing the sweet burst of each raisin. For the moment she was safe and out of reach, the car a blurred cave of sound, her whole being focused on the smaller cave of her mouth. Thank god her mother leapt out of bed at the crack of dawn and always remembered to feed her morning-challenged offspring.

"Don't forget your orange juice," said her mother.

"Thanks." After the muffin, the juice went down in sharp bitter gulps. Suddenly Sal cried out, doubling over as pain engulfed her stomach.

"What's the matter?" her mother gasped.

"It hurts," Sal whimpered, clutching her stomach. "When I eat."

"Did the muffin hurt?"

"Not as much."

"You could be getting an ulcer," said her mother grimly. "It's because of all that junk food you eat. I'm booking you an appointment with Dr. Rajani."

"It's okay. I'll stop drinking orange juice." Hugging

her stomach, Sal slouched lower in her seat. She hated doctors — they had an unnatural fetish for orifices, always wanting to poke around where no one else wanted to go.

"You'll do no such thing," snapped her mother. "You need your Vitamin C."

"Or my teeth will fall out and I'll get scurvy," finished Sal. "Isn't that what happened to Vasco de Gama?"

"Before my time," said her mother.

"Scurvy finished him," Sal said bleakly, watching water funnel down the side window.

Her mother chuckled. "Well, scurvy isn't finishing you off. I can probably get you in to see Dr. Rajani after school. I'll leave a message with the school office."

"He won't want to check my gall bladder or give me a hysterectomy, will he?"

"He'll probably prescribe something for you to drink," her mother said comfortingly. "Here's another muffin." Pulling over to the curb, she set a paper bag in Sal's lap. "And take my umbrella — the forecast is predicting rain all day."

"But what about you? You're wearing makeup." Sal stared stupidly at the umbrella her mother was holding out to her. "And you curled your hair."

"Take the umbrella," repeated her mother, tapping the wheel. "You're already sniffing. I don't want you home missing school because you're sick."

Hurt flared, a whiplash burn. "Of course," Sal snapped, grabbing the umbrella and her clarinet case. "We can't have S.C.'s best student missing a single day of school, can we?"

Closed umbrella in hand, she plunged into the downpour and slammed the door. Just ahead of her mother's car idled a van, its side door open. A woman stood on the curb holding an umbrella, waiting to hand it to the boy who was swinging himself from the van's back seat into a wheel-chair.

"Sally Hanson!" cried Ms. Wallace. "Is that you or a drowned rat?"

Brydan appeared in the van doorway, panic trapping his face as he caught sight of Sal.

"A drowned rat," said Sal, turning from Ms. Wallace's welcoming smile toward the rainsoaked gloom of Saskatoon Collegiate.

For the next several days, Sal was kept busy slurping Ranitidine and working on Myra Hurgett's terror campaign. Envelopes kept showing up in her textbooks or taped to the outside of her locker. Every time she turned around, someone from Shadow Council — Rolf, Ellen or Judy — seemed to be stepping out of a crowded hallway toward her, three fingers raised. Sal's response was automatic, a wave of shock that reverberated through her like a languid guitar string, then a bleak vague feeling, colorless and use-less as the four stone faces carved into Mount Rushmore. "Follow" was always the command, the Shadow Council member turning and starting off down the hall as if her compliance was part of the assumed order of things.

And she always followed; it seemed as natural as breath-ing. So did her listless unthinking manner as she scuffed along behind the Shadow Council member who was busily scouting out a quiet place to hand over the latest envelopes. She wasn't told what these contained. Each one arrived with her instructions clipped to it, detailing the target as well as the time and place of delivery. As per Willis's suggestion, the terror campaign was given a grassroots appearance —

there was no predictable pattern to the targets, and Sal was handing out an average of five envelopes a day. She never saw any of the duties take place, but overheard students talking: "... did you see Ryan Havel trip her in the cafeteria? She was plastered with Jell-O..." Or "... she let out a scream that shattered the trophy case, man. I think she actually thought the paint was blood ..."

Twice during this time, Sal crossed paths with Myra Hurgett in the hall. The first time the girl was still her normal bubbly self, cruising with the rest of the champagne-giggles crowd, but by Thursday afternoon she was walking differently, her eyes wary and darting, books held protectively over her chest. That night Sal dreamed of bodies walking in fear down endless hallways — the bodies of everyone she knew hunched inward, protecting themselves against the envelopes that kept appearing in her hand — and silence, dense unbroken silence. Friday morning the dream remained with her, unshakeable as she entered the school. Braced for the usual eruption of stomach acid, she approached her locker cautiously but no one stepped out, three fingers raised, to meet her. As the morning passed free of envelopes to deliver, the violence in her stomach gradually settled. Perhaps Shadow Council had gotten its fill and the goddam thing was over; maybe she could finally get back to some pretense of sanity.

Then, just before lunch, she entered the seldom-used girls' washroom at the back of the Tech wing and discovered a sobbing Myra Hurgett, her face pressed against the tampon machine. As Sal entered she whipped around, her face a cataclysm of fear. Equally startled, Sal froze, ready to bolt backwards out the door. Myra's face was a blur of make-up, her eyes swollen and bloodshot. With a jolt of surprise,

Sal realized the other girl wasn't pretty, not really — her appeal had always been in the effortless way she carried herself, a carefree glee now defined by its absence.

"*You*," Myra whispered, staring. "What do you want? Haven't you done enough already?"

So the grassroots camouflage had been a bust. Myra had guessed the true identity of her tormenters from the beginning, and she probably thought Sal had hunted her down now to deliver some kind of ultimatum.

"Don't worry," Sal stammered awkwardly. "I just want to use the can."

Myra turned, moaning, toward the sink, and Sal slipped gingerly into the closest stall. Heart thudding, she locked herself inside. Everything she touched vibrated as if about to explode, and the sound of her urine hitting the toilet water frightened her so badly she almost vomited herself inside out onto the cement floor. Crouched on the cold seat, she listened with radar-enhanced hearing, but there was no sound of anyone leaving the washroom. Reluctantly she emerged from the stall to find Myra waiting by the sink, her face washed and a tense determination shaping her mouth. The air pulsed, radioactive. Approaching the sink, Sal began to wash her hands.

Tugging two paper towels from the dispenser, Myra handed them to her. Sal hesitated. Was the lottery victim allowed to accept kindness from a target? *Hell*, Sal thought, suddenly furious. Was the victim allowed to own a single moment of her own mind, or was the inside of her head available only for the nauseating sludge of self-contempt?

"Thanks." Drying her hands, Sal dropped the paper towels into the garbage. Slowly her eyes climbed the wall, brick by brick, until she met the question of Myra's gaze. "It's over," she said tersely, her own eyes flitting away. "I think."

"You mean it?" Myra's face hesitated, afraid to leap toward hope.

"Just keep away from Linda Paboni on the volleyball court," said Sal. "Let her score every point she wants."

Myra nodded, her eyes vague. "The bitch."

"The bitch has friends," Sal said, turning toward the door. "Or whatever passes for friends in this place."

"Do you?" asked Myra suddenly, and Sal found herself riveted to the spot, unable to will herself forward.

"Do I what?"

"Have friends."

"Ask me a year from now."

"But it's not fair."

"Nine thousand people got wiped out in an earthquake in Turkey last week," said Sal. "Was that lottery fair?"

Myra's mouth opened, then closed.

"Just don't tell anyone what I told you, okay?"

"I won't," said Myra. "I swear on everything that's important to me. Cross my heart."

Their eyes held and Sal found herself looking into the beginning of friendship, a friendship that might or might not survive being put into deep freeze for the next nine months.

"Have a good year," she said harshly, turning this time without hesitation toward the door.


"Inside the Question" suspended on lofty drawn-out notes, high above the mundane. The trumpet line arced slowly, a bird dreaming its way toward the sun, while the clarinet hummed and rippled beneath it like grass in the wind, repetitive restless sequences of notes. The two melodies scarcely seemed connected, one so high, the other breathing across the surface, each pulling its own thoughts into sound. Yet the longer Sal played, the more she felt them singing toward one another, parallel rhythms of bliss.

"That's gorgeous," she sighed, resting the clarinet bell on her knee and staring at her musical score. "How did you ever think of it?"

"At my uncle's farm," said Willis. "Lying on my back in a field and watching the enormity of sky above me. There's a family of hawks in the area and I'd watch them hovering, the way they drifted weightless, like a mind set free. I'd lie there and watch the hawks hover and try to feel the sound of it — the song of that kind of dreaming. A hawk's reverie. One day I brought my trumpet with me and played while I watched."

"Did you feel like you were flying?" Sal's voice was husky, as if she'd gone deep into the dream of it and was speaking herself awake.

"There's a way of calling beauty into yourself," Willis said slowly. "Of opening to it. Out in that field, I'd feel as if I was calling all the blue of the sky down into me. You ever feel like that?"

Sal nodded.

"We're more than just this," Willis said, touching his arm. "When I play trumpet, I can feel it."

"Soul?"

"Soul, mind, dream — whatever you want to call it. Sometimes I can hear it in your playing too. You've been practicing."

"Yeah." She didn't tell him the way practicing felt when she was alone — repetitive, useless. Like lifting weights, climbing stairs, bricks in a wall.

"You should try writing music." Willis blew an experimental riff. "I'd like to hear what you'd come up with."

"Why?"

"Why not?" He met her eyes, expressionless, and they were back to square one, the basic tension that underlay everything between them — inside the question: *Why are you doing this, Willis? Why are you spending time with the victim?*

"Why can't anyone in this school talk to the lottery winner?" She couldn't say *victim*, not out loud. Not yet. "I could still deliver Shadow's messages if people were talking to me. What's the big deal with no one talking to me?"

"Your loyalties would be divided." Willis fiddled with his trumpet valves. "What if a duty targeted one of your friends? Sooner or later, you'd squeal."

Sal mentally ducked all thoughts of Myra Hurgett. "You could make me sign a contract. In my own blood. Threaten me with a zillion demerits if I told."

"Uh uh," said Willis. "You have to be set apart. Your *friends* have to set you apart. All connctions have to be broken. The victim exists in limbo. It's the only way."

"So Shadow can get its rocks off."

"It's just for one year. No one takes it personally. Wait and see — next year no one'll even remember."

"I'll remember."

"I know you will," Willis said quietly. "Why d'you think I'm here?"

Sal wondered if he knew he was lying — if he was presenting this lie to make her feel better, or if it was simply to improve his own self-esteem. "Inside the Question" had two parts — the trumpet couldn't soar as spectacularly without the low hum of the clarinet to give it contrast. Where was the astonishment of sky without the horizon line of earth to worship it? Just like everyone else, Willis Cass loved a victim. He needed her.

And she needed him. "So, why d'you think I'm here?"

For the first time he looked startled, his dark eyes faltering.

"I could blow your cover," she continued. "Squeal to Shadow, earn you a few demerits, maybe even get you kicked off."

A flush blew across his face, and he worked up a rueful smile. She saw it — the interest she'd piqued, the fear.

"Okay," he said. "So why are you here?"

She shrugged. "I'm not sure. Maybe I like it inside the question."

He nodded, and the same pause touched them both.

"Why don't you try it?" he asked. "Write some music for two parts and bring it next week." Rifling through a stack of textbooks, he handed her a book of composition paper.

"Not that much," she said, panicky. "Just one or two sheets."

"I've got lots at home."

Sal opened the softcovered book and stared at the empty pages of musical staffs. What kind of joke was this? Until a few weeks ago, she'd never even thought of practicing.

"Up there where the hawks fly," said Willis. "All that blue. I'm in limbo too."

Their eyes met. *No*, she wanted to tell him, *it's not the same*, but he wouldn't comprehend. Willis Cass had never been forced to live her kind of truth.

# Chapter Thirteen

Sal sat on her footstool in the corner, a silent pair of eyes. Today most of Shadow Council had been late in arriving, and for the first time she'd been able to observe them coming through the door. As each member entered, she'd been startled to see them give the Sign of the Inside, even Willis. Gesture completed, his eyes had flicked toward her position in the corner where they'd rested a millisecond too long on her face. Then he'd folded his body casually into the burgundy armchair and drawled, "I am calling this shadowy meeting of S.C.'s ruling elite to order. Get your brains in gear, comrades. We are now officially think-tanking."

It was Monday lunch hour. The weekend had been a bust — one long miserable trek from Superstore to Canadian Tire to Sears as Ms. Hanson had caught up on shopping. Both Sal and her mother loathed shopping, and the experience hadn't brought them any closer. On top of this,

Dusty had decided he was no longer speaking to Sal, and the weather had been cold and rainy, keeping her indoors. Sal's head buzzed and her eyes ached from too much TV. Hunched on the footstool, she sucked at the permanent raw spot clarinet #19 seemed to be donating to the inside of her bottom lip. The minutes dragged as the Celts' business was discussed. Every time there was a knock at the door, she was called into the circle to sit on the couch, then summarily ordered back to the footstool when the teacher or club rep departed. Finally the air changed its pulse as the Celts took off their masks, Shadow Council emerged, and the session mutated into a general foraging session for potential targets and the best possible methods for destroying lives. Because that was what Shadow Council was, Sal thought, studying them — a predatory horde that fed on other people's fear. What they did in this room was natural instinct for them, something they considered their right, their privilege. This session where they bartered, casually tossing malice back and forth, was like a hawk dreaming. To them, it was beautiful.

"Make Jean Maharaj strip in front of the entire cafeteria at rush hour, and make it my duty to jump her," grinned Rolf.

"Give Brad Carter a repeat performance, only this time he streaks through a faculty meeting without a paper bag," sang out Linda.

"Get a skinny minor niner crawling around under the chairs at the next assembly, gluing people's shoes to the floor," sniggered Ellen.

The hawk's song was ecstasy to the hawk. To the prey that lived beneath it, the sound meant terror, but who had the right to tell the hawk it couldn't be hawklike?

"Assign the chess club the duty of making a hundred

toilet-paper carnations and sticking them all over Ms. Tuziak's car with a *Wish I Were Married* sign," said Marvin.

Ms. Tuziak was a front-office secretary, not Shadow Council's usual prey. A cautious interest stole across Willis's face. "Why Tuziak?"

"She and our esteemed Principal Wroblewski are having an affair," said Marvin. "I saw them coming out of the Patricia Hotel together on Saturday afternoon. Real chummy."

Thoughtful whistles pierced the air.

"The Pat?" Willis said scornfully. "Wroblewski should get some class. Okay, let's get down to business. Who's next on the target list?"

Rolf flipped through his binder. "Fawzia Evans, Chris Busatto, Ken Goodwin and Alexandra Horseley."

*Chris Busatto!* Sal's teeth dug into the inside of her lower lip, tearing off a flap of freshly healed skin. Kimmie's older brother was a shy mumbler who talked inside his mouth and kept his eyes at knee level. Giving him a duty would be almost as mean as giving one to Tauni Morrison.

"Okay." Willis stroked his chin. "Everyone focus. Fawzia Evans. Grade nine, right? Who's been watching her?"

"I have." Ellen squirmed nervously, tapping her knee. "She's a library freak. Shelves books every lunch hour."

"Why was she chosen?" asked Willis.

"Random," said Rolf. "This was a Walk-the-Halls selection. I closed my eyes, took three steps, then opened them. Whoever I saw first went down on the list."

"Marvelous," said Willis, clapping several times. "Random patterning negates a single source."

Rolf gave a contented beam.

"So we think of a library duty," Willis continued, link-ing his hands behind his head. "Something in her natural biosphere. Something to do with shelving books."

The air thickened with thought. It was obvious from Shadow Council's overworked expressions that they didn't spend much time in the library.

"Put the books upside down?" suggested Ellen tentatively.

Grunts met this proposal, and a disconsolate silence again took over the room. Leaned against the wall, Sal sucked a steady stream of blood from her lower lip as she sent her gaze back and forth across the group. Beneath her concern for Chris Busatto, a thought kept rippling through her brain like an underwater fish — something she couldn't quite pull into words.

"Non-fiction," said Linda suddenly. "Dewey decimal system. It's got subject headings."

"So?" asked Willis.

"So we get her to trade them around. Stack the geology section on the Shakespeare shelf, Shakespeare in the second world war section. Poetry in architecture, that kind of thing."

"Brilliant," said Willis, clapping again. "Understated. Subtle chaos. How about you and Rolf work out the details on that one?"

Linda nodded, her mouth twitching with satisfaction. Glancing at Marvin, she made a few chop-chop gestures. He chop-chopped back.

"Next target," said Willis.

"Chris Busatto," said Judy. "I studied him. He's in grade eleven, kind of a blah kid. Puts in his time and gets the hell out."

Sal chewed deeper into her lower lip. Was it possible they'd chosen Chris because of her friendship with Kimmie? *Ex-friendship*, she reminded herself bitterly. Shadow Council would have nothing to gain by trying to get at her through her ex-best friend's brother. Besides, Rolf had said this had been a random selection. Chris had merely been in the wrong place at the wrong time, like Fawzia Evans.

"A blah kid," mused Willis, stroking his chin. "What about the assembly suggestion? Crawling under the chairs. There's a Future Options assembly coming up for the grade eleven and twelve students later this week."

"And he goes around gluing shoes to the floor?" Linda asked dubiously.

"No," said Willis. "Asking for donations — any kind of donation. To the future of Wroblewski and Tuziak."

A grin of sheer ecstasy rippled through the group.

"How big is Busatto?" asked Marvin.

"My height," said Judy. "Short for a guy. He's chubby though."

"Even better," smiled Willis. "Next target?"

So that was it — Chris had been processed for execution as casually as a fruit fly. Nothing had been mentioned about the personal details of his life, his night terrors, sleep-walking, and frequent appointments with the school counselor. Probably Shadow Council didn't have access to this kind of information. Should she raise her hand and say something, expose Chris's weakness? But wouldn't the smell of blood bring the hawks in for a quicker kill?

*He's a blah kid* — all things considered, this was probably Chris's best camouflage.

"I've been watching Ken Goodwin," said Rolf. "Grade eleven, tattoos, nose stud, general goof case. No mercy on this one."

"Demerits?" asked Willis.

"For breathing," said Rolf. His smile traveled around the circle.

"Think subtle," Willis advised. "We want class, here."

Sal could feel their brain waves lengthen into deep thought. Again, the submerged fish swam across her brain. What was it? What exactly was she not getting? She'd been staring so intently at the group in front of her that her perception of light and dark had begun to reverse. How she wanted Shadow Council to overreach themselves — to trip, stumble and plummet from their self-proclaimed heights. *For breathing*. Fighting the neon surge in her stomach, she raised her hand.

Willis's eyes gleamed briefly. "Victim may speak."

"Why don't you pull another Diane Kruisselbrink?"

"Gotch?" someone snorted.

"Make it a whole room. A classroom."

They were watching her now, hovering on the edge of getting it.

"Transport an entire classroom outside," she finished, holding her breath. It was too big, too grandiose. They would never be able to pull it off.

A tremor ran around the circle as Shadow Council gulped the idea, hook, line, and sinker.

"What's his schedule?" asked Willis.

"Periods one to four — Tech, Calculus, Chemistry, Phys Ed," said Rolf. "Periods five to eight — English, Physics, Geography and History."

"Tech wing won't work," said Willis. "Too many windows."

"Math is on the south side," said Judy. "English is —"

"There are trees all along the south wall," broke in Ellen. "From inside you can't see anything but sky."

"His Calculus classroom is next to an exit," said Rolf. "But how do we convince an entire class?"

"We don't," said Willis. "That's the target's duty. We decoy the teacher, the target motivates the class."

"What if it rains?" asked Ellen.

"Even better," grinned Willis.

"An entire class might squeal," said Linda dubiously.

"Only the target will know the command came from Shadow," said Willis. "It'll be part of his duty to keep that quiet. If the class succeeds, it'll be their glory. If they fail, they'll be acclaimed for trying."

Lifting his right hand, he undulated it slowly through the air. Sal's eyes narrowed as every member of Shadow Council copied the gesture. With a satisfied smile, Willis leaned his head against the back of his throne and closed his eyes. "Okay, last target. Who's got the profile on Alexandra Horseley?"

"Grade ten," said the guy sitting beside him, an infinitely forgettable jock. "Brown-noser and drama buff. She's got a small part in *A Midsummer Night's Dream*."

As the group slipped again into thought, Sal finally saw it — the fidgeting, the head scratching, the chin stroking, and incessant hand signals. The Sign of the Inside wasn't Shadow's only secret sign. There was a whole other level of language going on, a constant body code passing between them.

Willis played with his chin. "Keep studying her, Larry. Find out what her lines are. Maybe we can rewrite a few of them for opening night."

"And make her say them in performance?" Judy asked, wide-eyed.

"Why not?" grinned Willis.

"It's just ... kind of not subtle, isn't it?"

"Depends on how we rewrite them," drawled Willis,

again undulating his right hand through the air. "Power is unlimited, if you keep a gentle hand on the reins."

Sal's stomach rocked. Did he mean her? No, no, he couldn't. Their Friday lunch hours were like stepping into a different category of being, nothing touched them there, not even Shadow Council.

*Was anything truly untouchable?*

"Good work, guys," said Willis. "Our duty for the day is done. You are now free to go and bless the masses of S.C. with your undeniable presence." Carelessly, he rippled his right hand. "Remember who you are."

"*Shadow*," the others whispered simultaneously, the sound creeping up the back of Sal's neck.

When she handed the envelope to Chris Busatto, he was sitting in an empty corridor, eating his lunch from a cafeteria tray and reading a copy of *The Chocolate War*. It was Tuesday noon hour, a full twenty-four hours since Shadow Council's last session. She'd been given the envelope containing Chris's instructions that morning before homeroom but had delayed delivering it, knowing the duty wasn't due to take place until the following day. It had been easy enough to track Chris down in the halls. Though they'd rarely exchanged more than brief hellos, she'd breezed past his chubby form hunched in front of the Busattos' TV enough times. Chris rarely unplugged himself from the TV or computer. For a brief period last year, he'd gone into complete shutdown, directing an invisible channel changer at anyone who'd spoken to him and switching them off.

He wouldn't be able to switch Shadow Council off. Delivering this envelope to him would be the equivalent of telling him that he'd been born with a nuclear missile in his gut, set to go off at the first sign of happiness — something he'd always suspected would be his fate, but vaguely, like death.

"Hey, Chris," Sal said quietly, coming up behind him. "I've got something for you."

Fork in mouth, he turned around. As he caught sight of her, his eyes widened. She could almost hear the glass shattering across his brain.

"It's for tomorrow. You know — the assembly?" Holding the envelope out to him, Sal tried to smile encouragingly. She wasn't supposed to talk to targets any more than was absolutely necessary, but Chris was sitting, fork sticking freestyle from his mouth as he raised both hands protectively. The guy was in shock. "It's just something you've got to do once," she said quickly, "and then it'll be over, they'll leave you alone."

Chris opened his mouth and the fork fell out. "What is it?"

"Open the envelope and see."

"If I open it, I'll have to do it."

"Of course you have to do it. C'mon, Chris, it won't be that hard." Thrusting the envelope at him again, she rattled it impatiently. Didn't he know how hard it was for her to do this? He looked so much like Kimmie, they could have been twins. Just standing next to him was bringing back memories of pizza parties, sleepovers, and long summer afternoons at Riverdale Pool. It wasn't fair, making her suffer extra like this.

"No," Chris whispered. "I won't do it, I won't."

"Don't be silly. Of course you will."

"No." Chris shook his head emphatically, like a bouncing toy. "I won't, I won't."

Sal's stomach lurched, and she tasted bile. Why had she left her Ranitidine in her locker? "C'mon, Chris, it's just one thing and then you're done. No problem-o." Placing the envelope firmly on his tray, she set off down the hall. There — her part in this was done, she could wash her hands and leave the rest to fate. No one was special, there were no exceptions. Chris was just going to have to take his turn playing victim like everyone else.

The envelope whizzed past her feet, a spinning blur.

"Chris!" she wailed desperately, chasing after it. "You have to do this or they'll punish you. That'll be ten times worse."

"My psychiatrist says I don't have to listen to other kids bugging me." Chris stared at her over the top of *The Chocolate War*, wide-eyed and curiously defiant. In all the years she'd known him, this was the first time she'd heard him speak clearly.

"Well, your psychiatrist is wrong."

"Maybe I should get you an appointment." Raising his book, Chris blocked her out, and Sal's shoulders caved in an avalanche of defeat. She'd done her best, he'd have to face the music himself.

"Maybe," she sighed, stooping to pick up the envelope.

She had to turn him in. Sal knew this was what Shadow Council would expect her to do under the circumstances. If she didn't, Chris Busatto wouldn't be the only one suffering the consequences. In a situation like this, it was everyone for herself — Chris certainly hadn't shown *her* any consideration, and neither had anyone else. Envelope in hand, Sal headed toward the Celts' clubroom. There was the door, looming in an endless nightmare of doors, and

here now was the knock — three short and two long —
the knock of agony and defeat.

The door opened and she found herself looking into
Linda's scowling face.

"We're not open," the girl snapped. "I don't recall sum-
moning you."

"Chris Busatto refused his duty." Sal's hand shook as
she extended the envelope. Here at last she had a way of
proving her loyalty and appeasing Linda's constant suspi-
cion.

"What d'you expect me to do with it?"

"But he wouldn't take it." Confused, Sal faltered.
"D'you want me to throw it into the garbage?"

"Who is it?" Coming up behind Linda, Marvin slid an
arm around her waist. She leaned against him, smiling.
They seemed to be alone in the room.

"It's the *victim*," said Linda. "Apparently, Chris Busatto
refused his duty."

"So get her to do it," said Marvin, nuzzling her neck.

"That's an idea," purred Linda, her eyes traveling Sal's
face.

"But I don't have any demerits," protested Sal.

"Five demerits," singsonged Linda. "It's your duty to
make sure the targets do their duties. If you fail, you get
five demerits. Five demerits equals one duty. Presto, you
get Chris Busatto's duty."

"But I've got English that period." Sal's mind scattered like Pick-Up Sticks. "I'll have to skip."

"And whose problem is that?"

The door closed, and Sal rode out the detonation of
her stomach. It wasn't fair. She'd done her part, it wasn't
her fault the target had backed out. Why was she being

punished for his actions? There had to be a predictable system of penalties, built on a reliable version of right and wrong. Sure, the definition of morality was bound to change depending upon the tyrant in charge, but there had to be some kind of order, some way of protecting your ass.

Maybe that was the point — the victim's ass belonged to everyone.

Slowly Sal tore open the envelope and slid out the enclosed note. As she scanned it, she could hear Willis's voice dictating the contents inside her head: *Time: Wednesday afternoon, Period 7. Location: Future Careers Assembly, Auditorium. Duty: Crawl under the chairs with a paper bag, soliciting donations for the red-hot love nest of Wroblewski and Tuziak. Avoid all teachers.*

Blinking back tears, she headed to her locker for another dose of Ranitidine.

# Chapter Fourteen

On hands and knees, Sal studied the row of feet before her. The pair dead ahead were giant size, genetic defects from the twilight zone. Reaching forward, she tugged at the sweat sock bagging around the left ankle. The startled foot shot forward and a head appeared, dangling upside down in front of her.

"Excuse me," said Sal, holding out a paper bag. "I'm soliciting donations for the red-hot love nest of Wroblewski and Tuziak."

"Who?" hissed the face, adjusting the glasses that rode its forehead.

"Wroblewski and Tuziak," repeated Sal.

The upside down features contorted into a grin. "No kidding."

"Anything you've got."

"Just a sec." The face disappeared, then reappeared with

several others, all grinning profusely.

"Aren't you a cute little doggie," cooed a pair of vermilion lips.

"Donations?" Sal pressured, ducking the hand that reached to pat her head. The auditorium lighting system was a washout below knee-level, the faces before her indistinct, distorted by shadow. Mouths that hovered above eyes definitely gave her vertigo.

A pen cap and a wad of gum dropped into her bag.

"Thanks," said Sal, backing up and shifting sideways toward another pair of runners, smaller this time and crossed at the ankles. "Soliciting donations," she repeated to the quizzical face that dropped in front of her, curtained by a dark fall of hair. "For Wroblewski and Tuziak's red-hot love nest."

Cherry-red lips pursed and giggled. "Let me see if anyone's got something." The hair ascended out of sight while Sal crouched, trying to shrink her butt into invisibility. How often did teachers patrol the back row? She tensed, waiting as curious faces ducked in and out of the space in front of her, and finally objects began descending into her outstretched bag — an expired bus pass, a few cinnamon hearts, a condom.

The cherry-red lips dropped down in front of her again. "That enough?"

"Are there any teachers nearby?" Sal hissed.

"Mr. Whittley and Ms. Lalani are at the end of this row."

Sal considered. That put them about fifteen chairs to her right. Not great, but she'd already worked her way up and down most of the back row and she had to penetrate the solid mass in front of her at some point. "Let me through," she said, and the running shoes slid apart to grant her passage. Pressing forward, she discovered that she was too tall to crawl under the chair seat and was going to have to slither on her stomach. As she flattened herself, the girl to her right shifted her legs so that any view coming from the end of the row would be blocked. Rocked by a small explosion of gratitude, Sal tapped the new pair of ankles directly in front of her and held out her bag.

"Soliciting donations for the red-hot love nest of Wroblewski and Tuziak," she hissed.

"Wroblewski and Tuziak?" grinned a mouth that reeked of tuna fish. "Since when?"

"Since Saturday afternoon at the Hotel Pat," said Sal. "Donations?"

"I'll check with my buds," said the face and disappeared. Pressed against the auditorium floor, Sal waited. Her back was getting sore, her neck was developing a crick, and she kept bracing herself against the inevitability of someone using her butt as a foot rest.

A bouquet of delighted faces appeared and objects began raining into her bag — a lighter, a SAVE THE TREES button, a package of Kleenex, a tampon. As she wriggled onward into the next aisle, legs extended on either side, protecting her from the roving eyes of teachers, and when she reached out to tap the next pair of ankles, she found a face already waiting, upside down and grinning.

Before she had a chance to recite her line, the face quipped, "I heard. Believe me, I've got just the thing for Wroblewski and Tuziak." Once again, junk paraphernalia came pouring into her bag. She moved forward, legs on both sides shifting to protect her passage, and again discovered that the students ahead of her had already been contacted and were ready with donations. As she slithered deeper into the mass of bodies suspended on creaking seats above her, the pattern repeated itself, word of her approach rippling ahead so that the next row was always prepared for her outstretched bag. No one shrieked or kicked back in surprise, not once was her butt poked or violated. Though not a single member of the grade eleven or twelve class would have spoken to her in the halls, here in the semi-dark auditorium where she was forced to grovel, snake-like and utterly humiliated beneath their asses, the senior students of S.C. grinned down at Sal, patted her shoulder and rearranged their bodies to shield her from hostile view. Several students offered her sticks of Juicy Fruit, and one guy proffered a half-drunk can of Sprite. At one point, she was carefully redirected to escape contact with a teacher sitting three rows up.

On and off, Sal could hear Mr. Wroblewski introducing speakers from various colleges and universities. His aloof, thin-lipped expression floated through her head as she held out her paper bag, urging the faces before her to consider the contributions they could make to Wroblewski's and Tuziak's future happiness. S.C.'s principal wasn't well-liked by the student body. Though Sal had never run afoul of him personally, she had no sympathy to waste on someone who supported teen curfews and had threatened to install surveillance cameras in the school halls. As she crawled beneath the creaking sea of chairs, her heart gradually retreated down her throat and she almost began to enjoy the shadowy mass conspiracy, ground-level in the dark. Then, approximately fifteen rows into the crowd of coughing fidgeting students, she tapped a pair of sloppily laced Reeboks and watched them slide apart to reveal the upside-down grin of Shadow Council's president. Five centimeters apart, they stared at one another, Willis's grin quickly fading as Sal stuck out her bag, repeating the phrase she'd been instructed to give. "Excuse me. I'm soliciting donations for the red-hot love nest of Wroblewski and Tuziak."

"You are fucking not," Willis hissed emphatically. "It's supposed to be Chris Somebody-Or-Other."

"He refused the duty," Sal hissed back, "so Linda said I had to do it. I think she has a key to the clubroom. She and Marvin were in there today at lunch hour."

Willis's face contorted. "Give me that bag," he said, plucking it from her hand. "Consider yourself officially relieved of this duty." Without another word, he ascended out of sight.

Stunned, Sal dissolved into the floor. Relief had sucked the life right out of her and she couldn't move, couldn't remember how to operate without the adrenalin rush of fear. Slowly, she worked the dead weight of her legs up into the aisle behind her, then backed her upper half out from under Willis's chair. As she struggled to her feet, hands helped her negotiate the narrow aisle, guiding her toward an empty chair.

"Sit here," someone whispered into her ear, "until this goddam bitch of an assembly is over."

Swamped by exhaustion, Sal took her seat along with the rest of the human race. Darkness rolled thickly through her head. While Mr. Wroblewski gave his closing remarks, she rubbed floor grit from her face and worked a gum wad out of her hair. When the bodies surrounding her erupted from their chairs, she allowed an unfamiliar arm to tuck itself through hers and guide her to the auditorium door. Wearily, she turned to express her gratitude, but the arm had already untucked itself and vanished, leaving her standing once again alone and apart in the busy corridor.

It was late, the halls cleared of the after-school rush. Sal had been waiting in the girls' washroom across the hall, peering through the narrow slit of the open door until she'd seen all three members of Shadow Council's executive enter the Celts' clubroom. As she stepped carefully into the empty corridor, the washroom door closed behind her, the draft surging across the hall and dislodging the Celts' clubroom door. Whoever had gone in last had neglected to fasten it securely. Voices filtered through the gap, speaking quickly and angrily.

"You acted without consulting me. I'm the president, you're overstepping your bounds."

"What's the big deal, Willis?" The voice was female, obviously the vampire queen's. "She's just the victim. Why does she matter so much to you?"

"I know who she is," Willis retorted. "It's precisely because of *who* she is that we need to make sure we treat her exactly by the rules."

"Because she's a *special* victim."

"I was never in favor of that. We should have chosen the victim the regular way, according to lottery rules. From now on, everything connected to this victim will follow the rules *exactly*. That stunt with the three scrolls was a cretin's wet dream. It was so obvious, I was surprised she didn't catch on right then and there."

"It was a majority decision. Even the president has to abide by that."

"I *am* abiding by it, in case you haven't noticed. I also

happen to be abiding by the rest of the rules."

"Shadow lives to break rules. We break rules every day, all day long."

"You can't rule by chaos. You lose respect."

"We've got their respect by the balls," sneered Linda. "They're all terrified of Shadow. That's the way to run them."

"I agree with Willis." For the first time Rolf's voice broke in, quiet but steady. "We need some kind of rules, otherwise kids won't know who to obey. And since the victim has to obey us more than anyone else, the rules have to be clearest for her."

"Oh," jeered Linda. "Another one for the victim's fan club."

"She did the assigned duty," said Rolf. "I don't see why you're so pissed off. She hasn't caused any of the trouble her brother did."

Pressed against the wall, Sal breathed sudden knives of air.

"Yeah, and you know the way Shadow dealt with him," Linda said. "*Fear*. And it worked."

"She's already scared enough," said Rolf. "She's done everything we told her to do, no complaints."

"It's genetic," said Linda. "Whatever was in her brother will pop up in her, just you wait."

"Until it does," said Willis clearly, "you lay off, understand? And turn in your clubroom key — I'm the only one who's supposed to have one."

"Ooo — you going to give *me* demerits, Prez?"

"Maybe we should put that to a majority vote," came Rolf's thoughtful voice.

In the long ensuing pause, Sal breathed her way, millimeter by millimeter, down the hall.

Yanking the headphones from her brother's ears, Sal leaned into his startled face and shouted, "Why didn't you tell me?"

She crouched over him, her chest heaving. High-pitched voices vibrated in her head. The bike ride from school had gone by in a blur — not a traffic light, not a stop sign had come between her and her destination.

"Tell you what?" Flat on his back, Dusty eyed her warily. It had been a week since they'd spoken. Retro-Whatever still carried the small sharp angles of their last explosion.

"Your big secret." She had to raise her voice to be heard over the booming headphones. "Whatever happened between you and Shadow."

His eyes glimmered, then closed. "How'd you hear about that?"

Tossing the headphones aside, she propped his eyelids open with her fingers. "For your information, I just so happen to be this year's lottery winner, and all I know is that it has something to do with you and Shadow from years back."

Dusty's enlarged eyes stared up at her. "So that's why you and Brydan aren't talking, why Kimmie hasn't been around."

She nodded.

"Let go of my lids, man."

"Will you tell me about Shadow?"

"If you let me blink."

Backing off, she settled into the beanbag chair and watched him retrieve his glasses from a nearby speaker. The air sang with secrets. She felt vivid and deep, riding enormous possibility.

"Shadow," Dusty said softly, slumping against the opposite wall. "I had a feeling they'd come after you. That's why I've been on your case so much lately, but you wouldn't tell me, you wouldn't say."

"You didn't tell me anything either," she pointed out.

"You've got enough on your mind. I didn't want to bother you." Eyes closed, chin sunk onto his thin chest, Dusty spoke as if to no one, as if his thoughts couldn't carry beyond the tired boundaries of his own mind. "I guess we all keep Shadow's secrets in the end."

She'd never seen him like this, not even after their father had died. "Dusty," she whispered, leaning forward. "Were you the lottery winner?"

He shook his head. "Lizard."

Sal's jaw dropped. "But he *joined* them."

"He joined in his grad year. He was the winner in grade nine."

She sat swallowing assumptions. "So what does this have to do with Shadow and you?"

"He was my best friend. I couldn't let him go through it alone." Dusty rubbed his eyes tiredly. "I tried to stick it out with him."

"Did they come after you?" Sal asked quickly.

"Yeah," murmured Dusty, "but that wasn't the worst. It was the way they went after Liz. He begged me to ditch him, said he had to pay because I wouldn't shun him. What was I supposed to do?"

"But you're friends now," Sal protested. None of this made sense. How could something so enormous disappear into the past without leaving any evidence? Or had she just been unable to read the signs?

"We picked up again after grade nine," Dusty said quietly. "Never talked about it — he wouldn't — but I gave Shadow some flack the next year. Didn't last long, there wasn't any point to it. No one else gave a damn. I couldn't believe the way everyone seemed to get off on obeying them." He shrugged. "What's the point if you're the only one? Can't be a revolution on your own."

"What kinds of things did you do?" Sal grinned with pride but Dusty's eyes remained closed, his face expressionless. He was zoning out, she realized. The way Tauni Morrison did when she hit overload.

"Acts of random intelligence," mumbled Dusty. "Protest posters, a speech in the cafeteria, vandalizing the Celts' clubroom with graffiti. Got suspended for the last one. What are they doing to you?"

"Mostly I play gopher," Sal said. "I think it's the usual stuff. Willis makes them stick to the rules."

"Willis?"

"Willis Cass. He's the president."

Dusty opened his eyes to narrow slits. "Brother of Warren Cass? Son of Woodrow Cass, as in Cass, Burrows and Shody Solicitors?"

"I don't know who his father is," Sal said slowly.

"Warren Cass," Dusty said intensely, "was Shadow president the year *after* Liz was the lottery winner. That also happens to be the year I gave them all that flack — grade ten, the grade you just happen to be in this year. Warren Cass really hated my guts. Looks like he passed it on to his brother."

"I don't think so; hatred isn't genetic."

Dusty looked dubious. "The Casses are an ugly breed."

"Willis ..." Sal paused, considering, "... is protecting me. The rest of Shadow would run me into the ground, but he makes them stick to the rules."

"Why?'

"I don't know. He's different."

"Then why is he on Shadow?" exploded Dusty. "Believe me, if you're on Shadow, you *are* Shadow. No exceptions."

"I don't know," Sal repeated. "Nothing fits the way it used to, there is no black and white. The way I see it, everyone at S.C. is living both sides of the same coin. We all support Shadow, run off and stomp on some victim whenever they tell us to. At the same time, we're all victims-in-waiting, and any one of us could become the next target. The victim and the assassin are living inside each one of us, we all play both parts. *We* keep the whole thing going, we're doing this to ourselves. Every year, the entire student body holds its breath until one kid gets chosen to be the symbol for what's happening inside everyone else."

Dusty slouched lower, picking at the carpet. "I wish I knew what to do," he said heavily. "Like you said, everyone at S.C. is an extension of Shadow. If you go to administration, you'll pay for it every minute until you graduate. Believe me, if I'd guessed they'd go after you because of what I was doing, I never would've kicked up shit. This is my fault."

"It could've happened to me anyway," Sal said quickly. "There's always the off chance I could've ended up the winner from a legit Shadow lottery."

"What's that got to do with it?" Dusty grunted.

"You ever buy lottery tickets?"

He shrugged. "Sure."

She leaned forward, chasing her thoughts. "It's part of the same mentality, isn't it? Positive or negative, it's the belief that chance is god, it has the right to rule your life. You spend two bucks on a specific number and that number changes your life, makes you a millionaire. Or Shadow pulls your name, and you win loneliness and degradation for a year. It has nothing to do with *you*, though. You don't win a lottery through doing something noble, or coming up with a great idea. It just happens to you. A lottery winner could be anyone. A lottery winner is nothing."

Dusty nodded, blinking rapidly. "You're not nothing, Sally-Sis."

She waved an impatient hand, still chasing thoughts. "Everyone should commit random acts of intelligence like you did. I think it's cool you stood up for Lizard. I'm sure it helped him — he survived, didn't he?"

"Barely," Dusty said. "Sometimes I'm not sure I know him."

"But he knows *you*." Sal was glowing, full of sudden certainty. "Sure, he joined them in grade twelve, but he's *your* friend, so they didn't destroy him entirely. You keep him sane, Dusty, just like you keep me ... believing."

"Believing in what?"

"In something. I don't know what exactly. But you know what I know for sure right now? It's just one year and I can do it. You know why? Because of you. Because you showed me how to be. I learned everything I know about what's good and decent in life from watching you."

Dusty sat blinking in utter astonishment.

"And you know what else?" Tears running down her face, Sal sat sobbing and utterly triumphant. "You turned into who you are because you *earned* it, Dusty, not because you pulled some stupid number out of a hat. I think you're the best brother I could ever *ever* get in a million, trillion, zillion years."

Crawling across the room, Dusty pulled her into a bear

hug. "You're starting to talk like a little kid," he said husk-ily. "That means you need sleep bad."

"Want some hot chocolate first." Sal rubbed her runny nose against his shirt.

"Marshmallows?" asked Dusty softly.

"Lots'n lots'n ..." Sal sighed, drifting on the rhythm of her brother's breathing. It was happening — she was start-ing to drool with fatigue.

"I think I can manage that," said Dusty, patting her head.

# Chapter Fifteen

Sal cycled through the early morning streets, watching the earth come gently awake. Honey and blush pink stroked the horizon, light opened in the last of the poplar leaves, the wind was a late dream grumbling across the pavement. Breathing in the cold scent of frost, she veered sharply through a break in the hedge around Wilson Park. She was late as usual — no, later — and the Concert Band's warm-up cacophony was erupting loud and enthusiastic in her imagination. Bringing her weight full onto the pedals, she felt the bike leap forward in response. If she hurried, maybe she could make it before Pavvie mounted the podium and swan-dove into the first downbeat. Perhaps today she would actually escape the tragic shake of the head he reserved for her habitual late entrances.

At the other end of the park, a lone figure sat hunched on one of the picnic tables, reading a book. Sal zoomed toward it, wondering who would be out this early on a chilly mid-October morning. Not a dog owner — there wasn't a sniffing, squatting canine in sight. Curious, she rang the bell on her bike, slowing as the figure glanced in her direction. In the dim morning light the face was blurred, the features indistinguishable except for the shadowy black line of the mouth.

Hitting the brakes, Sal went into a short skid. When she righted her bike, Tauni Morrison was still watching but from a long way off, as if Sal was an image flickering across a soundless TV, there and not there, halfway to real.

"Hi," said Sal, standing uncertainly with her bike.

Tauni watched her, the black smudge of her lips saying nothing.

"I'm on my way to band practice," said Sal, "but I'm late anyway. Mind if I sit down for a minute?"

Shifting to the very edge of the table, Tauni pointed to the opposite end. "There," she said in a tight clipped voice. "Sit there."

"Sure." Leaning her bike onto its kickstand, Sal edged carefully onto the other end of the table. "I, uh, I've been thinking about you."

Giving a loud startled laugh, Tauni angled her body away from Sal. "Now why would you do that?"

"You're different," said Sal. "From other people."

"Of course I'm different!" the girl exploded, her face twisting. "Not that anyone will believe me."

Startled, Sal stammered, "What d'you mean?"

"I'm autistic," said Tauni, her voice strained and overly loud, as if pushing against an invisible barrier. "But I'm high-functioning, so —"

Abruptly, she stopped speaking. Leaning forward, she opened her mouth as if about to throw up, but what emerged instead was a series of odd sounds. "Ack, ack," she cried, as if her tongue had been cut off at the root and she could no longer form sound into words. Her eyes were closed, her face contorted with intense effort. Strange creaking sounds came out of her, like the unoiled hinges on a door. Rigid with uncertainty, Sal sat watching. Was this a heart attack or a stroke? Should she bike to the nearest pay phone and dial 911?

But the odd creaking noises had already stopped. Now Tauni was sitting silently, her eyes closed, moving her mouth tentatively, as if making sure everything was in place. Taking a deep breath, she opened her eyes and turned in Sal's general direction.

"Damn vocal apparatus," she said, her voice wobbling. "No coordination. I hit overload and can't get the words out. Can't speak, and then I can again." Shrugging, she gave another loud laugh. "Doesn't help that speech is a foreign language. Actually, sound is the second language and speech is the third."

"What's your first language?" asked Sal.

"I can't explain," said Tauni, a delicate sadness crossing her face. "Not in words."

*Autistic.* Sal had always associated the term with zombies, spaced-out people. Perhaps it fit the girl she'd talked with in the library study carrel, but the person sitting next to her now was verging on genius. Why was Tauni Morrison so different from one moment to the next?

"But you go to school," Sal said. "You read books, you won an award last year. And you're talking to me."

Tauni nodded furiously. "Of course I read books. I've read so much about autism, I know more than most professionals." Wrapping her arms about herself, she started a gentle rocking motion. "Autistic means you've got perceptual and motor difficulties. Your brain is physically different. I'm high-functioning. Most of the time I look normal, so people expect me to be normal. Then when I'm not, they get angry. Things like fluorescent lighting are a major problem — all that buzzing and flickering. I hit overload, the world explodes in my face, and people blame it on my attitude. My parents are the worst." She laughed again, loud and long. "They tell me I should play sports and go to school dances. Dances are chaos and loud. They expect you to touch and be *social*." A pained grimace took over her face. "And how am I supposed to play sports when I can't find my feet? Sometimes, when I'm really fried, I can't climb stairs. Stairs are evil."

"Oh." A vague disappointment settled over Sal. She hadn't realized there would be a label to explain the girl with the black lips — she'd been looking for mystery, not psychology. "I just noticed," she said slowly, "that you seem to hear things other people don't. Like music that comes out of nowhere. Singing."

Tauni's rocking slowed until she sat motionless, staring across the park.

"I've been trying," said Sal, then stopped. How did she explain what had no words, how did she describe her search for the blue voice? But whom better to discuss this with than the girl who experienced speech as a third language, the girl who couldn't find the mouth in her face?

"I'm trying," she began again, "to find a voice, a voice that sings only inside my head. The voice is blue. I heard you singing once, and I was wondering if you could help me find it. Will you listen if I try playing my clarinet?"

There was a pause, the wind twisting a long moan

through the grass, and then Tauni nodded. Carefully, as if lifting secrets out of the air, Sal took her clarinet case from her knapsack and assembled the instrument. The reed bled its familiar bitter taste onto her tongue — it was new and would probably squeak. Nervously, she screwed the ligature into place.

"I don't really know what I'm doing," she said, flicking a glance toward the girl at the other end of the table. "I'm looking for something that got lost a long time ago."

The wind writhed through her jacket, leaves whipped across the park, and Tauni continued to sit motionless, staring at nothing. Who knew what she was thinking, if she was listening or had gone off somewhere unreachable in her head? Sal knew about those unreachable places, how they could take you in and feel like home.

Then a tremble crossed Tauni's face and she sighed, her eyes slanting sideways at Sal. "I know about lost things," she said softly.

Something caught in Sal and held, a note waiting to be sung. Hesitantly, she fit the clarinet between her lips and blew into it. As she'd expected, the sound was breathy. The reed squeaked and an ache filled her, so immediate she almost cried out. Who was she trying to kid? The blue voice would never come to her again, it had moved on long ago, in search of better hearts.

"Ah, forget it," she muttered, groping for the clarinet case.

Tauni shifted, turning slightly toward her. "Don't stop. Try to find it," she said, her voice creaking with effort.

Sal paused, the clarinet case open before her like a wound. What if she tried and it didn't work? Could she bear another whiplash of loneliness? On the other hand, what was one more? She'd survived all the others, and the girl watching her from the other end of the table had certainly kept trying when her voice had stalled, squeaked and acked. Slowly, Sal raised the clarinet to her mouth. The sound she was seeking needed more faith, she thought, more gut, more of *her*. But how did she let go of the fundamental disbelief she had in her own worthiness? How did she lean into herself with hope, with *trust*?

Closing her eyes, Sal breathed and sent herself into the beginning of sound. At first she didn't know where to go — an ocean of possibility was opening on all sides and she was a mere ripple arcing through it, a tiny swimmer questing an endless watery blue. Where was the path she was supposed to follow, what was the right note to play? Then it came to her like a quiver of light riding the deep. There was no right path, only possibility. And that possibility was waiting for her, it wanted and needed *her* to make itself real.

A gladness leapt through Sal, a sighing ache, and then sound began to unfold like a dream coming awake. Slow notes flowed from the clarinet, a kind of conversation, a speaking that came from a deep wounded part of herself. This part had no words, only sound and the song that came out of that sound. Swimming deeper and deeper into the song of herself, Sal rose and fell on an ocean of notes until she forgot she was holding a clarinet, forgot she was anything but a long singing wave of blue. Sound lifted directly from her body — it was blue, it was honey and blush pink, it was a vivid scintillating flash of orange. Then it was black as Tauni Morrison found the mouth in her face and began to sing, voice pulsing from her in wave after wave of endless, wordless, merciful blue.

How long they sat together, floating on the blue voice, Sal didn't know. Suddenly the air changed, the song vanished, and she found herself back on the picnic table, the clarinet hesitant and squeaky in her hands. *Ack*, Sal thought. *Ack*. Her lower lip throbbed and she tasted blood. When she slid the clarinet from her mouth, she discovered the reed was stained a blotchy red. Looking up, she noticed the spot where Tauni had been sitting was empty, the girl with the black lips now halfway across the park.

"Hey," she called, "what's the matter? Where are you going?" But the girl headed on into the cold complaining wind. Bewildered, Sal stared at the clarinet in her hands. Dizzying snatches of the music she'd been playing shifted through her head. Why did beauty come and go like that? And why did she need someone else — Tauni or Willis — to touch that kind of sound, when all she wanted was to keep it deep within herself where it would never leave her, never go away?

But maybe this was what the blue voice was telling her — it wasn't a keepsake, it was a relationship that played itself out between people. Did she really want to spend the rest of her life holed up alone in her room, drooling onto her pillow, holding her most meaningful conversations with herself? What about the conversations she'd shared with Willis, and her talk yesterday afternoon with Dusty? Neither she nor her brother had released their deepest secrets — there was obviously something Dusty hadn't told her about his experience with Shadow Council, and she hadn't told him the mean things she'd been forced to do, the truth of Diane Kruisselbrink or Chris Busatto. Still, it had been a beginning, and when she'd woken this morning she'd felt as if a new place had opened inside, there was more space to move and breathe and know herself.

Thoughtfully, she pulled the cleaning swab through

the clarinet's gut and dismantled the instrument. The clarinet lay in its case, its parts separate and silent as the secrets she kept within herself. What if she brought them together, what if she let them sing for someone else? What kind of music would that be? Could anyone stand to listen?

Shoving the clarinet case into her knapsack, she rode the acid wheels of her stomach toward Saskatoon Collegiate.


The phones rang, a three-way echo in the quiet house. Sprawled on the livingroom floor, Sal listened for the click of the answering machine in the front hallway, but the chorus continued. She'd asked her mother to turn on the machine before leaving for her evening board meeting, but she must have forgotten. With a sigh, Sal listened as the phones went into their fourth and fifth rings. Why should she answer? No one had phoned her in a month. If she didn't pick up and her mother missed an important call as a result, it was her own fault for forgetting to turn the answering machine on.

The phones stopped ringing and Sal drifted listlessly back to *A Separate Peace*, a novel she was reading for English. It was a good novel, as far as novels went. She wasn't really into reading but she could sure identify with that moment in the tree, Linda Paboni poised for a dive into the river while Sal stood next to the trunk, jouncing the branch . . .

The phones were ringing again, the clamor of the hall phone overlaid by the electronic burble coming from the coffee table to her right. Sitting up, Sal glared at the livingroom phone. The damn thing was a replica of the Canadian flag, the speaker a long-stemmed maple leaf. Each ring gave out the first four notes of "O Canada." Dusty had bought it in a fit of patriotism during a grade eleven history trip to Ottawa, and they'd been stuck speaking intimate and intricate things into a red plastic leaf ever since.

The phones went into their seventh ring and she reached, groaning, for the maple leaf. She would be polite, but that was all she owed her mother's friends — no long, involved discussions about school, her social life, current boyfriends, etc., etc.

"Hello?"

A long pause came back at her. Great, someone with strep throat.

"Okay," she bargained with the silence at the other end of the phone. "I'll count to ten, and then you have to tell me the biggest darkest secret of your life or I'm hanging up. One, seven, five, two —"

"Sal?" The voice was frayed with nerves, but familiar.

"Who is this?"

"It's me. Brydan."

Her mouth opened like the ripple after a stone is dropped, the circle of shock widening without end.

"You still there?"

She could hear him, heavy-breathing into the other end of the phone. "Sort of."

"Yeah, me sort of too."

They waited, another silence stretched taut between them.

"Okay," Brydan said finally. "Here goes. I never knew I could be such an asshole. I always thought courage would come easy, like eating apple pie — y'know, feel-good stuff. Well, it's more like swallowing Javex. I've never felt so nauseous in my life."

"You're saying it makes you feel nauseous to call me?"

"I get sick just thinking about what Shadow's going to do to me."

"I never asked you to drink Javex for me. Maybe you should just hang up."

"Sal, no." Brydan's voice arced with desperation. "I've thought every day about making this call. D'you realize it's been a month today? Every single day for a month I've been breaking into a cold sweat thinking about calling you. God, I know I'm an idiot, but I want to explain. I want you to know why."

Sal sat, the plastic maple leaf pressed to her ear, drinking her own Javex. "Okay, so why?"

"I knew," he said hoarsely. "That afternoon we cashed my lottery tickets, I knew you'd won."

"Lost," said Sal.

"Okay, lost. But I thought I could handle whatever pressure Shadow would dish out. I thought it'd be apple pie and glory, you and me coasting in my wheelchair through the rest of the year."

"I can walk on my own two feet." She wasn't going to let him off easy, overwhelm him with gratitude. She hadn't asked him to call and make her feel like cleaning fluid.

"Geez, just hand me another cup of Javex, would ya?"

"Yeah, well I'm feeling somewhat nauseous talking to you too."

"They threatened me." Brydan spoke quickly, spitting static into the phone. "Someone must've seen us at Shoppers Drug Mart and reported to Shadow. That evening they showed up at my house and took me for a long ride in a van."

"So what happened?"

"They bought me a Slurpee, then drove around and talked

about no-brain stuff — the Roughriders, TV. You know."

"They didn't mention me?"

"Only at the very end, when they dropped me off. That was when they told me to give you the three-fingered salute at band practice or my tires would be slashed every day for the rest of the year."

She didn't need details, the scene was playing clearly in her head. "Who was there?"

"Marvin Fissett, Linda Paboni, Larry Someone-Or-Other. Rolf de Regt. A couple other guys I don't know."

"Was Willis there?"

"Willis was driving."

Another dropped stone, another circle of shock widening into forever. "Brydan," she said quickly. "I never blamed you, not really. If this had happened to you instead of me, I probably would've done the same thing."

"But I want things to be different!" he exploded. "I want to be friends like we —"

"We can't," she said. "Nothing is like it was. They'll murder you if you hang around with me, and then they'll murder me."

"But —"

"But maybe," she said carefully, "we could make up a secret code, y'know — for talking? Hand signals, gestures. That's what they do."

"Who does?"

"Shadow."

"I don't want to be like them, Sal," Brydan said quietly. "Not anymore."

Frightened admiration blew through her. "So what's your suggestion?"

"Actually," he said, stumbling over the words, "d'you

want to meet for lunch tomorrow?"

Tomorrow was Friday. "I can't," she wailed. "I can't explain, but that's the only time I'm ever busy."

"What about after school?"

"You got some more lottery tickets to cash?"

There was a short pause. "I stopped buying them."

She spun on a Frisbee of happiness. "Meet me by the bike racks, okay? Or maybe Wilson Park — no one'll see us there."

"I'll meet you at the bike racks," Brydan said carefully. "So, see you tomorrow?"

She hadn't used the phrase in so long, it felt awkward.

"Yeah, see you tomorrow."

# Chapter Sixteen

Room B stood open, the notes from "Inside the Question" dreaming their way through the doorway. For once Pavvie was nowhere to be seen, the empty music classroom holding itself still and silent, as if listening to the hawk's reverie. Sliding clarinet #19 from its shelf, Sal hummed along, then stopped in surprise as she realized that the melody she was singing differed from the one Willis had assigned her — more urgent, it dug into her throat with a short insistent pulse.

Abruptly the trumpet cut off and Pavvie's voice could be heard, rushed and excited. "It is good, very good. I have been listening to you practice. The girl, Sally Hanson, she is getting much better. You are ready for an audience — I think the assembly next week. The band is playing and I will introduce you as a surprise duet. What do you think?"

Riveted to silence, Sal stood waiting for Willis's reply.

The two of them, Shadow president and victim, playing a duet in front of the entire student body — sheer panic must be blasting Willis's brain at the prospect. How was he going to ooze his shadowy self out of this one?

Willis's voice emerged carefully out of the long pause. "I think that's a great idea, especially if we keep it a complete surprise. But I'll have to ask Sally first. I don't know if she's played a duet in front of a large audience before."

Stepping into the doorway, Sal gaped at him open-mouthed. Dark eyes inscrutable, Willis returned her gaze, one eyebrow quirked upward.

"Yes, yes, here she is." Pavvie smiled benevolently from a chair in the opposite corner. "We were talking about you and Willis playing at the assembly next week. Practice now, and I will listen when you are warmed up."

Without waiting for her response, he nodded himself enthusiastically out of the room. The door shut behind him, closing Sal and Willis into a watchful silence.

"In front of the whole school?" Sal said weakly. "Do we have to?"

"Only if you want to."

"Won't you get demerits?"

"No rule says Shadow can't interact with you," Willis said easily, tilting his chair back. "In fact, you're supposed to interact with us on a daily basis."

"Oh c'mon," Sal moaned, collapsing into the chair beside him. "This is different."

"So am I different." A stubborn look closed Willis's face. "No one tells me what I can do. You can't let other people dictate your existence."

*Easy for you to say*, Sal mused. *Who was it crawling under everyone's asses at the last assembly, and now you want to put me center stage?* Then she thought, *And stand beside me.* Because that was what he would be doing — standing beside the victim, in front of the entire school. Whatever his motive, it was an obvious statement.

And her, standing beside him — what kind of statement would that be? Desperation? Kissing ass? She was only the victim, did her motive matter?

Ducking her head, she muttered, "What if I squeak?"

"You get nervous at the beginning, but it goes," Willis said. "The music will take you in and you'll forget the audience. You're playing a lot better than I thought you could. And we'll be warmed up from playing with the band, don't forget."

Nodding, she stared at her closed clarinet case. A bleak numbness seeped through her, and she felt like a wooden puppet. Was that what she was? Was she always going to let fear pull her strings?

"All right," she said, "but we've got to practice extra. At least a couple of times."

"Give me your address and I'll come over," Willis agreed. "Then we can practice as long as we want."

They warmed up, then slipped into the slow floating notes of "Inside the Question," Sal's new reed squeaking several times before releasing her into clear singing sound. She played, the melody starting somewhere deep in her body, then flowing out through the clarinet, and when the sound left the instrument she was still part of it, suspended mid-air in a moaning breathless pulse.

"Beautiful, yes beautiful!" came Pavvie's voice and she looked up to see him smiling in the doorway. "I will sit now and listen," the band teacher said excitedly. "You play again, yes?"

They played several more times, Pavvie leaned forward, chin on hands, his face so intent Sal could feel him mid-air, floating with the sound and the dream.

"Right here," said Pavvie, pointing to Willis's page. "You need to pull back a little, give the clarinet more room — it is her moment, yes?" Leaning forward, Willis nodded slowly. "And here," said Pavvie, pointing to Sal's musical score. "Here you let go and let your soul sing. You know how to sing, let it sing!" His eyes beamed directly into hers, then skittered shyly away. "Yes, yes, you two will play this surprise, and we will not tell a soul in advance, eh? Not even the band. We are supposed to play three pieces for the assembly, so the band will play "In the Mood," then you will play "Inside the Question," and the band will finish with "Call of Fate." Not even the band will know until you get up to play."

"Great." Willis's voice walked the tightrope of his thoughts. "Thanks for your comments, Mr. Pavlicick. You're right about giving Sal more room."

"You don't need much help." Pavvie rose to his feet, still beaming. "Well, classes in five minutes. I must go."

"Shit!" hissed Willis, losing his guarded demeanor as Pavvie exited. "I've got Physics in the north hall at one." Packing his trumpet, he stood to leave. "The assembly's on Wednesday. How 'bout we practice Sunday afternoon and Wednesday morning before school? Sunday at two?"

"Yeah, sure." Hastily, Sal wrote down her address and handed it to him.

"Great," said Willis, pocketing it. At the door, he hesitated and turned back. "Oh — about the Chris Busatto thing. I took care of it. It won't happen again."

"Okay." Sal blinked rapidly, unsure where to look. "Whatever."

"See you Sunday." With a wink he was gone, and Sal was left staring at the empty doorway, wondering what the hell they thought they were doing. Just exactly how did one go about laying out the delicate beauty of one's soul in front of fifteen hundred predatory peers? How could she expose and protect herself at the same time, how was she going to survive inside that question? And how would Willis? He would be prey then, just as she was.

As she stood to go, her eyes fell on a small spiral-ring notebook that lay beside Willis's chair. Wondering if it was his, she flipped it open to see every line filled with his familiar intense scrawl. Though no title identified the contents, she knew immediately what she held.

*Sign of the Inside* — *brush left side of nose. We are the gods* — *ripple right hand through the air. Report for duty* — *raise middle three fingers of right hand.* As she scanned the first few pages, phrases leapt out at her. *I am the master* — *stroke chin. Outsider* — *crook left index finger. Low level* — *grunt and slap knee.* Here it was, line after line — Shadow Council's secret language, the body code she'd been watching them play out between themselves for over a month. Did Willis know he'd dropped this notebook? Had he left it intentionally for her to find?

Somehow, she doubted it.

Swallowing Javex, she slid the notebook into the back pocket of her jeans.

The after-school crowd poured jubilantly through the exit, leaping headlong toward the weekend. Pushing her way through the melee, Sal paused inside the doorway, gnawing the raw mush of her lower lip. Private confessions on the phone were one thing, a public encounter in the middle of several hundred potential spies something else entirely. Brydan had had all day to stew in regret. Would he be out there waiting, or would she find herself unlocking her bike and pedaling off into the familiar desolation?

The bike racks buzzed with the usual banter, students exchanging weekend plans, slipping on knapsacks and cycling off down the sidewalk. Keeping her head down, Sal fumbled with her chain-lock, unlocking and relocking it as the racks gradually emptied. Her heart ticked off seconds like a clock, the voices that surrounded her faded down the street and she stood alone with just two unclaimed bikes. Still Brydan didn't show. Why would he do this to her, set her up for a day-long torture of expectation, then leave her to dissolve into absolute loneliness?

"Sal!"

Glancing up, she saw him cruising toward her, his face flushed but determined. "Sorry I'm late, my math class got held back."

The late afternoon sunlight dusted his hair with gold, and she could see every pore in his face. Leaned against the closest bike rack, she tried to disguise a massive adrenalin rush. "How come?"

"The class next door ended up on the front lawn — someone's idea of a practical joke when the teacher got called out. A kid coming in late told us about it, so we swarmed the windows to watch."

"Could you see anything?" She'd delivered the envelope to Ken Goodwin on Wednesday. Obviously it had taken him some time to work out a game plan.

"Nah, too many trees in the way. Couldn't see a thing, but we got held back fifteen minutes for disrupting the class."

He gave her an apologetic smile, his eyes flicking nervously across her face. "Hey, what d'you say we blow this popsicle stand?"

As they started off down the sidewalk, she ducked her chin against the wind and tried to ignore the startled glances coming their way. Someone across the street gave a wolf howl, and a long low whistle from the school lawn reverberated sickeningly through her gut. Beside her, the quiet slap of Brydan's gloves on his wheels kept them moving grimly forward.

"So," he said finally, as they turned the corner toward Wilson Park. "How was your day?"

It was, she thought, a heroic, if plastic, effort at conversation. "I've been drinking a lot of Javex. You?"

"ODed on Javex. Then I switched to Drano. I thought about trading in my stomach for a toxic waste container."

"God, I feel like such a catastrophe." The words burst out of her, agonized and astonishing. She tried to choke them off, but they kept coming. "Every time I turn around, I bring more shit into someone's life."

"It's not you," Brydan said quickly. "It's Shadow."

"But it's been like this for years." How did she explain about her father, her hit-and-miss relationship with her mother, and the fact Dusty couldn't grow up and get a life because he was stuck worrying about his kid sister's problems? All her life she'd been a problem to other people — the evidence was stacked sky-high around her.

Brydan paused at the entrance to Wilson Park. Curving his body around the flick of his lighter, he dragged deeply on a cigarette. "Okay, brace yourself," he said. "Here it comes, the deep-six meaningful philosophy of my life." He wheeled across the dry crackle of leaves, following the logarithm of his thoughts. "When I was in the hospital after the accident, I got pretty low. I mean, what a way to come down off acid — stuck in a hospital bed, Christmas lights everywhere, your body sawed off below the knees. I kept staring at those stumps and thinking, *This is you, man. From now on, you are nothing more than what you haven't got*. I wouldn't do rehab or talk to anyone — the doctors, my parents, even my sister Cheryl. Hell, she was the one who was driving — I blamed her for the wreck of my life.

"Then Christmas Eve, after my family gave up on me and went home, this old lady came and sat down beside my bed. She was a volunteer. You know the type — looks like somebody exploded a pack of rouge in her face. She must've been at least eighty, cheerful as a Hallmark card for over eight decades. She was wearing a Santa's hat and carrying a bag of presents. *Oh swell*, I thought, *the great-great-GREAT-granny from hell*."

Coasting beside him, Sal dragged her toes through the withered grass. Brydan's words were comforting, a relaxed thoughtful flow, but they weren't taking her where she wanted to go, away from the ache inside herself.

Blowing a wobbly smoke circle, Brydan continued. "'Isn't that a nice tattoo you've got there, sonny,' the old lady said to me, and then she started fishing enthusiastically inside her Santa's bag of presents."

"Tattoo?" asked Sal, picking up interest.

Brydan shot her a sideways grin. "You know hospital pyjamas. I was wearing mine backwards — another way to bitch, I guess. Anyway, I had the string ties across my front and it showed off the dragon I've got tattooed on my chest. It's small, but it's got a rose in its teeth. I call it Harry Potter. Sometime I'll show you."

"Yeah, sure." Sal flushed, thinking more about chests than dragons. "Must be a great character reference."

"Depends what you're applying for," Brydan grinned. "Anyway, this old lady handed me a little wrapped present, all pretty with a big red bow. 'Merry Christmas, sonny,' she said, and I was so mad and pissed off, I yelled, 'Go to hell, you old bag. Can't you see I just want to die?'"

"Geez," Sal muttered, without thinking.

Brydan nodded. "My first Christmas without feet. Yeah, I was on a downer, but that didn't throw the old lady one bit. 'Ah, but you're not going to die,' she said with a fiendish grin, leaning into my face. 'You see how old I am? You're going to last even longer than me. You'll be so old, you'll be defecating dust balls before they finally lay you in the ground. Think about it, kiddo,' she said, poking my arm with her long skinny claws. Damn near took off the skin, too. 'You want to be this mean and nasty for an entire century?'"

Sal giggled uncertainly and Brydan tilted his head back, dragging intently on his cigarette. "Then she came up with something that really blew me away. 'Remember this, kiddo,' she said, getting out her claws and poking me again. 'You're not a burden, you're a privilege. There's some that know this truth about themselves, and the rest ache their whole lives long trying to find it. Now you get working on yourself until you believe what I just told you, and then you go out there and grab everything life has to offer you.' Then she got up and toddled off to poke and harass everyone else in the ward into crawling back into some self-respect. That was one cool old lady."

They'd stopped at a picnic table. Leaning her bike onto its kickstand, Sal sat down and stared across the park. "So you're telling me I'm a privilege?"

"I'm telling you that when I started believing I was a privilege, the world threw off the slime it was wrapped in, and nothing was ever the same again."

"Yeah, but ..." *With you, it's just your feet* — she couldn't come out and say that to Brydan. How did she know what his feet meant to him? Maybe losing your feet was just as bad as watching the brains of someone you loved blown across the horizon of the rest of your life.

"But what?" Brydan asked immediately, right on her, and for a moment she considered it — opening to the words that would describe that long ago, helpless shattering. But what would be the point? It couldn't change what had actually happened, and just thinking about mentioning it was sending her head into dizzy dangerous swerves.

"I've got something to show you," she said, diving into an abrupt change of subject. Pulling Willis's notebook from her pocket, she shoved it at him. "It's full of Shadow's secret code, the way they talk between themselves."

Slowly Brydan perused it, so quiet she could hear the ember flare as he dragged on his cigarette. "I've seen them pulling some of this stuff. I never realized —" He stared off thoughtfully.

"Realized what?"

"It was all so meaningless," he said almost helplessly. "You see them do this code thing, and it makes them seem so — I dunno — so goddam glamorous and important, with their hand signals and meetings and duties. But when you find out what it actually means ... What kind of idiots go through all the effort to make up a secret hand signal for 'We are gods'? It's like Saturday morning cartoons. 'Low-level'? 'Under-human'! Y'know what this is — just another version of 'my dick's bigger than your dick.' That's all it is."

"I guess that's the reason for the code — so we won't figure out they're no different than the rest of us," Sal mumbled, trying to ignore the heat that engulfed her. Why couldn't someone invent a female brain that wasn't always thinking about sex? But then again, would she want it?

"Why d'you think we need them?" Brydan asked. "I mean, we must need them for something, or we wouldn't be paying them any attention, right?"

Sal leaned into the thought, feeling very intent. "What d'you mean, *need* them?"

"I mean, what do they do for us?" asked Brydan. "If they didn't exist, who would we be without them?"

And suddenly she knew, the answer coming to her as clearly as if the words had been spoken by Willis Cass himself.


It was Dusty who opened the door that Sunday afternoon, then stood without speaking in the doorway, ignoring the rain that splattered against his face. Sitting halfway up the staircase to the second floor, Sal had a good view of the encounter taking place in the front hall — her brother's merciless gargoyle glare and just beyond him, Willis, hunched in his windbreaker, the wind blowing back his hair so that his sideburns could be seen outlined clearly against his face. She'd agreed in advance to let Dusty answer the door — he'd kicked up a mini-uproar that morning when he'd heard Willis was coming over, and she was more than a little curious to see how he'd handle the shadowy president. Now, watching the two silently stare each other down, she found herself more interested in her brother — the cold open anger in his gaze, the fall of long thin hair

down his back, his faded AC/DC t-shirt. Everything about
him said "low-level" and "under-human" but there he was,
his tall skinny body defending the front doorway for her
like a bare electric wire.

"Could I speak to Sal?" Willis asked finally, his voice
carefully casual.

"Maybe," said Dusty.

Willis stared back, unblinking. "You looking for an
apology for times past?"

"I'm looking for a guarantee," said Dusty. "You know
what for. Though a guarantee from scum isn't much of a
guarantee, is it?"

Willis blinked, then nodded. "You'll have to take my
scummy word for what it's worth, I guess."

Dusty spat. "Shadow's honor?"

"Shadow's honor," said Willis, shifting to avoid catching the goober on his shoe.

Turning to look over his shoulder, Dusty hollered, "Sal!"
and just as they'd agreed, she came thumping down the
stairs, pretending to be completely unaware of the encounter
that had taken place.

"Hi." It was difficult to feel shy after watching that
front-door scene. Leading Willis past Dusty's glower and
her mother's welcoming handshake, she took him downstairs into Retro-Whatever. This scene had also been
planned in advance — she'd left the overhead light off for
effect, and now watched gleefully as Willis rotated at the
center of the room, following the ooze of the lava lamp
across the orange shag ceiling, walls and floor.

"This," he said slowly, "is a completely alternate reality."

"My brother and his friend Lizard did it."

"Lizard?" Willis asked faintly. "As in Lewis Jones, former

member of the Celts?"

"Yeah, they're still best friends," said Sal. "Lizard practically lives here. We keep him on a *leash* in the backyard."

"Oh good." Willis avoided her eyes. "I'd like to get out of here in one piece."

He'd brought his own music stand and began to set up in front of the two chairs she'd arranged at one end of the room. Flicking on the overhead light, she sat beside him and ran through a few scales. She'd been warming up, on and off, for hours, and after a few squeaks, the reed settled into a comfortable vibration against her lower lip. For the next hour, they ran through "Inside the Question," trying out all of Willis's practice patterns — breaking the melodies into riffs, playing it straight through as eighth notes, inverting intervals, attempting it backward.

"You can't play it like this," Sal protested halfway through the last version, dissolving into giggles. "The hawk crashes into the ground, doesn't it?"

"Your part doesn't though." Willis lowered his trumpet to his knee, oddly quiet.

"I am the ground," Sal shot back, sudden bitterness catching her. "I can't get any lower."

"I never thought of your part as the ground," said Willis. "More like a river, with the hawk's reflection floating across the surface."

"So my part is actually you, upside down?"

"Maybe."

Their eyes met, and she was trapped inside the intensity of his gaze.

"What would you do, Sally Hanson," he asked softly, "if you were me? What would you do if you were Shadow president, and the feel of it climbed like snake slime up your throat? If everywhere you went, people either avoided you or sucked up to you because getting on your good side meant keeping off Shadow's duty list? I look in the mirror and my face gets further and further away, there's so much shit piled in front of it. I reek, I can't bear the stench of myself or any of my so-called friends. The only place I can get away from it, the only place I can truly see myself now, is when I look at you."

"Me?" croaked Sal.

"You haunt me like the hawk's reflection in the river," Willis said hoarsely. "You're my shadow, my other option. The choice."

"I never chose to become the victim," she spluttered.

"No, but I would be," said Willis. "If I kicked up flack on Shadow or resigned, that's what they'd do to me — turn me into you. I'd be choosing to become you."

Did Willis really see other people as low-flying versions of himself? White-hot phrases exploded in Sal's head, she felt the rage her brother's body had radiated at the front door. "You might become the *victim*, Willis," she said softly, tasting the pride in her voice, savoring it. "But you'd never become me."

He flinched, then took a deep breath. "What d'you say we ask your brother to sit in and listen to us? And your mother? We could use a practice audience."

Her mother had gone out, but Dusty tucked himself into the beanbag chair and listened remorselessly, his eyes closed, his body motionless. When they'd run through "Inside the Question" several times, he finally straightened and began pulling on his knuckles, cracking them one by one. Instantly Willis stiffened, as if coming to attention before a superior.

"Y'know," said Dusty quietly, studying his hands. "They use all kinds of shit and garbage as compost to help flowers grow. And you're blooming, Sal, you're a beautiful yellow rose."

Unfolding his long thin body, he silently left the room, and Sal knew this was as close as Willis would ever come to receiving a compliment from her brother.

# Chapter Seventeen

Monday morning brought another barrage of envelopes, delivered to her locker by Judy Sinclair. "Deliver before 9 AM, no exceptions," said Judy crisply. Avoiding Sal's eyes, she handed over the envelopes.

*As if*, thought Sal, *I'm a machine, or something not quite here. That's what they're all pretending — I'm not real, just a symbol. And you can do anything you want to a symbol.*

Judy's hand fluttered nervously across her carefully curled hair, then touched the center of her forehead. "And there's a meeting at noon," she added tersely. "Don't be late."

Sal recognized the code from reading Willis's notebook. Shadow Council used a system in which the human face was overlaid with a clock to indicate meeting times — touching the center of the forehead meant twelve o'clock, the chin six o'clock, and so on. But why would Judy use this signal with the victim? The only code Sal supposedly knew was the Sign of the Inside. Did they suspect she'd picked up Willis's notebook, or were Shadow Council members so caught up in their secret coded world that they sometimes forgot who was "inside" and who was "outside"?

The name and homeroom of each target had been paper-clipped to the respective envelope. Ditching her curiosity about the contents, Sal concentrated on delivering the envelopes before classes began. Sometimes she knew what kind of misery they contained, sometimes she didn't — what did it matter? Her job was simply to get them to the targets on time. By now she'd learned to erect an effective barrier against the expressions of startled dislike she received as she handed out duties. This morning's only twinge of regret came as she delivered the final envelope to Jenny Weaver, last year's victim, and watched the look of weary resignation cross her face. So it was out of the fire and back into the frying pan with everyone else — surviving a year as victim didn't guarantee anyone a leap onto Shadow Council's protected list.

Twelve o'clock found her at the Celts' clubroom door, giving the victim's knock — three short and two long. When she was admitted, she discovered her usual corner stacked with posters for an upcoming garage sale fundraiser that was being held for the drama department. Dragging her footstool to another corner, she watched as each Celt claimed the quota of posters for delivery, then took up a position in the circle formed by the couch and chairs. Immediately the hand signals and foot tapping began, Willis undulating his right hand through the air and everyone following suit.

"Quick meeting," Willis said, loosing a wide grin.

"We've got the masses running enough duties right now, but Ellen's come up with a beaut of an idea I knew you'd want to hear about."

"Yeah, okay," said Ellen, flushing under the concentrated gaze of her fellow predators. "Well, it's the school crest that's painted on the auditorium wall. Y'know S.C.'s motto — 'Veritas, Justitia et Libertas.' Well, I just thought we should get someone to paint it over as 'Wroblewski, Tuziak, and Ecstasy'."

The circle showed its approval in various ways. Linda spluttered with mirth, Rolf chewed his pen and grinned, and various right hands undulated. In one way or another, a ripple of pleasure made its way around the entire group, taking everyone in.

"But we need to Latinize it," Judy said quickly. "Let's see — Wroblewskas, Tuziatia et Ecstasas."

"Even better," approved Willis. "Now the only question is the target."

"An art major," said Larry. "Or someone who knows calligraphy."

"Dayna Mascarenhas is good at that kind of thing," said Judy.

"So is Bill Artem," added Rolf.

"You know who else is good at it?" Linda spoke so casually, Sal almost missed the stalking quality in her voice. "Our old friend Diane Kruisselbrink is a maniac for calligraphy. She does most of the lettering for the Posters Committee."

"She's already been targeted once," said Judy, frowning slightly.

"But picture it," Linda grinned. "Diane Kruisselbrink on a stepladder in the auditorium, sweating over the lettering for ecstasy."

A breathy laugh ran around the group.

"We've got to get it on film," muttered Marvin.

"It'd mean getting her in at night," mused Willis. "You think she's worth the risk?"

"She's got no friends," said Linda. "Who's she going to tell?"

"Those are the kids you've got to watch the most," said Willis. "The ones with nothing to lose."

"Vote," snapped Linda. "Everyone in favor of Diane Kruisselbrink, raise your hand."

Seven hands rose into the air, Willis and Judy abstaining.

"Carried," said Linda. "Rolf, write up the duty."

"I won't deliver it." The words left Sal's mouth before she knew she was thinking them. Sailing across the room, they smacked Linda Paboni right on the kisser. As Shadow's vice president turned toward her, a look of utter astonishment on her face, Sal's stomach went off like a field mine. "Not Diane Kruisselbrink," she stammered, bent double and rocking around her gut. "Please don't pick on Diane Kruisselbrink."

"You do as you're told," snarled Linda, leaning forward in her chair.

"Not Diane Kruisselbrink." Sal's mind had blanked, it was all she could think to say. "Just not Diane Kruisselbrink," she repeated desperately.

"Why not Diane?" asked Rolf, chewing his pen. The room was suddenly so intent, Sal could feel the bricks listening in the walls.

"Because she's a walking wound," she mumbled. "That's what you want to turn everyone into, isn't it? Well she's already there, so go after someone else."

"You know how many demerits you've just earned, victim?" Linda asked. "Looks like you've landed the duty of repainting the school motto."

Hunched on the footstool, Sal dug her fist into the acid scream of her stomach. For a long moment, no one moved. Then Willis cleared his throat.

"This was supposed to be a short meeting — pick up posters, in and out. Our next full-member session is next Monday at noon. We'll discuss this then. Everyone dismissed."

"I think Exec and the victim should hang around," Linda demurred.

"Can't," said Willis. "I'm already late for a Student Council Exec meeting. Everyone's officially dismissed, including the victim. *Now*."

Riding the emphasis of his last word, Sal clutched her stomach and bolted for the door.

For once she was early, in her place and warming up before most of the Concert Band members arrived for Tuesday morning practice. It hadn't been intentional — one of her mother's pointed comments delivered through the bedroom door had set Sal off pell-mell to beat her parent out the kitchen door, and the rush had carried her, pedaling furiously, all the way to school. Now, seated alone in the music room's first row of chairs, she felt odd, as if she'd stepped into another, unfamiliar part of her brain where everything was reversed. One by one, students rushed through the doorway with their instruments, and she watched them as they must have watched her so many times. It was like looking in a mirror — she could predict their every movement as they dumped their coats and books in the heap by the door and turned to scan the room, looking for someone to connect with. Then their gaze met hers, and she could almost hear the door slamming in their brain as their eyes went blank, turning inward or away. When Willis entered, he glanced immediately toward her seat, even though he must have expected to find it empty, and something leapt between them — wordless, full of fear. His face blanked and he mounted the risers to the back row, taking his place as lead trumpeter.

Brydan's eyes also fixed immediately on her, and a flush began crawling up his neck. They'd met again yesterday, followed the after-school crowd to the nearest 7-Eleven and defiantly slurped their Slurpees just outside the store door. No one entering or exiting had spoken to them. As the crowd of students that usually packed the parking lot had drifted away, Sal's Slurpee had settled into a cold defeated mound in her stomach. "Want to come play video games at my place?" Brydan had asked, but she'd made excuses, wanting only to crawl into bed, curl around the nuclear fusion of her stomach, and sink into an intense sleep drool. Now, as Brydan wheeled through the music room doorway toward her, she felt the pain in her gut flare briefly before settling into its regular slow burn.

Fetching his clarinet from the wall cabinet, Brydan backed into place with quick precise movements and began setting up. "So, how's the Javex?"

"How's the Drano?" she countered.

"Pardon?" asked the oboist to Brydan's right, turning toward him.

"I was talking to Sal." Keeping his head down, Brydan slid his clarinet joints together with unusual concentration.

"You were?" The oboist's eyes slid quickly toward Sal,

then back to Brydan. Shifting in her seat, she carefully angled herself toward the flutist on her other side. Brydan's face flickered with astonishment, then narrowed into thought.

"I guess I was that tight-assed last week, wasn't I?" he said ruefully, glancing at Sal.

"Time passes," Sal shrugged. "Things change."

"Hey," said Brydan. "Ape became man. That was one self-improvement course."

As soon as Pavvie released them, Sal ducked out of the music room, knowing from experience that she needed to get to her locker as soon as possible in case there were deliveries to make. As she'd expected, someone from Shadow Council stepped out to meet her, three fingers raised, extending a handful of envelopes. No words were exchanged. She accepted the envelopes, scanned the paper-clipped names, and headed off to the indicated homerooms. The deliveries progressed with the usual minor setbacks — she had to use the Sign of the Inside twice — but the procedure was complicated by the presence of Willis's notebook burning a hole in her back pocket and pushing her thoughts to a feverish pitch. She hadn't told Brydan of her plans for this morning, not wanting to face him with failure if she lost the courage to carry them out. Now she wove her way through the crowded halls, plucking her thoughts like daisy petals as she debated the enormous choice looming over her.

*Should I, or shouldn't I? Will Willis love me, or will he hate me forever? When Shadow finds out, will they kill me, or will they kill me? If I deliver every one of these goddam envelopes first, will they go easier on me for good behavior?*

It was an idiot's bargain, but her brain was a collection

of bare wires, white hot and fused into hyper-drive. All she knew was that she *had* to do this or something inside her, some fine rare specimen of hope, would go extinct. This was the DNA of choices, the decision that could bring her back to her truest self. At the same time it was the act of a lunatic, and the envelopes she'd been given to deliver were the only barrier standing between herself and all hell breaking loose. Each one passed from her hand like a farewell to sanity. Handing the final envelope to a Megadeth fan in classroom N8, she stood in the buzzing corridor, her brain stripped to one last daisy-petal thought.

*Everyone should commit acts of random intelligence.*

Her watch stood at 8:53, leaving her seven minutes before the bell. Sliding Willis's notebook from her pocket, Sal scanned the busy hallway ahead of her and swallowed a surge of bile. Never had her body felt so heavy, a dead weight. Slowly, she tore the first page from the notebook.

"Message from Shadow," she said, pressing it into the hand of a nearby student.

"What?" asked the girl, glancing at her.

"Read it," said Sal, moving on down the hall. Tearing out another page, she tapped a guy on the shoulder. She felt trapped deep underwater, her words slurred like a depth sounding. "Message from Shadow," she repeated and handed him the page. Noticing a teacher, she ducked her head and hurried on, then tore out another page and pushed it into the hand of the next student. On and on she went — the notebook was full of coded phrases, most of them never used, but relevant nonetheless. "Message from Shadow, message from Shadow," she kept repeating, handing out page after page until the notebook had been reduced to its front and back covers.

"What is this?" a guy demanded, turning and coming after her with a page in his hand.

"It's the way Shadow thinks and talks about you." She could barely get the sentence out, the words jumbled and oversized in her mouth. What was the matter with her? Why couldn't she speak like a normal human being?

"Get real," he said. "Really?"

"Really."

"No kidding." He wandered back to his friends, his lips moving as he scrutinized the list of codes. Watching him, Sal wondered if the wall was finally starting to crack, if the words he was reading would do anything except destroy what was left of her life.

The rest of the day progressed as usual. No one spoke to her, though she kept getting glances — eyes full of questions that darted away, too frightened to stick around for the answers. Twice that afternoon, she glanced up to see someone from Shadow Council headed grimly toward her, but she ducked each encounter, skipping her locker after school and taking off on her bike without waiting for Brydan.

The streets flew by, a blurred electric field. She kept expecting to see Shadow Council step out from behind hydro poles or rise out of the ground. How had she managed to escape their clutches for an entire day? But maybe it wasn't all that surprising. Even Shadow needed time to organize after something unexpected — they weren't supernatural, and they wouldn't have seen this coming. Except for her refusal to deliver Diane Kruisselbrink's second duty, she'd been docile and cooperative, handing herself to them like a lamb going to the slaughter.

The house was empty, her pillow waiting. Sal crawled in among crumpled packages of Doritos and Oreos and shattered into tears as the familiar smells of laundry soap and sleep rose to engulf her.

Sometime later she woke, ascending sharply into a chorus of phones. Stumbling downstairs and through the darkened house, she glanced out a window into more darkness. *What day was it? Tuesday, Tuesday evening.* No one home again, just her and her lonesomeness. Dusty was probably studying at the U — well, hopefully — and her mother working late at the office. No, Sal thought angrily. Her mother was an alien, zooming in from another planet to check on her offspring only when the guilt became intolerable. If things went according to schedule, that guilt would start hitting Ms. Hanson in approximately one hour. The clock on the kitchen stove stood at 7:23. It had been ten and a half hours, Sal realized with surprise, since Willis's notebook had been distributed to the masses.

Again the phones rang, yanking her out of her thoughts. Picking up the livingroom maple leaf, Sal mumbled, "Hello?"

"You bitch!" screamed a voice at the other end. "You did this to him. If he dies, it'll be your fault."

"Who is this?" Bewildered, Sal sank onto the couch.

"Kimmie Busatto. Don't you remember your old friends now you've turned so evil?"

"Of course I remember you." Sal struggled with the inside of her head, still dense with sleep. "Why are you talking to me?"

"You know why." The phone spat static. "How many envelopes have you delivered in the past two days? How could you do this to my brother? You know how upset he gets."

"Chris? But that was last week," Sal faltered. "He refused his duty and I had to do it for him."

"Not the past two days," Kimmie yelled. "Kids have been kicking and shoving him, ransacking his locker. Today a couple of guys picked him up and turned him upside down into a garbage pail in the cafeteria. He left school after lunch, came home and cut his arms. Wrist to elbow, Sal — the way you do it if you really want to die."

The living room dissolved into a vast roar. "No," Sal whimpered, lost in the whirlpool. "No."

"He's in the hospital now." Kimmie was no longer yelling, but the words still came at Sal like bricks. "The psych ward, and you did it to him. This is your fault, Sal Hanson. I thought after this year maybe we could be friends again, but not after this. No one'll want to be your friend after I tell them what you did to my brother."

"But I didn't know," Sal wailed desperately into the phone. "I didn't know those envelopes were about Chris. All I do is deliver them, Kimmie. That's all I do."

The only sound that came back to her was the dial tone.

The stairwell raced by, a panicky blur. Flicking on the overhead light, Sal headed straight for the stereo. After Kimmie's phone call, the headphones wouldn't be enough; she needed Dusty's floor-to-ceiling speakers reverberating from every corner of the room. Quickly she flipped through the stack of CDs on the shelf. Where was it, where was it? Here, at the bottom, it'd been a while since she'd listened to *The Wall Live*. Skip the first track, pump it up, pump it up. Yes, there was her favorite guitar line, blasting from the speakers, vibrating the carpet so each orange fiber stood on end. This was what she needed, this great booming force field convulsing her body into mad savage shapes — something huge, like a god, blasting her to smithereens. Yeah, when she was in the middle of this sonic boom, this fusion of sound and mind, nothing could touch her, nothing was real. Problems shattered the way a brick wall collapses — you just had to put your mind to it, and all the walls came down.

A blurred form brushed past her. Shutting off the stereo, Dusty turned toward her and shouted, "What, are you crazy? Now we're supposed to take you in for bionic eardrum replacements?"

"You like loud music," Sal yelled back, floating on the supersonic ringing in her ears. "Why can't I?"

"I like *music*," said Dusty. "That was like listening to the air show."

"I was just getting something out of my system." Sal fidgeted, frightened at the quiet in the room, the stillness of her own body. She had to keep moving, *keep moving*, or it would catch up with her and blow her wide open again. "Dusty!" she cried, faking a glittery smile. "I've got a good idea. Take me driving. I haven't had a lesson in weeks."

"Kinda late," muttered her brother, running a heavy hand through his hair.

"It's only 8:15, and I need practice driving at night." Catching his arm, she dragged him toward the door. "C'mon Dusty, please? Pretty please?"

"All right," he sighed, melting. "A short lesson, just around here."

They came out the back door into an evening that was oddly warm, a last pocket of summer. Standing at the curb, she waited as Dusty backed the car onto the street. Then they switched, Sal easing into gear, peering between headlight beams. Parked cars and street signs flashed by, there and gone, coming and going in the dark.

"Slower," said Dusty. "Remember, this is your first time at night."

"It looks so different in the dark." Shadows twisted and muttered at the back of Sal's head. She blinked, trying to focus. "I hardly know where I am."

"Maybe you shouldn't be driving," Dusty said. "Pull over, I —"

"No," she said quickly. "I'm doing okay. I stopped at all the stop signs, didn't I?"

"I guess."

"I know what I'm doing." The shadows in her brain were taking shape, on the edge of revealing their true form. She fought them with words that tumbled heedlessly, end over end. "I know exactly what to do, I'm a good driver. I won't let anything — no accidents, no dead people, no blow-up brains — stop me from being a good driver, right Dusty?"

"Sal," said her brother, reaching for the wheel. "Pull over, you're crying."

Impatient, she shoved his hand away and pressed down on the accelerator. The car engine grumbled, urging itself forward into the dark.

"I'm a good person, aren't I, Dusty?" Her voice skipped across the words as if they were red hot. With an angry fist, she swiped at the tears blurring her vision. Where was she? The street kept shape-shifting like something in a bad dream, something that didn't know itself. But she knew who she was and why she did things. She had everything under control.

"I'm a good person and a good driver too." Her voice

spiraled upward, fighting the craziness in her head. "I know just where I am and what I'm doing, and it's not going to happen to me now, it's not ever going to happen to me again."

"What are you talking about?" demanded Dusty. "Why are you pulling in here?"

Without warning, the shadows erupted from her mind and took solid form. A familiar darkness rose wide before her, the inescapable landscape of an eight-year-old's terror repeating itself yet again. Giving herself up to it, Sal twisted the steering wheel and swerved directly into memory. The screaming began, the endless *I hate you, I hate you*. Headlights arced, the car jolted as it swung into position, and then she saw it — the wall, the great brick wall of Saskatoon Collegiate coming toward her at top speed, and she was going to hit it head-on, smash it into shattering crumbling bits.

"Sal!" Dusty's hands came down on the wheel and his foot hit the brake. The car spun a wild donut, the wall veering to the right, then reappearing dead ahead. As the car squealed to a stop, Sal opened the door and ran full tilt toward the school. If she couldn't run the wall down with the car, she'd do it with her body — smashing her shoulder into it, grunting as the air was punched clean out of her lungs. Backing up, she ran at the wall again, screaming, "I hate you, I hate you. You're wrecking everything, nothing's like it used to be."

Then she was knocked to the ground, Dusty holding her tight as her gut exploded, the great inner wall collapsed, and she finally understood what happened seven long years ago.

"It was my fault," she sobbed. "I killed my daddy, I killed him."

They lay motionless, Dusty listening like a body-wide ear. "What?" he whispered.

"You know how Mom calls it an accident? Well, it wasn't." Sal's voice staggered under the weight of telling. "Daddy was driving to the store to buy beer, and I was mad because ... because I'm *evil* and I *hated* him. So I screamed, 'I hate you, you're wrecking everything, I hate you so much.'" Her voice faded, crawling into itself to escape its own sound. "He looked at me, so sad, like I'd stabbed his heart. And then he drove the car into the tree on purpose, because ... oh Dusty, because I said I hated him."

Suddenly she was writhing, convulsed with self-loathing, waiting for her brother to get up and leave her for the no-good, disgusting piece of shit she was.

"Sal." Dusty knelt over her, his long hair falling across her cheek. "Sal — are you listening?"

He was still there, he hadn't gotten up and walked away.

"Do you hate me?" she whimpered, covering her face with one arm.

"No, I don't hate you."

"Do you promise?" Her body released its last deep shudders, and she lay exhausted and spent. "You're not going to leave me and go away forever?"

"I'm not going anywhere unless you come with me." Dusty leaned closer, his warm breath traveling across her face. "But first you have to listen to me, okay?"

"Yeah." She was so tired, she was drooling onto the pavement. She wanted to crawl inside her brother's breathing and stay there forever.

"First of all," said Dusty, still crouched above her, "Dad

was an alcoholic. He was drunk when he killed himself. Second, he went bankrupt about half a year before he died. Third, he and Mom had been fighting and were probably going to get a divorce."

"But I said I hated him." Sal twisted to look up at him. "And his face was so sad —"

"I hated him too." Dusty settled onto his heels, combing back his hair with both hands. "I was a kid, what did I know about what was going on inside his head? All I saw was his alcoholism wrecking everything." He paused, rubbing his face. His wire-rim glasses glinted, tired stars in the dark. "Did you know he left a note?"

Sal gaped. "A suicide note?"

"Yeah."

She sat up, the blood roaring in her head. "So he planned it? With me in the car?"

"No," Dusty said quickly. "You just happened to be with him. He was so miserable, he wouldn't have thought about what he was doing to you."

"I wish he'd killed me too."

Tears began to slide down Dusty's face. "I don't," he whispered. "All these years, I don't know what I would've done without my kid sister."

The words were unbelievable, the world turning itself inside out once again. "But what did I ever do for you?"

"You were just there." Dusty hugged himself, rocking gently and staring off into the dark. "Bringing me into each day, then putting the day away again. Mom's been like a fading picture. I think she blames herself for Dad's death, thinks it was her fault, something she did. Maybe she's afraid of hurting someone else too, and that's why she keeps pulling back. Whatever, most of her life seems to be over, she just fades more and more into herself. But you've always been there, following me around, asking a million vivid questions, needing me, making me feel human. You love me, Sal. That's helped me love myself."

They sat, snuffling their runny noses into their sleeves. "D'you think," Sal mumbled, "that if I'd yelled 'I love you' instead, he might not have done it?"

"Who knows?" said Dusty carefully. "But it was *his* decision to make. You were just a kid — you didn't control him, you didn't make him do anything. He'd already written the note, remember?"

A sigh shifted through her, leaving a deep quiet place. "Why didn't you tell me this before?"

"You'd been through enough already. Mom didn't show me the note either. I found it on her dresser."

"So why does she lie about it?"

"We all lie," said Dusty, "to stop the hurt from hurting deeper."

He reached out a hand, and they pulled each other to their feet. The parking lot took shape around them again, quiet and ordinary in the dark. Saskatoon Collegiate loomed to their right. Sal stared at it in surprise. She'd forgotten where she was.

"Let's go home," said Dusty. He took her arm and she let him lead her to the car. Splayed in the passenger seat, she watched the school wall slip away as the car eased out of the parking lot. A great weariness lapped through her, peaceful, like water. As her brother tooled through the night streets, she wanted nothing more than to let him drive her through the rest of her life. Then, slowly, she realized what a mistake this would be. She needed to be more than what happened to her. She wanted to be made up of her own choosing.

"It's gone now," she said, touching Dusty's arm. "The wall inside me. I feel a huge open space where it used to be."

Even in the dark she could feel the smile that spilled across her brother's face. "Sally-Sis," he said, "that's the best thing anyone's said to me in a long, long time."

# Chapter Eighteen

She woke Wednesday morning to find the great inner space still with her. The wall hadn't rebuilt itself overnight. It was well and truly gone now that she no longer needed anything to stand between herself and her fear. *I'm not a murderer*, she marveled, leaning her chin on the windowsill and staring out. *When it happened, I was just a squirmy scared little kid. I didn't kill Dad — it was because I loved him that I said I hated him. I wanted him to be different, to be happy the way he used to be. I just didn't know how to say it properly. How could I? I was only eight and scared out of my mind because he was driving drunk.*

Her entire body felt different, no longer the prison of guilt it had been. *Not the hand of a murderer*, she thought, watching her finger trace a heart into the condensation on the window-pane. She touched her lips. *Not the mouth of killing words.* How was it possible that six words — *I hate you, I hate you* —

could have controlled her life for so long? But they had, causing such tremendous guilt she'd blocked them entirely from her memory. Only the guilt had remained, vague and undefined, affecting every aspect of her life. Sal breathed deeper, deeper still. The air felt so good, as if it somehow belonged to her again, as if she'd regained the right to breathe. Standing, she spread her feet firmly on the carpet, claiming space. Brilliant happiness blazed through her. She threw back her head and howled.

"Jeeeeesus!" came her mother's long-suffering voice.

"It's okay, Mom," Dusty groaned from his bedroom. "I'll check my textbooks. It's probably considered absolutely normal for fifteen-year-old girls."

"Maybe," said Ms. Hanson dubiously, retreating into the washroom with a firm click of the door.

*If only*, thought Sal, as she mounted her bike and coasted the streets toward Saskatoon Collegiate, *all the outer walls had gone down with the inner one*. But there was still her mother's Teflon-smooth barrier, not to mention Shadow Council's impenetrable divide-and-conquer system. Sal wasn't kidding herself about the latter — she knew it was still out there, waiting for her, every brick in place. And this morning, Shadow Council would be ready. It had been twenty-three hours since she'd handed out the key to their secret coded universe, and they weren't likely to have forgotten her refusal to deliver the second Diane Kruisselbrink duty. The summons would probably come at her locker. Perhaps Willis would deliver it himself, at their pre-school practice session.

But when she arrived, Room B was empty, and though she sat waiting until 8:45, Willis didn't show. No envelopes were presented at her locker for delivery, and when she passed Rolf in the hall en route to her 9:15 class, he brushed past her as if she didn't exist. The lack of response was unnerving and made her feel as if an attack was continually about to launch itself from anywhere and everywhere. Why hadn't Willis shown? Were they still going to perform the duet? Fidgeting through her first-period math class, Sal avoided the curious glances of other students. Band members weren't excused from classes to warm up for the assembly until 10 AM, and the waiting was interminable. Finally, the assembly participants were summoned over the PA. Filing into the music room with the rest of the band, Sal took her seat and ran through a few nervous scales. Pure high notes ascended from the back-row trumpets. When she'd entered the music room, Willis's eyes had flicked across hers, complete blanks, as if nothing had ever lived there.

Without the inner wall, there was nothing to block her fear. Shrugging off Brydan's attempts at conversation, Sal chewed the inside of her lip and surfed wave after wave of panic. Why had she ever trusted Willis? There had to be a catch to this duet, some way for Shadow Council to exact its revenge. Surely after the notebook incident, Willis would have told them about the surprise performance. That was probably why he hadn't shown for their morning practice — he'd been told to screw her up so badly the entire audience would break out jeering. The way she was feeling, it wouldn't take much.

Sucking her bloody lower lip, Sal dug herself deeper and deeper into her thoughts. Slouched beside her, Brydan sat without speaking. If he'd heard about the distribution of Willis's notebook, he wasn't asking and she sure wasn't explaining. Surrounded by the band's warm-up cacophony,

they tooted their clarinets half-heartedly until Pavvie
mounted the podium. With a moan, Sal sank further into
her seat. Time for the deadly pre-concert tune-up, the
moment that distinguished the afficionados from the musical scum. Setting the electronic tuner to concert B flat,
Pavvie listened carefully as each individual band member
adjusted his tone to its pitch. When her turn came, Sal
squeaked, then found she was flat. Pavvie nodded politely
and misery claimed her, rising thickly above her head. What
had she gotten herself into? Why had she agreed to a duet
with the school's chief predator? She was a third clarinetist, for chrissakes, with the emphasis on third rather than
clarinetist.

Listlessly setting the cap onto her mouthpiece, she
walked toward the auditorium beside Brydan, then followed him up the stage's side ramp. There was the usual
uproar as band members climbed the risers and adjusted
their chairs and music stands. Off to one side stood two
extra music stands, ready for the duet. Whispers and giggles erupted from the wings — the purpose of today's assembly was a pep rally in support of the soccer semi-finals,
and the teams were psyching themselves up. Beyond the
stage lights, the auditorium stretched into darkness, empty
except for the endless rows of chairs. Soon every teacher
and student would be parking their butts in a chair that
had been set in place by a member of the Celts. The club
had probably also set up the risers and chairs for the Concert Band. *Shadow touched you everywhere*, Sal mused.
Wroblewski thought he ran things? Just wait until he saw
the updated version of the school motto planned for the
auditorium wall.

A low rumble echoed through the building as classroom doors opened and students began filing toward the auditorium. Suddenly Sal's heart was thudding painfully, the clarinet slipping in her sweaty hands. Glancing over her shoulder, she saw Willis staring pale and expressionless at his knees. Gone was the wolfish grin, his mouth sucked into itself, tasting dread. The rumble coming down the halls crescendoed as students jammed into the auditorium. Chairs scraped and creaked, ripples of laughter rode the crowd. Stepping out of the wings, Mr. Wroblewski strode to the mike and began speaking, his comments a distant static in Sal's head. Then the stage lights were focusing on the band, Pavvie stepping onto the conductor's podium and rapping his baton. The band took a collective breath and launched into "In the Mood." Notes lurched, frightened and scattered, from Sal's clarinet. *No*, she wanted to say, *I never asked for this. I never asked to be lifted out of insignificance and mediocrity, I never wanted to be more than what I am.*

Chris Busatto's face flashed through her head, and her thoughts veered after it. What did his arms look like now? What was he thinking, what *could* he be thinking with the drugs they must be pumping into him? Did anything she had to face today, did anything Willis had to face, come close to the moment when Chris had placed that sharp edge against his forearm and decided to dig his grave inside his own body?

"In the Mood" ended with a flare of trumpets, the band lowering their instruments and reaching for the second piece of music. With a quick nod to Sal and Willis, Pavvie walked to the mike, his shy clipped voice resonating throughout the auditorium.

"This morning we have a surprise, a duet composed by

Willis Cass and performed by Willis Cass and Sally Hanson. It is called 'Inside the Question'."

Incredulous, Brydan twisted toward her, and the auditorium filled with an immediate buzz. Sal's next breath opened endlessly, like an accordion. As she stood with her copy of "Inside the Question," the stage lights faded in and out. Beyond them, darkness loomed like a huge swallowing mouth. Then a slight tug came at her sleeve. Glancing down, she saw Brydan's grinning face. "Ghost of Benny Goodman," he hissed. "Let 'er rip."

She walked toward Willis, who was shifting the extra music stands to the front of the stage. He picked up his trumpet, and she took her place beside him, facing the dense silence. "Ready?" he whispered, his eyes briefly making contact, an unreadable glint that left her as alone as she'd ever been.

*Alone*, she realized suddenly, *but not the same*. The inner wall had crumbled, and she was no longer staggering under seven years of inexplicable guilt. She didn't have to feel unworthy — the air was hers to breathe, this clarinet was hers to play any goddam way she wanted. Whatever Willis or Shadow Council had planned for this duet, they couldn't control the way air and sound passed from her body into a musical instrument. That was hers.

*First language*, she thought.

The first eight bars were Willis's solo. Lifting his trumpet, he took a deep breath and climbed a slow arc of notes. Sal slid her clarinet between her lips, listening and waiting, and then it came to her — an opening deep within herself, and from it, a line of pure longing that rose swiftly to greet her. Dreaming and insistent, the first notes passed her lips, and her fear of squeaking vanished. Sound filled her, she was riding the slow pulse of the wind in the grass, she was the hawk's reflection rippling across water — a second hawk at ground level, broken-winged yet dreaming of the possibility of sky. Oh, how she longed to soar, lift out of her skin and sing with the sun. Closing her eyes, Sal sent herself wishing into sound and it became the song of her father she was playing, the song of Chris Busatto, Tauni Morrison, Diane Kruisselbrink, and Jenny Weaver — all those who couldn't find the mouth in their face, yet would not be silenced. She played on, their voices rising through her, demanding an existence that was free of the hawk soaring above, and more than a low-level reflection. The music lifted through her, taking the shape of their faces — Diane Kruisselbrink, arms lifted for a mighty shove; Jenny Weaver's eyes darting here, there and everywhere, still searching for one true friend; Chris Busatto glaring over a copy of *The Chocolate War* and saying, "Maybe I should get you an appointment"; Tauni Morrison whispering, "Find your feet, find your feet"; and her father's gaze, hurt and staring, just before he gave that final twist to the steering wheel — all of them fighting back in their own way, saying, *I cannot live with this, it is not enough.*

And it wasn't enough, not for them, not for her — no one could live as the reflection of someone else's contempt. Longing twisted through Sal, calling her out of the expected. Leaving behind the part she'd been given to play, she soared into her own song, a smoky melancholy splendor. Beside her, the trumpet line faltered. Then Willis had also leapt free of his composition, and they were freewheeling together through sound, the glory and the ache. There were no words for this kind of knowing, it sang through the rise and fall of their lungs, the thud of their hearts and the sweating of their palms, sending its question into the S.C. student body: *Are you there, do you hear me, are you inside the questions of your heart?*

Then from the dark auditorium came an answering voice, the blue voice lifting out of the endless rows of chairs and dreaming its way toward them. It came to Sal the way it had always come — as if it knew her, as if it had always known her and the way her heart needed to sing. Pulsing with her clarinet, Sal let the blue voice fill her, she let all things become the timbre and resonance of deep evening blue. When the exquisite longing finally faded from her body, she opened her eyes and stood blinking in the stage lights, wondering where she was. A movement caught her eyes, pulling them downward, and she saw Tauni Morrison leaned against the front of the stage, black lips smiling, pale gaze fixed directly on her own.

With a gasp, Willis lowered his trumpet. Tumultuous applause and foot-stomping began, opening the air to praise. Amazement flooded Sal — they'd heard, they'd listened, and they were speaking back. But as she grinned at the crowd, Tauni raised both hands against the thundering noise. Stumbling toward the nearest exit, she bumped into the doorframe.

"Find your feet, find your feet," Sal whispered as the girl fumbled with the push-handle. "Doors open, walls don't."

Then Tauni was through and gone, in search of the solitude she needed to piece her reality together again. Throughout the auditorium, the S.C. student body was quieting, the applause dying out, only the odd whistle still piercing the air. Turning toward her seat, Sal paused as Willis touched her arm.

"Sally," he said quietly, his eyes faltering across hers. "Whatever you think of me, whatever comes next — thank you for this."

He hadn't betrayed her, Sal realized. He hadn't told Shadow about their surprise duet. So, not everything was etched in stone.

"Yeah," she said, breathing and breathing the great good air. "Thank you too, for helping me to live inside the question."

For two days, they left her alone. No further envelopes were presented to her for delivery, and no one signaled her in the halls. From the time Sal entered the school until the time she left, the only student who spoke to her was Brydan. Then, Friday evening around nine, the house erupted into a clamor of phones. Coming down the stairs she answered without thinking and picked up the front-hall extension to hear Willis's careful voice at the other end.

"Sal, is that you?"

She knew immediately and shrank into the tight cave of her breathing. Without waiting for her response, Willis continued, as if he was aware Dusty and her mother were out, leaving Sal the only one present to answer the phone. "It's the duty, we've scheduled it for tonight. I'll come by at one-thirty, in the back alley. Can you be outside waiting?"

"One-thirty," Sal whispered, the words creeping up her throat.

"There's no other time to do this." Willis seemed uncomfortable, his voice strained. "It has to be done at night. Make sure you bring your house key to get back in."

"Yeah, sure."

"See you then."

She spent the intervening hours walking an invisible blueprint of fear. Stupidly, she'd fooled herself into believing she was safe in her own house, that Shadow Council ruled Saskatoon Collegiate but it ended there. Now it felt as if the school halls and classrooms had been superimposed over her home, a transparent nightmare that followed her as she paced the solid reality of her bedroom, the kitchen, and the long lonely halls. Even Retro-Whatever could do nothing to blast the images of dread growing so strong in her mind that her mother and Dusty, when they finally came home, seemed distant and unreal, a mere fantasy of safety.

At 1:25 she crept down the back stairwell, pausing at the door to the basement. She could hear Dusty and Lizard ensconced in Retro-Whatever, immersed in Led Zeppelin. Snatches of their conversation floated toward her. For a moment she considered hurtling down the basement stairs and revealing all, but what was the point of dragging a look of concern back onto her brother's face? Since that night at the school wall he'd been so different, relaxed and proud of her, as if the main problem had been solved and everything else she had to face was mere technicalities. And perhaps he was right. *Whatever's coming* ... Who knew what tonight would bring? Maybe she would paint her own version of the school motto onto the auditorium wall: *Shadowus, Celtus et Bullshittus*. What could they do to her, after all? They couldn't actually force her to paint the words they wanted, and they weren't likely to beat the crap out of her. Shadow Council never incriminated itself directly, and Willis would be there to protect her.

The night sky arced clear and cloudless, dreaming with

stars. Beyond the back gate purred the outline of Willis's car, a newer model that left Dusty's several decades in the dust. Opening the passenger door, Sal slid into the acrid smell of hash and Radiohead's hypnotic drone.

"So the victim has arrived." Marvin saluted her from the back seat with a beer. "Give the girl a drink."

"Can't," said Willis, easing his foot off the brake. "She has to be able to paint, remember?"

"Oh yeah." Marvin snorted. "Ecstasas."

He was echoed by a refrain of giggles. Checking the rearview mirror, Sal noted the shadowy outlines of Linda and Rolf passing a joint between them. She shot a careful look at Willis but he ignored her, keeping his gaze straight ahead.

"I think the victim should have *one* beer." Leaning forward, Linda pressed an opened Coors into Sal's hand. "Here victim, it's on me."

"Do I have to?" Again Sal glanced at Willis. Mouth tightening, he continued to stare straight ahead.

"Yes, you do," Linda declared, her voice slurred and overly loud. "It's part of your duty because I said so. Drinkie, drinkie."

Something about this struck the other backseaters as hilarious. Snickering, Linda sank back among their guffaws. Sal shot another careful look at Willis. Without taking his eyes off the road, he gave a minute shake of his head, and she set the can on the floor.

"Nice concert you gave on Wednesday, victim," snorted Linda, coming out of a long titter. "I really, really liked it."

"You guys want to get focused?" Willis demanded sharply.

"Focused like you're focused?" Marvin asked in a high

giggly voice and the three were off again, collapsing into one another, choking with laughter.

"Give me that." Swinging around, Willis grabbed the joint and tossed it out the window.

"Ooo — all work and no play makes Willis a dull boy," sang Linda. "And tonight we just want to play."

"Yeah, well, play later," Willis snapped, pulling up to the curb. "Everybody out, we're walking from here."

Fear thrummed in Sal's head and pounded a reggae beat through her body. Several residential blocks lay between the car and Saskatoon Collegiate, every house along the street darkened for sleep. Digging her chin into her jacket, she walked beside Willis as the three gigglers stumbled behind, negotiating their feet. Imperceptibly, Willis quickened his pace and they pulled ahead, two parallel silences.

"How are we getting in?" she asked as the school building loomed.

"Key," Willis said shortly. "Legend has it that a Celt was helping maintenance unload supplies. One of the staff dropped a key chain and the Celt scooped it up. He got all the keys copied within the hour, then left the originals where they'd be found in the same area. The school locks were never changed, and Shadow figured out which keys were helpful."

"Hey," came Linda's slurred voice. "No associating with the enemy, Prez."

Again Willis's face tightened, but he swallowed his thoughts. Far off, a siren wailed. They crossed the parking lot, the gravel scuffing loudly in the quiet.

"The door's open," said Rolf. "They're already in."

"Shhh!" hissed Linda, and another round of helpless giggling began. Staring at a slightly open maintenance door, Sal felt the hair rise on the back of her neck. Why were so many Shadow Council members present tonight? She'd assumed a few would be there — Willis, Linda, probably Rolf — but why had so many of them shown up to watch her paint a few words on a wall? Desperately she imagined herself taking a stand and refusing to enter the school, or simply turning and dashing off into the darkness. Then the doorway was looming and her body passing through it, silent and obedient as ever.

They entered a small loading area she'd never seen. Another door stood open to their left. "This way to the auditorium," sang Linda, but Willis pushed forward with an abrupt "I'll lead," and they followed him into a hallway lit only by an EXIT sign at the far end.

The hallway seemed larger in the dark, an endless gloomy row of lockers and classroom doors. As they started along it, Sal had the quick blurred impression of stepping into herself and beginning a long walk toward something that waited within. Beside her, Willis picked up the pace. They seemed to be circling the auditorium that sat at the center of the school. Doors led into it from the north, east and west halls. As far as Sal knew, they were always left unlocked, but Willis passed the north entrance without glancing at it and turned down the west hall. Gradually the three gigglers behind them fell silent. Everyone was wearing soft-soled shoes, and the eerie quiet gave Sal the feeling of walking through a shadowy underworld.

Abruptly, Willis stopped at the west door. Knocking three times, he turned to her and said, "What follows herein will be kept secret until you are laid in your grave, on pain of death." Then he opened the door and she followed him into a darkness so immense and complete, it seemed like a living presence.

*No exit signs*, she thought, squinting into the unrelenting dark. *Someone must have unscrewed the bulbs.*

"Begin," said Willis, and the auditorium's darkness was shredded by flashlight beams. Deliberately they crossed Sal's face, momentarily blinding her. Blinking, she watched as they turned toward the stage, bringing two objects into sharp relief — a wheelchair that sat center stage and above it, a human body cut off at the knees and dangling midair, a rope around its neck.

"Brydan!" she screamed, shock gutting her brain.

"Too late," said Willis, stepping in front of her and cutting off her view. "You disobeyed, and now someone has to pay the price. The bell tolls, the traditions are written in stone, blood is required for a traitor's —"

She lunged at him, shoving wildly. The body that dangled center stage seemed to be jerking. Was it still alive, was —? But Willis had stepped in front of her again, blocking her view of the stage. Suddenly she knew with absolute certainty that he offered her no protection and never had — Willis would always do whatever Shadow required to save his own skin. Whirling, she rammed her way through flailing arms and startled shouts. Then she was out the auditorium door and tearing down the long, gasping hallway. Darkness squeezed in and out of her head. Disoriented, she slammed into a wall and bounced off. *Find your feet, find your feet*, she thought. Endless doors flashed by, endless locked and empty rooms. Then, finally, she saw it — a dim light that could only be coming from the front-office glass doors. There would be a phone in there. If she reached it, she could call for help. It took a while for someone to strangle to death in a noose, not like head injuries. Maybe an ambulance could get here in time. All she had to do was smash through the

glass. If she put up an arm to protect her face, she would just
have to work up enough speed ...

"Sal, no!" Footsteps pounded behind her and Willis
grabbed her arm, swinging her around.

"Let me go," she screamed. "You're killing him, you're
killing him."

"Listen to me," Willis yelled into her ear. "Would you
just listen?"

Hands over her face, she sank quivering to the floor. It
was over now, the chance was gone — she was sure of it.
"Brydan," she whispered.

"It's not Brydan." Breathing heavily, Willis leaned over
her. "It's a dummy and a wheelchair, just a stupid trick.
Come back, let them play their infantile game, and then
they'll let you go. The whole thing will be over — half an
hour and you'll be out of there, I swear."

She stared up at him, stunned with disbelief. "Like you
swore to Dusty?" Struggling to her feet, she stood swaying
as the hallway looped figure eights around her. "More of
Shadow's honor, is that what you're offering me?"

"Dusty told you?" Willis hissed, his face contorting.

"Told me what?" She didn't know whether to move
forward or backward. Everywhere had become nowhere,
all the same dying place.

Willis paused, his face drawn and wasted in the dim
light. "We have to go back," he said, "or they'll come looking. They'll cover the exits. There's no way out."

He started down the hall and she followed. Slowly the
darkness sorted itself out, taking on the vague outlines of
lockers and doors, everything silent and closed into itself.
Without speaking, Willis turned down the west hall, toward the group clustered in the auditorium doorway. A

whisper went up and the figures disappeared into the auditorium.

"What's going to happen?" Sal asked as they approached the door.

"I don't know," Willis said, pushed it open, and passed through.

She stepped into the auditorium. For a long moment there was nothing, just a vast room echoing with darkness. Then a single flashlight came on, pinning the dummy that swung center stage. Dim figures shifted beyond the flashlight beam, closing in.

"Now is the time," a male voice began to chant, "a time for reckoning."

"Time for reckoning," other voices repeated, overlapping and out of sync. In the brief pause that followed, someone giggled. It was Linda, Sal would have recognized the vampire queen's titter in any darkness. Turning toward it, she filled with a rage so dense and complete she couldn't breathe, couldn't think. Suddenly she was bent forward and screaming, her whole life pouring between her lips.

"You're so fake, with your shadows, codes, and stupid games. You couldn't come up with anything real, you don't know what real is. I saw my father die, I saw his brains smeared across the car windshield, and you know what? I *survived* it. You think you can shut me up now with a dummy? You're the dummies. You're nothing but shadows, the biggest cowards this school has going. None of you are real. You are all just so full of bull*shit*."

She staggered as the fury evaporated, leaving her hollowed and spent. The flashlight cut off, and in the ensuing darkness, no one moved. The game seemed to be over.

"I'm leaving," she said hoarsely. Groping toward the

door, she leaned briefly against the frame.

"I'll drive her home," said Willis. "Everyone clean up. We're finished for tonight."

This time she led and he followed, even when she miscalculated in the dark and he took her arm to correct her. As the long labyrinth of hallways faded behind her, Sal had the feeling of emerging from some deep interior place. Coming through the loading area, she stepped out into the clear night air — a great darkness above, loaded with stars, and space opening on all sides. Exhaustion rippled the ground beneath her feet as she and Willis walked the several blocks to his car. Neither spoke, though he paced himself continually to her, tensing when she stumbled. Finally they reached the car and she climbed in thankfully, staring out into the trance of passing streets.

"What did you mean when you asked if Dusty told me?" she asked, her mind thick and slow-moving.

Willis's fingers tapped his hesitation onto the steering wheel.

"Just once," she said, turning to look at him directly. "Just once in your life give a straight answer, Prez."

Willis's eyes flicked toward her, then away. She had a sudden inane desire to undulate her right hand slowly in front of his face.

"Okay," he said quietly. "The stunt they pulled tonight is a tradition usually reserved for the victim until the end of the year. It's a scare tactic designed to shut you up, seal your lips. This year they decided to bump it up because you handed out the codes."

"And Dusty?"

Willis sighed. "Your brother gave Shadow a lot of flack when he was in grade ten. They pulled that stunt on him too, made him think they'd hung his best friend."

"Lizard?"

"Shadow got Lizard to drop some acid with Dusty just before, and your brother fell for the game completely. Of course, he figured it out later, but it was enough to crack him. As far as I know he never told anyone, and he stopped harassing Shadow."

"And me?" asked Sal. "What was this supposed to do to me?"

"What d'you think?" Turning down the back alley, Willis parked at the Hanson's back gate. "That beer Linda gave you was spiked with enough to send you way over the edge. Lucky they were too far gone to notice you didn't drink any."

She sat, cradled by the car's gentle throb, considering the vast loneliness of the universe. All these years, Dusty had remained best friends with a guy who'd betrayed him, and had never talked about it with anyone. And what about all the years she'd wasted, not trusting the one person in her life who'd turned himself inside out trying to protect her?

"Y'know, Willis," she said, getting out. "There are no *nice* jerks."

Closing the door, she went inside to talk to her brother.

# Chapter Nineteen

She stood before the yellow door, tracing the black iron outlines of the number thirty-four. How she remembered this door, the initial resistance as it opened, the quick give midway, and the inevitable slam as she and Kimmie tore through, en route to the water park, the rollerblading rink, or soccer practice. It was the only yellow door in the neighborhood — the Busatto's entire house glowed with dandelion yellow doors, shutters and eavestroughs. Yellow was the color of spring, starting anew, and forgiveness. Raising her hand, Sal took a breath of the impossible and pressed the buzzer.

Footsteps approached from the inside, pausing as someone peered through the peephole. Five heartbeats went by, deep, underground detonations. Then the door opened onto Kimmie's face, expressionless, carved in stone. Her eyes were swollen, her makeup smudged — Kimmie had always been abysmal at applying makeup. Without a word she stood holding the door ajar, grimly staring into Sal's uncertain gaze. The muffled sounds of late-afternoon TV could be heard from down the hall, laughter erupting as Oprah carried off yet another intimate, up-front, and personal interview.

"Who's there, Kimmie?" came Ms. Busatto's voice.

"Just the paperboy," Kimmie called over her shoulder. "Don't worry, I'll get it."

They stood watching one another, Kimmie's relentless gaze forcing Sal's downward. The silence grew interminable, a thick sludge. "I, uh ..." Awkwardly, Sal fished an envelope from her pocket. "I wrote Chris a letter, and I was wondering if you'd give it to him."

Kimmie glared at the envelope, making no move to take it.

"I didn't seal it," Sal said. "You can read it if you want."

Kimmie let loose a huff of air and began to close the door.

"Wait," Sal said desperately, jamming a hand between the closing door and the frame. "I'll read it to you."

Kimmie hesitated, then opened the door partway and stepped into the gap. Ignoring the pain in her hand, Sal slid out the letter. She'd worked all weekend on it. No one had seen it, not even Dusty.

"Dear Chris." She had to stop and clear the self-loathing from her throat. "I never should've done what I did to you. When I delivered the envelopes, I didn't know what was in them, I swear. But if I'd known, I don't know what I would've done. You're so brave, Chris — of all the kids in S.C., you're the only one who said no. I'm sorry I didn't have your guts, but I'm working on it. Maybe someday we'll all be as brave as you are. Until then, please get better and come back to S.C., because that school needs you more than anyone."

She lowered the letter and stood watching the toe of her left runner. The sky was an immense weight pressing down. It was all she could do to keep breathing. Then, slowly, incredibly, the letter began to slide through her fingers.

"Okay," said Kimmie, carefully avoiding Sal's eyes as she folded the letter into her shirt pocket. "I'll take this to Chris."

"D'you want the envelope?"

Kimmie snorted. "I don't think Chris needs to see another envelope for the rest of his life."

They stood, looking past each other, watching the wind wrestle with the afternoon.

"Well," said Kimmie.

"Yeah," Sal agreed helplessly. "Well, see ya."

"See ya."

Sal turned to go, and the yellow door closed behind her. Something had ended, something innocent — two girls ricocheting through summer afternoons with popsicles in their hands, shrieking about boys and water parks — and it had ended because Kimmie still believed in the victim. But that victim, Sal realized as she walked down the front walk, was Kimmie Busatto, not Sal Hanson. In spite of what had happened to her brother, Kimmie continued to obey Shadow Council. She hadn't told her parents what had really happened to Chris, and in her private thoughts she was holding the lottery victim completely responsible, exactly as Shadow wanted her to.

*I'm the obvious scapegoat*, Sal realized. It was simply easier to hate someone on the bottom rung than to take on the gods directly. As long as there was someone as tangible as a lottery victim to hate, Shadow Council could get away with anything. Year after year, the selection of another lottery victim would ensure that there was always someone to absorb the fear and hatred the S.C. student body actually felt for Shadow Council.

It was a system, thought Sal, turning onto the street. A system in which everyone played a part. And that part, she thought, walking more quickly, was defined by the people around you. In a system, you didn't think or choose, you just tried to fit in.

She felt a curious opening in the air then, as if another invisible barrier was beginning to dissolve. For the rest of her life, people would be trying to define her, close her in with their thoughts and expectations. But, she was finally realizing, it was *her* perspective that mattered the most. Ultimately, it was her own fear or desire that would lock her in or allow her to open to the utter possibility of herself.

With a determined lift of her chin, Sal took another breath of the great good air.


It was, admittedly, an odd conglomeration — Tauni Morrison seated at one end of a library table, reading a book called *Somebody Somewhere*, and Sal and Brydan crowded into his wheelchair at the other. After Sal made several futile attempts to engage Tauni in conversation, Tauni had set down her book and begun spinning her pen, watching the rotating Bic as if it held some clue to the meaning of the universe. Recognizing the signs, Sal had given up. Some days she wasn't sure if Tauni even knew who she was, and it was frustrating to be treated as non-existent. On the

other hand, she didn't have to live inside Tauni's world —
a place that could blow up in your face at any moment.
Watching a pen spin probably helped Tauni avoid overload.

Leaving Tauni to the whirling Bic, Sal focused on en-
joying the new wheelchair seating plan. It had been worked
out the previous Saturday night at Brydan's place, somewhere between playing computer games and clipping each
other's nostril hairs. That evening had been like a song
from the Cecil Taylor CD Brydan had been playing on his
bedroom stereo — music that picked up a room and
changed the shape of the walls. Everything transformed
itself when you listened to free jazz, Sal thought, leaning
against the steady thud of Brydan's heart. Rooms took different shapes, so did people and their souls. And there was
so much you could do together in a wheelchair if you put
your mind to it ... and your lips and fingertips. She hadn't
seen the dragon tattoo yet, but she was planning on it.
Maybe this weekend ...

"Hey, Diane!" Abruptly Brydan straightened, rocking
Sal as he waved his arm. Pulled out of her reverie, Sal focused on the figure of Diane Kruisselbrink, standing at the
library checkout. Hesitantly, the girl turned toward
Brydan's voice, then away again.

"Diane!" Brydan called again, waving furiously. "Over
here."

After their nostril-clipping session, she'd confessed the
underwear episode to Brydan and he hadn't condemned,
hadn't said much of anything. This, here and now, she realized, was his belated response.

"Thanks," she whispered, as Diane warily approached.

"You don't have to tell her you did it," Brydan whispered back. "It might not be the best thing."

"She probably knows." Sal leaned forward, halfway between eagerness and shame. Maybe she couldn't do anything about Chris Busatto, but this was a chance — a *real* chance — to touch someone else's loneliness and right a personal wrong. "D'you want to join us, Diane?"

At the sound of Sal's voice, Diane's eyes blanked and her face sucked inward, quick-drying into a prune. Suddenly frozen, she stood several meters from the table, strenuously observing her own feet. Bewildered, Sal stared at the motionless girl until a poisonous realization snaked across her brain. Of course — she was still the lottery victim. Just because she'd stepped into another place inside her own head didn't mean everyone else saw things from her new perspective. Diane would probably prefer to sit next to the plague. Chewing her lower lip, Sal watched the girl shuffle silently to the other end of the table and sink into the chair beside Tauni.

"Okay, so Rome wasn't won in a millisecond," Brydan whispered into her ear.

"Not there," Tauni said in a tight clipped voice, without looking up from her spinning pen. "Too close."

Without the slightest change of expression, Diane shifted one chair to the left. "Better?"

Startled, Sal realized she'd never before heard Diane speak. The girl's voice was deep and husky, a barroom singer's voice.

"Much," piped Tauni, glancing vaguely in Diane's direction before returning to the revolving Bic.

Hunched forward, Diane regarded Tauni thoughtfully. "Why are you spinning your pen like that?"

"I'm stimming." Again, Tauni looked up from the pen,

her eyes oddly focused but vividly alight.

"Stim?" asked Diane. "As in short for stimulate?"

"Yeah." The spinning pen slowed as Tauni shot a series of runaway glances at the invisible halo around Diane's head. "How did you know?"

"I have a cousin who's autistic," said Diane. "He stims on anything bright and shiny, and he loves spinning things. I take him to his therapy sessions with Dr. Verner."

"Who?" demanded Tauni, her voice intensifying, shooting upward.

"Dr. Verner," said Diane, watching Tauni closely. "She's the autism specialist in Saskatoon."

"D'you think I could see her?" Suddenly agitated, Tauni began rocking in her chair. "I have to see her, I have to. Maybe she'll believe me."

"Sure, she'll believe you." Diane's voice slowed, growing quieter. "Don't worry. I've got her phone number."

"But I can't use the phone." Tauni wrapped her arms around herself, rocking more intensely, and the words poured out. "I can't think and talk at the same time, and there's all those strange people on the other end, and it's always different. If I don't know who I'm talking to, I don't know how to talk to them. I don't know what the structure's supposed to be, and I don't know where the conversation's going. I can't talk on the phone with strangers. I can't, I can't! Phones are evil!"

"I'll phone for you," said Diane. "Don't worry, I know how to call Dr. Verner. I'll call for you."

Fascinated, Sal watched as Diane calmly talked Tauni out of her rocking state. Gradually Tauni straightened and looked around herself, as if coming out of a dream.

"I've started wearing ankle weights," she said brightly,

leapfrogging to an entirely new subject. "I read about it in a book. It's supposed to help me find my feet."

"You can't find your feet?" Brydan's astonished voice reverberated through Sal's back. Suddenly she was wobbling as he jounced his legs. "Hey, neither can I!"

Tauni didn't even blink. "I have no idea where my feet are," she continued in her quick high voice, missing the joke entirely. "Unless I'm looking at them. Same with the rest of my body."

The corner of Diane's mouth tucked in, and a strange burble came out of her. Startled, Sal realized she was giggling. "Sometimes," Diane said, her mouth tucking in deeper, "I can't find myself in all this fat."

Tauni's eyes darted toward Diane, and then she threw back her head, laughing uproariously. All over the library, students turned to stare as the girl with the black lips rocked, guffawing, in her chair. After a moment Diane began a slow heaving chuckle, and the two girls floated in laughter, separate from everyone else.

Sal turned toward Brydan and shrugged, about to speak, when someone tapped her on the shoulder. Looking up, she saw Willis standing just behind Brydan's wheelchair, three fingers raised. Their eyes met and she felt the studied vacancy of his gaze, the calculated cool that ruled every moment of his face. Then, briefly, his expression opened inward and a rare, private smile flickered across his mouth. One eyebrow quirked and he pivoted, walking swiftly toward the checkout desk.

"Don't go." Brydan's arm tightened around her. "You don't have to."

So this was it, Sal thought, watching Willis disappear through the library exit. The moment of truth, delivered by the Prez himself. Whatever was coming, at least Shadow Council had gained enough respect to send their most illustrious emissary. Standing, she tugged gently at Brydan's closest earlobe — once, for luck. "Don't worry," she said. "They're pretty scared because of what happened to Chris Busatto. I don't think they'll go after anyone for a while."

Coming out of the library exit, she was caught up in the inevitable adrenalin rush as she saw Willis standing a short way down the deserted corridor. In spite of everything that had happened, in spite of her calm, clear knowing that this was a guy who'd warned her not to drink acid-laced beer only because he thought his tiny warning shake of the head wouldn't be noticed, still she wanted to believe the Cheshire Cat grin taking over his face. Not just believe it — *trust* it. Stomping on the thought, karate-chopping and stun-gunning it, she walked briskly toward him, saying, "What is it? I've only got a minute."

He leaned against the wall, thick sideburns still begging to be stroked, one eyebrow carefully raised. "A message from Shadow."

"No scrolls?" asked Sal. "No blank envelopes, no silly plastic tabs?"

"Look, we're willing to take you back." A flush quickened Willis's face. "I made a deal with Shadow — they'll lay off on extra duties and respect you like a normal victim. Everyone else in the school will continue to shun you until the end of the year, and then all will be forgiven and forgotten. You'll be accepted back into the fold with open arms."

"The sheep fold?"

Willis's flush deepened. He fidgeted, scratching a sideburn.

"And if I refuse?" Sal asked, counting heartbeats.

Willis closed his eyes, breathed, and opened them again. "A new lottery will be held and another victim selected," he said quietly. "You'll be shunned by everyone at S.C. until you graduate, and when you leave this place, it'll follow you like a curse for the rest of your life."

Sal traced out the long silence of the empty hallway with her eyes. "Willis," she said slowly, "if I'd been a regular lottery victim, one that was chosen by the usual method, you wouldn't have bothered with me at all, would you?"

Willis shrugged. "Shadow wouldn't have been all over your ass. You would've been treated fairly, like a normal —"

"— *victim*," interrupted Sal intensely. "You *believe* in the victim and the lottery, you *believe* in Shadow, don't you? And you know why you believe in them? Because you *need* them. You need Shadow to keep you in your place."

"And what is my place?" Willis's eyes narrowed.

"Afraid."

"Afraid of what?"

"Of yourself," Sal said simply. "You're afraid of the possibility of yourself. As long as Shadow keeps you in your place, you don't have to think about who you could be if you were *choosing*. That's what the question is, isn't it? Who could I be if I wasn't always so afraid?"

Willis stared, his eyes gripping her face.

"Inside the question," Sal said softly. "It's a nice fantasy, isn't it?"

He nodded, his eyes closing, a tranced expression crossing his face. "See you there, Sal."

She left him, eyes closed, standing alone in the hall.

The last notes of "Child In Time" faded into a dense quiet.

Sprawled on the orange shag carpet beside her brother, Sal waited, letting her ears adjust to the ringing void of sound. They'd been dancing, whip-snapping their bodies to a frenzy until they'd dropped exhausted to the floor. There they'd lain, twitching and convulsing to the odd riff or favorite guitar chord as the CD ended. Now, breathing silence, Sal felt the full length of her body breathe with her — threaded with aches and sore spots, but without inner walls. Nothing hidden, nothing to fear.

Rolling onto his back, Dusty released a long enigmatic fart, the result of curried chickpeas for supper.

Sal sniffed loudly. "My, that was a hefty one."

"My best," Dusty murmured contentedly.

"Yeah, well, d'you mind keeping your best up your butt?"

"Mocked, scorned and unappreciated by my own blood."

"You got that right."

They lay, breathing in sync, counting the orange threads that dangled from the ceiling.

"So," Dusty said casually. "How's it going with Brydan these days?"

Heat bloomed in Sal's face.

"That good, eh?"

"I didn't say anything," she mumbled, rolling onto her stomach.

Dusty laughed softly. "I'm not color-blind."

She tossed a throw cushion at his grinning face.

"Thanks," he said, tucking it under his head. "So, Shadow's not after him for hanging around with you?"

"Not yet. It's like we've dropped off the face of the earth — no one talks to us, but no one bothers us either. If they've picked a new lottery victim yet, I haven't heard about it."

"You going to shun the new victim?"

"No, but I bet the victim will shun me. I'm the lowest rung on the S.C. ladder until I graduate, right?"

"We'll see," said Dusty. "You never know, anything can happen."

"Yeah," said Sal. "It's not even Remembrance Day, and look what's happened this year already."

Her brother let out an emphatic sigh.

"So," Sal continued softly, "you don't have to worry about me anymore, Dusty. I think I'm going to be all right."

"You think?" Dusty said, not looking at her.

"I think."

"Geez," Dusty said, "whatever am I going to do with all my time?"

"Study," said Sal. "Do housework for Mom. Get your goddam muffler fixed."

"Mmm. Not wild about those options. Think you could develop a few new problems so I can go back to worrying about you?"

"Nope," said Sal. "You're just going to have to grow up and stand on your own two feet. But thanks for worrying about me until I found the mouth in my face."

"Huh?" Dusty turned a confused expression toward her.

"Never mind," she said, grinning. "It's a woman thing."

"You know what the mouth in my face would like right now?" Dusty stretched into a long groan. "A cup of hot chocolate with about a zillion mini-marshmallows floating on the top."

Sal lost herself in a temporary fantasy of marshmallow

foam, the silky swim of chocolate on her tongue. It had been days since she'd tasted blood or stomach acid. Her mouth was gradually returning to her as a good place to be.

"Mom home?" she asked, getting to her feet.

"Yeah, I saw her office light on when I came in." Dusty looked up at her quizzically and Sal grinned down at him fondly.

"Allow me to make you and your mom the two best cups of hot chocolate in Mountain Standard Time," she said.

Taking his hand, Sal pulled her moaning brother to his feet and helped him lug his aching body up the basement stairs.

# *Epilogue*

The note progressed, hand to hand, along the back of the room. Sal kept it in her peripheral vision, vaguely curious, wanting to maintain her Pony Express techniques by proxy, if only for nostalgic reasons. At the front of the class, Ms. Demko turned from the chalkboard to pick up a textbook and the guy across from Sal froze, crumpling the all-important missive into his fist. As the teacher turned back to the board, he slid the note onto his desk and scanned it. His eyes darted surreptitiously toward Sal, flicked away, then returned. Her heart began a slow painful thud. Was the note for her? Had Shadow Council finally recovered from the Chris Busatto tragedy and begun moving back into high gear?

Suddenly, the guy was leaning across the aisle and shoving the note into her hand. Wrinkled and moist from so many sweaty palms, the back was plastered with the usual graffiti. Flipping it to the front, Sal read the original salutation: *THIS NOTE IS INTENDED FOR THE EYES OF GILLIAN SPADA ONLY.*

It wasn't for her. Sal's heart quickened, and her stomach gave a brief acid surge. Fixing her eyes on Ms. Demko's back, she leaned forward and slid the note into the waiting hand of the girl seated in the desk ahead of her. The girl caught the eye of the guy across the aisle and nodded, then sent the note onward. Unable to believe what had taken place, Sal glanced at the guy across from her, but he was keeping his gaze riveted to the chalkboard. Slowly, she let her eyes trail across the rest of the class.

The wall was alive. It could think, breathe, learn. Brick by brick, it could change and choose, just as she'd changed and chosen. Dusty was right. Anything could happen, it had just happened, and it would continue happening for the rest of her life.

Smiling, she leaned back in her chair and hummed a quiet blue song.

═══════

Also by award-winning author BETH GOOBIE:

 *Before Wings*

In Adrien, Beth Goobie has created a memorable character
— intelligent, strong, irreverent, stubborn, funny,
independent, fragile — who learns to confront the reality
of her own death and to "believe" in life.

*"Beth Goobie just might be the best YA writer in the
country ..."* — TIM WYNNE-JONES

- • CLA Young Adult Book Award Winner
- • Saskatchewan Book Award Winner

1-55143-161-0 • $19.95 CAN; $16.95 USA; cloth
1-55143-163-7 • $8.95 CAN; $7.50 USA; paperback

# I.S. 61 Library

## DATE DUE

| | | | |
|---|---|---|---|
| | | | |
| | | | |
| | | | |
| | | | |
| | | | |
| | | | |
| | | | |
| | | | |
| | | | |
| | | | |
| | | | |
| | | | |